SPEAKING OUT
LGBTQ YOUTH STAND UP

edited by

Steve Berman

A Division of Bold Strokes Books

2011

SPEAKING OUT

ISBN 13: 978-1-60282-566-6

THIS TRADE PAPERBACK ORIGINAL IS PUBLISHED BY
BOLD STROKES BOOKS, INC.
P.O. BOX 249
VALLEY FALLS, NY 12185

FIRST EDITION: SEPTEMBER 2011

CREDITS
EDITORS: STEVE BERMAN AND STACIA SEAMAN
PRODUCTION DESIGN: STACIA SEAMAN
COVER DESIGN BY SHERI (GRAPHICARTIST2020@HOTMAIL.COM)

Acknowledgments

First and foremost I want to thank all the authors who contributed stories to *Speaking Out* and allowed me to share their voice with readers.

I owe a debt to my publisher Len Barot, who shared my enthusiasm for this anthology. The BSB staff were a joy to deal with, especially Stacia Seaman.

Thanks are due, as well, to dear friends who have encouraged my fondness for queer young adult fiction: Tracey Shellito, Holly Black, Casey Fiesler, Aimee Payne, Kristopher Reisz, Wayne Wilkening, the brilliant Ellen Kushner and her lovely partner Delia Sherman.

For Brent Taylor, the boy who first comes to mind
when I think of bold, sassy, and awesome.
Never change, Brent. You never need to.

and

For Nicholas Horne, a young man whose wisdom and
kindness are treasures that he is always willing to share.
I am lucky to be his friend.

CONTENTS

INTRODUCTION

If I ever encounter a time machine, I want to have this book on hand.

I'm daydreaming as I type this—the look on a fifteen-year-old Steve's face as future (or is that present? damn, time travel plays havoc with adjectives and tenses) me hands him an anthology of stories, all showcasing the self-esteem every LGBT kid needs. No, deserves. I'd probably be all mumbly-mouth, telling teenage Steve to read this story first…no, that story. Well, I'd recommend he avoid the intro or else the entire space-time continuum might collapse around New Jersey (a risk in any era, let me tell you). That fifteen-year-old me would be able to face high school, then college, then his twenties without much of the fear of being alone, being different, being gay. He would know that the voice he used to entertain himself with odd stories could be heard by many who understood the daily trials (harassment by bullies, hiding from parents and straight friends).

Voices are meant to be heard.

Such are the thoughts stirring in my head as I read the authors' stories. I want to have read them ages ago, to have grown up with them, as so many kids grow up with fairy tales (which are all so boringly hetero). Not that I believe the stories in Speaking Out are cautionary tales like "Red Riding Hood" or "Hansel & Gretel." I'd like to think of them as *incautionary*—the authors you'll discover when you turn the page want you to be brash and assured no matter what your gender or sexual identity. These are new tales for a new era.

My hope is that by the time you set this book down, you'll be encouraged to speak up, to speak out. In 1987, six gay activists in New York began promoting AIDS awareness with the slogan SILENCE = DEATH. But silence also means bullying and seclusion, inurement and loneliness.

Those of you who have come out, be heard. Those of you who know someone who is LGBT, let them be heard (and if you only suspect they are queer, listen *harder*). Those of you who are peering out from the closet, trust your voice. Be heard.

All of us involved in *Speaking Out* are ready not only to tell our stories but to listen to yours.

Steve Berman
Spring 2011

SPEAKING OUT

RIGOBERTO GONZÁLEZ is the author of eight books of poetry and prose, including the YA novel *The Mariposa Club*. The editor of *Camino del Sol: Fifteen Years of Latina and Latino Writing* and the recipient of Guggenheim and NEA fellowships, winner of the American Book Award, and The Poetry Center Book Award, he writes a Latino book column for the *El Paso Times* of Texas. He is contributing editor for *Poets and Writers Magazine*, on the Board of Directors of the National Book Critics Circle, and is Associate Professor of English at Rutgers–Newark, State University of New Jersey.

Whenever I travel and give readings or presentations, I always make sure my audience knows that there's an out and proud gay Latino in front of them. Even if it's obvious to many, I still speak openly about ethnicity and sexuality, because I discovered that modeling this courage gives permission to others to do so. This was something I learned when I was a shy closeted college kid, still embarrassed by my Mexican heritage, and especially by my name! But I kept running into people—presenters on stage—unafraid and confident about where they stood: "As an out lesbian..."; "For gay men like me..."; "My queer Chicano community..."; "My beautiful black gay brothers..." I don't remember these people's names, but their strength made it possible for me to be strong, which is why I keep my message gay-positive. I never know who's in the audience, waiting for an opportunity to become visible. The last time this happened was in Decatur, Georgia. At the end of the presentation, a teenager came up to me and asked in a timid voice: "Excuse me, Mr. González. Could you recommend some books about people like us?" People like us need to keep spreading the word.

LUCKY P
RIGOBERTO GONZÁLEZ

Nemecio and Paloma. The names click together, royal and golden, like an emperor sitting next to his empress. Like Maximiliano and Carlota, the two rulers of Papi's Mexico. Like Romeo and Juliet, the two lovers of Mami's Shakespeare. Except that Papi's rulers and Mami's lovers all die in the end, their glory cut short by worlds that don't allow the richness of their names to soar. The burden of the double weight always brings such couples down.

Nemecio and Paloma. I am in love with their names as much as I am in love with each of them. My name is Pedro Pérez, common and everyday as a name like Bob or Fred. In fact, that's who I'm named after—Fred Flintstone, Pedro Picapiedra in Spanish, because Papi identified with Fred's big flat feet, the same big flat feet that got him rejected from the military. So he pursued his other passion, operating heavy machinery, bulldozers and such, breaking ground and gravel just like Fred Flintstone, minus the slide down a dinosaur's back at the end of the workday.

So there I am, sitting at my desk designing a heart large enough to fit the elaborate handwriting I use when I write the names of my two crushes, Nemecio and Paloma, leaving myself out because I don't feel there's room for a cartoon character name like mine. How comic: Pedro Picapiedra and Nemecio, Pedro Picapiedra and Paloma. Nemecio and Paloma. Much neater.

The match is more dignified, like Maximiliano and Carlota, like Romeo and Juliet.

"Are you with us, Pedro?"

I must look startled because my classmates begin to laugh. And it seems unfair to be shaken out of a daydream only to wake up in a vulgar high school geometry class with poor old Ms. Kaneko standing over me, probably wondering if this time she should tell my mother, one of the English teachers at the school.

Ms. Kaneko, taking pity, walks back to the chalkboard and finishes her lesson while I slip back into the fantasy of fitting my two loves into a single heart.

As soon as the dismissal bell rings, I bolt from my seat before Ms. Kaneko has time to stop me. I hear her utter the two plain syllables of my name, but they're drowned out by the scuffle of bodies because this is the last class period of the day.

"Pedro!" I hear my name again, more clearly this time because it isn't old Ms. Kaneko saying it but Nemecio as he walks out of the remedial math class across the hall.

Not only can Nemecio stop me in my tracks, he can stop my breath. He's as elegant as his name, with curly dark hair and long thin feet inside long narrow shoes that remind me each time I see him that I have inherited my father's features—thin hair, big flat feet.

"Are you headed home?" he asks. He smiles at me and I want to knock my head against the lockers.

No, I shouldn't be headed home because I'm on the yearbook committee, and my task is to make sure everyone's names are spelled correctly. If this were a typical California high school with names like Tiffany Smith and Lewis Johnson, it wouldn't be too big of a deal. But we have names like Nemecio Villaseñor and Paloma Manríquez, names so proud of their tildes and accent marks that they have to be checked and double-checked before the yearbook goes to press.

"Yes, I'm headed home," I say, and in my head I calculate how late I will be after I rush back to the school as soon as Nemecio and I part ways.

"Cool," he says. He smiles, and I'm pleased that this pleases him.

As we walk side by side through the hall, I feel the jealous eyes on me and it makes me feel superior. Nemecio has chosen me again to be his companion from the front steps of the school to the corner of Third and Ralston. That's six city blocks of walking on air. He doesn't ask me every day, but at least once a week he lets me cling to him like a static-heavy sock on a shirt, hoping perhaps that my mother, looking out her classroom on the second floor, will see us together. Or that my father, getting out of work at that hour, might drive by and raise his eyebrows in approval. Or that I will somehow remember to mention Nemecio's name at dinner. *I walked home from school with Nemecio this afternoon. You know him, right? He wants that summer job at the construction company.* Or maybe, just maybe, he actually wants to spend time with me. Why should *that* not be a possibility?

If I could wave a wand I would grant Nemecio's wish and have him in my life past the school year and into the summer months so that Papi will utter his name in the house and it will be as if his breath spread the scent of Nemecio's cologne.

I take a long slow whiff and nearly faint from the manliness of it.

"Are you all right?" Nemecio asks.

I clear my throat. "Yes. Allergies."

"I get those, too, once in a while," he says.

I want to hug him for lying. But instead I hug my books, just like a schoolgirl. And I grin, suddenly wishing that there were more people to bump into during our short walk, or that more people would step out of their houses or look out their windows. I want more witnesses to my stroll in a state of bliss.

Nemecio stops and looks over at me and says, "You're in a good mood today."

I blush and shrug at the same time. "I am?" I say.

"Yes," he says. This time I smile.

"Care to share?" he asks, and he mirrors my smile. He has done this before, and that's where it usually ends. But today he goes one step further. He reaches over and flicks his finger gently on my chin.

Did he just touch me? I must be standing there too wide-eyed for words, so Nemecio decides to move on.

"Well, I'll see you on Saturday for Spanish tutoring," Nemecio says. "Say hello to your father for me."

"Okay," I say, a little too faintly. I watch him walk away until he turns the corner and I can no longer hold on to the sight of his snug pair of jeans. And then it's like a spell is broken because I have to hightail it back to my second love, Paloma.

"Where have you been, Pedro?" Paloma says. She's got her reading glasses on and a pen sticks out of her gorgeous brown hair, right where the ear is hidden.

"Small emergency," I say. "But I'm here now."

"Fine."

She picks up a clipboard with a list of names, a few rows crossed out already. When she hands it to me I catch the scent of her perfume. I suspect she dabs it on her wrist like my mother does when she and Papi go out to a wedding or to a social function put on by the construction company. The smell ropes me in each time Paloma comes near me.

When I start on my task, I realize there are five more people in the room, each one under Paloma's supervision. How easily I forget that anyone else exists when I'm around her. It's strange. When I'm with Nemecio I want everyone to notice. When I'm with Paloma I make everyone disappear.

"By the way, staff," Paloma announces. "We're our own team at the Senioritis Games."

The rest of the group groans. I'm excited because I'm only a junior but will be allowed to play since I am part of the yearbook committee.

"Now, now," she says, and I want to throw myself at her feet because she commands such authority and respect. "We have to model school spirit. We don't have to win or anything, but we all have to participate. Pedro, since you're the only one who didn't roll his eyes at my announcement, you can be my co-captain." She winks at me.

I blush. And something inside me wants to stand up and take a bow, but everyone's moved on, including Paloma, who adjusts her glasses as she looks down on the table to compare two photographs. I purse my lips and look down at my list of names. Andrea. Lorenzo. Sara. Luis. None of them as interesting to consider as Paloma. Or Nemecio.

Walking to the corner of Third and Ralston for the second time is lonely. It's not yet spring, so the afternoon temperature drops and I wish I had remembered a sweater or a hoodie. And without Nemecio by my side I feel slightly vulnerable. Once I walked with Paloma, who usually drives to class, but that one week it was in the shop she had to walk just like the rest of us who lived nearby.

"You walking my way?" she asked.

"Toward the mall?"

She nodded. "My ride's there. Linette, my sister. She works at the nail salon."

That was the most personal information I had ever gathered about her at one time, and I still hold on to it dearly.

"I can walk you all the way to the mall," I offered, feeling protective.

"You don't have to," she said. "But thank you. That would be nice."

Unlike the times I walked next to Nemecio, who was mostly smiles and very little chitchat, Paloma laughed and swung her head about as she talked about this and that, a disposition so different from the times she was acting as the head of the yearbook committee. But the real surprise came when we reached the parking lot of the mall.

"You are such a sweetheart, Pedro," she said. And then she leaned down to kiss me on the cheek.

I still carry that kiss, even when I'm walking next to Nemecio. At night, I place pillows on both sides of me and I fantasize that I'm sleeping between them and that when I toss in my sleep I sometimes throw my arm to my left, and then switch to the right, neglecting no one, comforting all.

At dinner, Papi and Mami make eyes at each other all evening, which means that they will be up in their room that night having sex. They used to call it "trying to make a baby," but since no other baby has been made since I was born sixteen years ago, they're now resigned to the fact that they do it because they like it. "But it's much more special because we're married," Mami explained to me once. And I rolled my eyes at her.

"I can take care of the cleanup tonight," I offer. And Mami giggles.

Papi gets up and tries to touch Mami's behind and she gets all shy and proper all of a sudden.

"Artemio, stop it!" she says, giggling some more as she swats his hand.

"Oh, for crying out loud," I say. "Would you two just go up to your room already!"

This time Papi laughs. "Don't worry, son. Your time will come."

The condescending tone annoys me. Thankfully, they have left me alone about it, but I know they still think I'm confused, that I haven't figured out if I am gay or straight, as if those were the only choices. Papi probably hopes that I'll turn out straight because I'm the only child and what a shame it would be if I didn't have a son to inflict our legacy of thin hair and big flat Flintstone feet. Mami probably hopes that I'll turn out gay because that will mean I will never leave her side the way Johnny Méndez never left his mami after her husband died. He cooks for her and wheels her out to the porch when the sun is shining and he tells her every chance he gets how beautiful she looks even though she's an old woman with very little hair and bad teeth.

What's in a choice, anyway, except loss? I don't want to lose either Nemecio or Paloma. Well, okay, they aren't really mine, but they bring something out in me that makes me feel I'm alive. Why would I want to let go of half of what gives me pleasure?

When the groaning and moaning noises start to get a little loud upstairs I walk over to the couch, reach for the remote control, and turn the television on. Artemio and Maribel. I'll let them have their dance on their side of the house as long as I can have mine.

The phone rings and I roll my eyes at that, blushing a little because it's not as if the phone will notice.

"Hello?" I say.

"Pedro, it's me," Adam says in his unmistakable high-pitched voice.

"What's up?"

"What you doing?" he says, his voice lilting.

"Watching TV." I quickly add, "But you can't come over because my parents are having sex."

"Oh, I hate that," he says, which sounds like a strange thing to say because he's been wanting to have sex with me since we were in junior high. We weren't friends then because the black kids and the Latino kids didn't really mix, but everything changed in high school because of sports and the dozens of clubs.

"You hate that my parents have sex?" I ask, just to toy with him.

He squeals. "No, dummy, I hate that I can't come over. I'm bored out of my mind."

Like me, Adam is an only child, and this is one of the many parallels in our stories.

"Maybe I can come over there," I say.

"Not tonight," he says. "My mother's church group is here organizing some picnic, and you know she doesn't let me bring anyone up to my room."

I shake my head. I wish I could tell Adam's mother that nothing's going on between us, but she probably wouldn't believe me. Her son is effeminate, therefore he messes around with boys. The truth is I'm not sure he's messed around with anyone. No one from around here anyway, and certainly not since we became friends a few years ago. He would have bragged about it.

"Hey," he says. "I saw you walking with Nemecio."

I grin. "Really? Isn't he hot?"

"Too hot for words," Adam says. "He's not gay, is he?"

There we go. Labels, labels, labels. But it's an argument we've had too many times before, so I let it go. "I don't know," I say simply and sigh.

"He's still yummy," he says. "You know who else is yummy?"

I half pay attention to Adam rattle on about this guy and that guy as I surf the television. One thing is swirling your impossible loves in your head, another is actually talking about them. It can get uninteresting fast.

"I'll tell you who else is yummy," I say.

"Who?" Adam says, perking up.

"Paloma," I say.

"Who?"

"Paloma, the head of the yearbook committee. She's cute, she's hot."

The pause that follows tells me Adam's making a face. Behind me, Artemio and Maribel walk by in their bathrobes.

"Who's on the phone?" Mami asks.

"Adam," I say.

"Hey, Adam!" Papi calls out.

"Your parents are done, I see," Adam says.

"Yes, but I still can't play. I want to crack open the Spanish textbook," I say.

"That's right, you're tutoring the hottie! Woof! Woof!"

I'm annoyed at how Adam refuses to acknowledge my sexuality, so I tell him I have to get off the phone.

"Maybe I'll come over tomorrow and get some tutoring myself," he says. "I want to master my lips in Spanish, if you know what I mean."

"Talk later, Adam," I say, and hang up.

"You're still tutoring that tall lanky kid who wants to work at the construction company?" Papi asks. He sits down on the recliner and opens up a bottle of beer.

"Yeah, are you going to hire him?" I ask.

"Don't know yet," my father says. "It depends on our budget. Besides, he's a bit on the scrawny side, isn't he?"

My mouth drops open. These are hardly the adjectives I've been using.

"Nemecio is a very healthy-looking young man," Mami offers from the kitchen. "And I'm glad he's getting the help he needs for school."

"He needs to pass a Spanish language class to graduate," I say.

"He doesn't know Spanish?" Papi says.

I sigh. "Nope."

"With a name like Nemecio?" Papi says. "Wow."

Mami comes over with a glass of wine in her hand. "Now, now, Artemio. Don't get all Mexican militant on the kid. Blame the parents for that one."

"A shame, that's all," Papi says, and he turns to the TV.

"Paloma says the same thing," I say.

"Paloma?" Papi says. "Pretty name."

"She's also the smartest young woman in the school," Mami adds. "Our valedictorian, in fact."

I beam with pride and try to hide it by changing the subject. "She says it bugs her when people don't know what her name means. She said one time a girl thought it meant *pigeon* instead of *dove*."

We all laugh at that and I know Paloma would have appreciated that in this household we all know how beautiful and special her name is.

"I like her," I say. It's an admission that breaks up the laughter. My father's the one who doesn't miss the opportunity to steer things his way. My mother squints, looking suspiciously at me.

"Really?" He puts his beer down. "Have you told her?"

But now I'm at a loss. Instead of answering the question, I look down at the remote control in my hands. I try to swallow, but there's something caught in my throat.

"I'm sure that Paloma knows that Pedro appreciates her very much." Mami reaches over to tousle my hair and I move away.

"That's not what I mean," I say. "I like her. As in, I think about her all the time and when she's near me my entire body goes warm."

Papi is about to smile, probably thrilled that he won some kind of wager with my mother, but I refuse to give him the satisfaction either. So I quickly add, "It's the same with Nemecio."

Papi's face grows serious. The three of us sit there unsure of what to say next. If anything, I seem to have confirmed that I'm still confused. But it's not confusion I feel, it's exhilaration. Since junior high they have been trying to get me to come out, either as gay or straight. They don't ask directly but through a series of leading questions to which I give noncommittal answers because I know what they are up to. I'm not stupid. And tonight I came out all right, as neither gay or straight.

"Well," Papi finally says. And I want him to say the right thing for once, like, "That's wonderful. Maybe you will find the love of your life, male or female." But instead he says, "You know you can't have two relationships at one time. It gets a little messy."

"Artemio," Mami says, throwing one hand up in the air.

"What?" he says, unaware of how dumb that comment sounded.

"I'm not looking for two relationships at once," I say. "That's not how it works."

"It?" Papi asks.

Yes, what do I mean by "it"? My desire? My body? My affection.

Mami puts down her wine and comes around the couch to

sit next to me. "I think I understand," she says, and she plants a kiss on my head.

Papi pipes up: "I'm not sure that *I* do."

I'm left speechless, but thankfully Mami steps in. "How it works is that love guides the path," she says.

"Exactly," I say, more confident suddenly. "It's about love, not about labels."

"And you can love a girl the same way you can love a boy?" Papi asks. I can hear the skepticism in his voice.

I scramble off the couch and declare proudly: "I can love. That's what matters."

"Love is good," Papi says, though it sounds more like a surrender than a moment of clarity.

I drop the remote control on his lap and head up to my room. As soon as I close the door I throw myself on the bed.

I suppose I shouldn't blame my parents for not understanding completely. Sometimes I don't quite understand it myself. I just know that it feels right. Being attracted to males *and* females feels right. If I were lying to myself about something, I would know it, wouldn't I?

❖

The next morning Mami is in her upstairs office grading papers and making lesson plans, and Papi is already gone to the construction site. He works on Saturdays, but only when he needs to and only until noon. I've got the whole kitchen and living room to myself and I appreciate that privacy for once after last night's moment of awkwardness. I eat some of the scrambled eggs Mami left on the stove, drink my OJ, and then wait at the table with the Spanish textbook in front of me until Nemecio finally knocks on the door.

"Adelante," I say, playing it cool. Looking at Nemecio always makes my heart flutter. I try not to breathe in too deeply.

"Gracias," he says, though he says it in three syllables and this lazy pronunciation lessens the impact of his arrival.

He takes his place at the table and we spend the next thirty minutes going over conjugations and the differences between masculine and feminine nouns and pronouns.

"I just wish it all came back to me during the test," he says with an exasperated sigh. "Shit, all I want to do is pass this class."

This is the most I've heard Nemecio confide in me.

"Don't worry," I say. "It'll be all right." I have the urge to reach over and put my hand on his back but I resist. Instead I add: "You just have to concentrate."

Nemecio blinks a few times as if he's shaking off the last flakes of self-doubt and then reaches for the textbook. *"Conocer,"* he says. *"Saber."*

To know. As in to know someone—recognition. And to know. As in to know something—knowledge. In English it's all one and the same. In Spanish, it's a little more complicated. I know I like him, I know I like her, and they seem to like me, but I'm not sure they know that I like both of them.

After about an hour, we take our usual break and I take out two sodas from the fridge. I always label the cream soda with a sticky note on it saying *DO NOT TOUCH* because I save it just for Nemecio. It's his favorite flavor. I make sure and remove the note before I hand him the soda.

"Thanks," he says. "Hey, you roll with that girl from the yearbook, what's her name? Paloma?"

"Yes," I say, beaming. Her name in his mouth sounds glorious.

"What's her deal, do you know if she's got a boyfriend?"

Suddenly my smile drops. One thing is matching them in the air, another is matching them so that they exclude me in real life.

"I don't know." I feel like a creep for not saying the truth. "She sometimes goes to meet someone at the mall." Okay, now I'm aiming for the Pinocchio nose.

"Well, if you find out anything," Nemecio says, "let me know."

He sits down again and lets out a tiny belch. I sit down across from him and I feel as if I can break out into hives now. The idea that Nemecio can become my rival frightens me.

"Hey, so are you planning to work at my father's construction company this summer?" I ask, hoping to reel him back into my corner.

"I would love to. Has he said anything about it?"

"He has," I say. "And I'll keep you posted. I'm sure he has you in mind." If I tell one more lie I swear I'll start losing my teeth.

"Cool," Nemecio says, cheering up. "That's way cool. Thanks for looking out, Pedro."

Nemecio reaches over and places his hand over mine and then winks. My throat goes dry so I take a long and acidic swig of soda and I start to choke.

"Are you all right?" he asks.

I pat my chest. "I'm fine," I say through a frog voice. "Just fine."

On Sunday Adam comes over after church. He goes to a Baptist service with his mom, who drops him off on her way home. She doesn't seem to mind that our family doesn't attend

Mass even though we call ourselves Catholic. When he knocks at the door Mami answers in her bathrobe and lets him in. He's seen her in her hair curlers so often she doesn't even hide it anymore. I'm in the living room writing down my birthday wish list even though it's not until July. But since I began asking for more expensive gifts, I have to let my parents budget early.

"Ooh, the birthday list," Adam says. He sits down next to me. "I'd ask for tickets to the Lady Gaga concert."

"Maybe," I say.

"Do you want something to eat, Adam?" Mami asks. "We've got plenty of chorizo and eggs left."

"I'll take a breakfast burrito, Mrs. P." Adam says, and then adds: "And a glass of milk, please."

"Okay, porky," I say.

"What? I have to keep my strength up. You know the Senioritis Games are just around the corner."

"And you're a junior, just like me," I say.

Adam swivels his neck. "And just like you I get to be an exception because I'm part of the journalism club. Don't even try it, missy!" He gives me the hand.

Mami chuckles from the kitchen.

"Excuse me," I say. "Well, it should be fun."

Mami comes over with Adam's breakfast when I write the word *car* on my list. "In your dreams," she says and it's Adam's turn to chuckle.

"Thanks for the love, everybody," I say. "Anyway, if I can't get a car, then an iPad will do."

"Right," Mami says. "Let's try to aim for the reasonable, Pedro, your father's been having some problems at work. He won't even be able to afford any extra help over the summer."

"Are you serious?" I say. "I thought he said he didn't know about that yet."

"He knows now. It's terrible. He's going to have to work longer hours."

"And what about Nemecio?" I say.

Mami looks at me, puzzled. "What about him?"

"Where's he going to work?"

Mami shrugs. "I don't know, I wasn't aware he was promised a job at the construction company. Did your father tell him?"

Adam pipes up. "No," he says. "But Pedro did."

"Shut up, Adam!"

"Hey," Mami says. "A little more respect for your friends."

"Sorry, Adam," I say.

Adam bites into his burrito, Mami takes a sip of her coffee, and I'm squatting in front of the coffee table watching the list blur in front of me. I don't care a fig about the car or the iPad. What I want is to make Nemecio as happy as Paloma makes me.

At the yearbook committee meeting we leaf through the mock-up and congratulate each other on making the deadline. Now the yearbook will definitely be available by the Senioritis Games. At the mention of the games, another group groan bursts out.

"Oh, come on, guys," Paloma says. She's wearing a white sweater that indeed makes her look like a dove. "Let's not confirm for the whole school the stereotype that the yearbook committee is nothing but a bunch of wimpy nerds."

"I'm fine with it," Franklin says. He's an overweight kid with glasses.

"Well, I'm not. When I look out I see a very intelligent group of people who can also be capable of undertaking an athletic challenge or two," Paloma says with conviction. It's inspiring, the way she rallies us. "Besides, some of the games don't require physical agility, they require a good eye and a good mind—and that's us. We're the yearbook committee!"

"Yeah!" I blurt out. Franklin rolls his eyes at me.

"That's team spirit." Paloma walks over to me and wraps her arm around me. I know I'm turning red.

In my room. In the dark. In my world of fantasy. I can be with whoever I want. I make believe my bed is a raft floating in the open sea. We are all limbs and fingers and mouths twisting and turning in the cradle. We are glowing beneath the bright sun and our skins, once different shades of beige and brown, burn into each other because there is a single gold fleece connecting us from one extremity to the other. There is no starting point, no ending point, just a single mass of unrestrained bliss.

Before we know it, the yearbook arrives. Before we know it, it's time for the Senioritis Games. Before we know it, it will be the end of school and graduation and Nemecio and Paloma will fly off to their respective futures, leaving me all alone. This last dose of reality makes me anxious, so I focus instead on today and the thrill of leafing through the fruits of our labor. The sizable yearbook order allowed us to go hardcover this year, and the glossy senior portraits are the best gift we could give to the graduates. I immediately turn toward the M's and the V's to locate the beautiful face of my beloved Paloma and the handsome face of my darling Nemecio, both posing full of color and toothy smiles that make me melt into the chair.

❖

We haul the boxes to the Senioritis Games on the football field, adding to the excitement that's already bubbling inside the high school students. The distribution takes only minutes since everyone's hands are hot for the book, and just as quickly come the requests to memorialize the books with impromptu messages, love notes, and shout-outs.

I resolve that the only people I will ask to sign my yearbook are Nemecio and Paloma, but then I add Adam and Mrs. Kaneko and even Franklin, and soon I toss that silly resolution out the window and even ask the foreign exchange student from Amsterdam to sign my book though I had never really talked to her before today. It's easy to get caught up in the moment.

The flurry of yearbook exchanges is disrupted by the announcement of the games. The first is an all-student hobble across the field with the yearbook balanced on top of our heads. Nobody makes it but everyone has fun trying to catch the book before it drops to the ground. Adam comes in second on the musical chairs and Nemecio wins the potato sack race. And when we start the team competitions, there's no shame for the yearbook committee since we place well in the water balloon toss. For once no one gets hurt, no one is shamed, and I'm all but ready to declare this the best day of high school as I stand there next to Paloma until the next game is announced: the mint relay.

Here is how it works: students line up boy-girl-boy-girl, everyone biting into a toothpick. A mint shaped like a lifesaver is placed on one toothpick and that person has to pass it on to the next, toothpick to toothpick until it reaches the end of the chain. No touching allowed, though the faces come uncomfortably close to each other, and bodies need to twist and turn in order to make a successful mint transfer. Oh, boy.

I freeze next to Paloma. Near mouth-to-mouth contact with the love of my life? Where's the big California earthquake when I need it? Someone give me a fire drill at least. But no, the box of toothpicks gets passed around. I'm psychically preparing myself for the intimacy, trying to figure out if I should close my eyes or keep them open. I suppose the eyes have to stay open, otherwise how do I catch the itty-bitty candy hole on this itty-bitty stick? Jeez, the game is naughtier than I thought.

"We have to have even numbers for this one," the game monitor shouts out. "We need another body. Any group have a spare?"

"I'm a spare," Nemecio says, walking over from his group. He positions himself next to Paloma.

Okay, this was an unexpected plot twist. Now Paloma stands between me and Nemecio. The symbolism isn't lost on me, but I'm also sure this isn't right. And the stars probably felt the same way because here comes the clincher: the order will be determined alphabetically by last name. Manríquez, Pérez, Villaseñor. Everyone else in the yearbook committee, it turns out, comes before all three of us. I move to reflect the new order. I stand there between Paloma and Nemecio. Now I can die.

I have no idea what the game monitors were thinking, but this new challenge in which girls are standing next to girls and boys next to boys and sometimes three girls stand in a row and sometimes three boys—even four—adds another level of bravado. But we've come this far, there's no turning back, and the winner of this challenge takes it all. Who's game? We all are, apparently.

Since Paloma, Nemecio, and I are at the end of the chain, there's plenty of time for the butterflies in my stomach to age into pterodactyls. Paloma doesn't seem to mind but I can sense Nemecio's anxiety. Paloma has kissed me on the cheek; Nemecio has only touched my hand. This should be interesting.

The cheering, the laughing, the pointing, the poking fun is at an all-time high as each pair of bodies does its contortionist dance. I watch Adam betray his mortification because he's stuck between two girls, but he pulls through, receiving the mint and then passing it along, toothpick to toothpick. I can imagine we will have to perform some type of exorcism at home because he has never been this close to a girl, let alone two.

Franklin gets to pass the mint to Paloma and he sweats it out as well, swiveling his neck over her as she tries to secure the transfer by bending her knees and arching her back. I want to giggle at that except that it means I'm the next recipient of the mint. I turn to Nemecio, who looks like he's having the same thought. I mean, one thing is exchanging flirty touches in private, another is contact in public. But then his body relaxes and he smiles at me. He shrugs it off. "Hey," he says. "It's all in fun."

Time stands still. And that's when it hits me—the one-sidedness of the situation. The way I see things is not the way either Paloma or Nemecio do. And I'm not just talking about the fact that I'm attracted to both males and females but that *this* male and *this* female don't know I'm attracted to them, even if one or both or neither is attracted to me. I know who I am and I know now that if it were real, the affection between me and either one of them would be mutual and unmistakable. Suddenly I feel liberated and devastated all at once. Silly me, I was stressing out over choices that were not there to be made, not yet anyway and certainly not with either Nemecio or Paloma. In a few months, they'll be gone along with all the fantasies I built around us. Lucky me, now I can seek my true soul mate, whoever he or she is, because being who I am means having no fear to express my love to that one special person.

Paloma turns to me with the toothpick in her mouth, the mint glowing at the end. She leans forward and cranes her neck.

How incredibly small this accidental thing that will pass among the three of us, and how incredibly large the possibility that the next time I bring my mouth close to another mouth it will be an undisguised deliberate kiss.

Sam Cameron is the author of the forthcoming novel *Mystery of the Tempest*, about a gay teen detective and his twin brother in the Florida Keys. After several years of military service, home is now a houseboat in Florida with two sun-loving cats.

My cousin attends a very prestigious preparatory school where a recent flap evolved over two lesbian students who wanted to attend a Sadie Hawkins dance. I met one of the girls during a trip to campus and she confided that she felt out of place at the school not just because of her orientation, but because of the divide between day students who commuted in and the students who boarded all year long. I'm happy to say that the girls did attend the dance and had a great time. This story features a couple just as much in love as my cousin's friends.

DAY STUDENT
SAM CAMERON

Being a day student means you can visit the common areas of the dorms, but you need an escort to go upstairs where all the fun stuff happens. It means you miss out on a lot of activities, like Sunday Football and Pumpkin Carving Day, because you have to stay home to watch your little brothers and you need to save the train fare anyway. It means you can hear residents laughing through the open windows as you trudge by Goodwin House with a fifty-pound book bag on your back, but you don't get to stop.

Being a day student means you hang out in the cemetery behind Goodwin House a lot, longing for what you don't have.

"People are going to start thinking you're a necrophiliac," says my boyfriend, Charlie, as he sits against an old tombstone and does his algebra homework. "Little do they know you're a dormaphile."

"That's not even a word," is my response. I'm busy watching the second-floor windows with my handy pocket binoculars. One of the seniors is sitting at his desk, golden head bent over his laptop. A few windows over, a freshman is ironing his white Oxford shirt. I wonder what it's like in there when lights go out. Boys in silk pajamas, boys in tiny underwear, boys naked in the communal shower—

Charlie makes a thoughtful noise. "Dormitorium, dormitorius, dormire…"

I drop the binoculars. Charlie's incredibly cute when he starts practicing Latin. So cute that I want to tackle him and kiss all the freckles on his nose. We could make out right here, in the dead brown leaves of autumn, on top of the grave of H. P. Lawrence, 1840–1899. The big stone wall means no one would see us, and it's not really that cold out—

"No, no, no," Charlie says, alarmed.

"I didn't say anything."

"I know that look. You want to get into my pants."

We're in our Endicott Preparatory Academy uniforms—blue wool trousers, matching jackets, white shirts with red and blue striped ties. The ties came off the minute we left campus. Charlie's also wearing a sleeveless sweater vest and a blue overcoat. He gets cold easily, but I consider it my sacred academic duty to warm him up whenever possible.

I drop down to the ground and crawl his way with lechery in my heart. "No one would see us."

He lets me get practically on top of him before he pushes me off, laughing. "No! I have to get home."

For him, it's a thirty-minute train ride. For me, it's forty-eight minutes on a good day. There are fifteen day students in the sophomore class, but most come from the town of Endicott out here in the leafy suburbs of Boston. Charlie and I have the longest commutes. It's a good time to do homework, Charlie says. I think it's a good time to doze on his shoulder, lulled to sleep by the train wheels and floating on the smell of Irish Spring soap on his skin.

Things would be so much easier if we lived in Goodwin, the oldest of the nine dormitories and the one with the smartest, cutest boys in it. We'd have more time to socialize and do school activities and just, you know, hang out in front of the big-screen

TV under the oil painting of Admiral Howard Goodwin. Both of us are on scholarship, however. The rich reaching out a generous hand to the poor, but not so generous that we get residential costs covered, too.

It's not like I could move from home, anyway. Ever since Dad ran off to California with some old girlfriend, it's been just my mom and me and my little brothers, the six of us in a small rented duplex. Mom knows I'd rather live on campus. She also knows it's not really about the guys. Endicott Prep is a stepping stone to the Ivy League. Academics are important, but you also need connections. Connections that come from living with the sons of millionaires, not just sharing classes with them. Endicott is all about rich vs. not so rich, residential vs. day student. No day students have ever gotten admitted to Harvard.

I want Harvard just as much as I want Charlie.

And okay, yes. The boys in Goodwin are amazingly cute as well as rich.

Charlie climbs to his feet, brushes dead leaves from the back of his legs, and gives me a hand up. We're just about the same height and size, but he's the kind of handsome that makes you catch your breath. If there are any handsome genes in my family, they got left back in Ireland during the potato famine. Charlie says looks don't matter. We met the first week of freshman year at a Rainbow Club meeting, and we've been inseparable ever since.

Which is why it's a bombshell when, several weeks later, Charlie announces that he's got bad news for me.

❖

"Breakup kind of bad news?" I ask, my mouth suddenly pasty and dry. "You-want-to-see-other-people kind of bad news?"

Even though it's the middle of winter break and freezing cold outside, we're walking along Revere Beach. Summer, winter, spring, and fall, Charlie likes beaches. Revere Beach is a huge long curve of sand that was the first public beach in America. You can walk from the train station past big condo towers all the way to Kelly's Seafood to buy big plates of fried clams. Right now the sun is bright and the tide is low, seagulls screeching loudly whenever anyone throws them food.

"Don't be an idiot," Charlie says. His breath frosts in the air. "Why would I break up with you?"

I relax a tiny bit. "Well, yeah. There's no good reason on earth to do that. So what's your bad news?"

He digs his hands deeper into the pockets of his blue North Face parka, which looks like a mammoth sleeping bag. "It's about school."

"You're transferring, aren't you?" I stop him with both hands. "You're leaving. How can you do this to me?"

He shuts me up with a kiss. Charlie knows that's one of the quickest ways to distract me. But it's not effective now, even if his lips taste like the hot chocolate we had on the train.

"I'm not leaving," he says when we break apart. "My dad got a big raise and he can afford the dorm fees now. I'm moving into Goodwin."

That's when I take two steps backward, trip over a piece of driftwood, and break my left ankle.

❖

As it turns out, wearing a big bulky plaster cast on your leg means you have a handy excuse for not moving your boyfriend into the dorm of your dreams. It's not like I can carry anything up the stairs, after all. Charlie's dad drives him over on the Sunday before the term starts while I sit at home and yell at my brothers to stop fighting over the last chocolate-fudge Pop-Tart.

Charlie sends me text messages like *room is small* and *roommate is paul stanley* and *how come ur not answering?*

As graciously as possible I text him back, *brats r keeping me busy.* The brats have names—John, Joe, Jeremy, and Seth. I call them the Demon Spawn, except when Mom's around. I got the gay gene and they got the "make as much noise and mess as possible" genes. Though, to be fair, Seth is only five years old. He might turn out okay.

When Charlie calls later that night he says nothing about how fabulous his day has been and instead concentrates on me. How's my ankle? How am I going to get to walk on crutches with all the snow that fell yesterday? He says he will meet me at the train station and help me carry my book bag.

"I don't need help," I tell him.

"Don't be silly. It's almost a half mile to campus."

Mom isn't home yet, and the Spawn are fighting in the living room over who gets to watch their favorite show on TV. I can hear thumping through the walls of my bedroom, but I'm not moving off my bed. "No problem. I don't have a lot of books."

"Since when?"

"Mom called the school. They're going to let me keep one set here and use another set in the classroom."

Charlie sounds doubtful. "I should meet you anyway."

"Don't you dare," I tell him. In the living room, the thumps have gotten louder. If the Spawn put more dents into the wall, the landlord's going to have a fit. "Sleep in, have breakfast, I'll see you in history class."

He's quiet for a long moment. "I think you're trying to punish me."

I hear breaking glass and shrieks of annoyance. "Don't be

silly," I say. Then I hang up and go see if anyone has severed an artery or cut off an important body part.

❖

The next morning is all about me drowning in sweat. Hobbling to the train station on crutches isn't so bad, but maneuvering up and down the platform stairs really sucks, and the heat blasting out of the train vents makes the whole place like a mobile sauna. I nearly die of heatstroke. At Endicott Station there's another set of stairs to go down, and the sidewalk isn't shoveled very well. Maybe I'll slip and fall and then I can sue someone. The crutches dig into my upper arms because I keep using them wrong— you're supposed to support your weight with your hands, not your shoulders, but I'm clumsy either way. I take the shortcut behind the field house to avoid the dorms but that just means I get to history ten minutes late, after everyone else has already taken a seat. Twenty boys with fresh faces and clean uniforms look up when I lurch in with my red face and sweat-stained blazer.

"Mr. O'Malley!" says our teacher, alarmed. "Are you all right?"

I collapse into the only open seat and ignore Charlie's worried look. "Never been better."

After class Charlie pins me in a private corner, kisses me silly, and says, "You're an idiot, Matthew." By the end of the day he's arranged for one of his new housemates to drive me to the station. Only seniors can have cars, but I'm still surprised to see that my chauffeur is Tom Porter.

"It's not a problem," he says, popping open the front passenger door for me. "I usually go downtown after school every day for coffee."

Tom drives a Lexus, how's that? Five-speed, keyless ignition, heated leather seats. He's also the captain of the Endicott lacrosse team and has a perfect GPA. And, oh yeah, he looks like someone who just strolled out of an Abercrombie and Fitch ad—square jaw, slick hair, devastatingly handsome.

Luckily Charlie's in the backseat, a silent reminder that I don't really want to throw myself on Tom and make an idiot of myself.

"So you two are a thing, huh?" Tom asks as we pass under the campus's iron archway.

Charlie tenses a little. I say, "Yes. That's a problem?"

"Nah," Tom says. "Nobody cares. But here's the thing. Every year one of the residence halls has to host the Valentine's Day dance. This year it's our turn, but nobody wants to take charge. But now we've got a gay guy. So you're good at parties and decorating, right?"

"That's a stereotype," I say sternly.

But Charlie says, "Absolutely! I'd love to."

Traitor.

Tom grins a little. "Yeah, I know it's a stereotype. But we're desperate."

Charlie says, "I'm on it."

It takes three minutes of automobile comfort to get to the train station. Once we get there I go for the casual "thanks" and try not to trip over my crutches into a snowbank. To my surprise, Charlie gets out of the car as well.

"Where are you going?" I ask.

"I have homework to do," he says cheerfully.

"You don't have to take me home. You've got a party to plan now, after all."

He says, "Shut up. You'd volunteer, too, if you were the new guy."

I can't really argue with that.

❖

For the next two weeks, Charlie rides home with me and we do homework and other things in my bedroom, the door locked in case the Spawn try to break in. That's very nice. The downside is that he doesn't get back to campus until late and he's missing out on the group dinners. He says I'm more important. Meanwhile, he cajoles his housemates into picking me up in the morning at the train station and taking us back there in the afternoon—if not Tom Porter, then Steven Slater, son of the famous senator, who drives a Ferrari. Sometimes one of the other seniors. Sometimes even Mrs. Winthrop, who is the Goodwin dorm mother. She has a beat-up old Hyundai with broken heating, but she always brings fresh doughnuts to share.

The trouble with Charlie's housemates is that I like all of them, and I'm ridiculously jealous that Charlie's living there, and every day I get a little more resentful. Which is awful of me. Mom works double shifts at the hospital without complaining, and I'm whining because I don't get to live at my fancy-shmancy prep school? Time to get a grip on reality.

Charlie says, "Come see my room" and "Let's stop for some of Mrs. Winthrop's hot chocolate," but I always find a way to avoid going to Goodwin. If I don't visit, I can ignore the fact Charlie lives there and I don't. Silly, right?

It doesn't help at all that Valentine's Day is coming up fast. I don't have much spare money to buy Charlie a gift, and I don't know what to get him—a nice pen, a framed picture of us, dinner at some restaurant? None of those sound right. Meanwhile, he has to start staying on campus to work on the party arrangements. I ride the train home alone and do my homework alone and babysit the Spawn all by myself, and not even constant text messages can keep me from brooding about all the fun Charlie's having on campus.

❖

Things get absolutely worse the day that Farrin Harrell drops by the basement office of *The Endicott Gazette,* our official biweekly newspaper. It's study period and I'm trying to write a scintillating article about proposed changes in the library check-out system. I'm not a natural journalist. It's just something for my résumé. Farrin is a drop-dead-gorgeous blonde who also happens to be Tom Porter's girlfriend. She writes a column called "Fashion and U" for *The Endicott Chimera,* our rival publication.

"Matthew O'Malley," she says, propping her size-0 butt against my desk. "Why haven't you ever let me sign your cast?"

I'm sort of flummoxed. Number one, she never asked. Number two, why would I want her signature? It's not like we're friends. She's famous only in her own mind and in the halls of her dorm, Milford House.

"Do you want to sign it?" I ask.

She grabs a marker from the desk. "I'm very artistic."

So I prop my foot up and she starts writing something. Her glossy long hair shields her work. She smells like some ritzy perfume that might be popular but to me just smells cloying. She says, "Tom says that Charlie's doing great work for the party. It's going to be the best dance in years. Are you two coming as a couple?"

"Absolutely," I say, although we haven't really talked about it. I just assumed. My cast should be off by then, and even if it isn't, I can still dress up and hobble around.

"You'll be our first same-sex couple," she says. "You'll be so cute."

I can't tell if she's being serious or mocking. "We specialize in cute."

"Just remember, when it comes to Valentine Queen, that doesn't mean one of you gay people," Farrin says casually. She keeps drawing. "Tom and I are hoping to win. It's the first step in the trifecta: Valentine's Day, President's Ball, Senior Promenade. Three crowns. Silly, right? But it's like when you get married at Cinderella Castle at Disney World. Just for fun, but romantic, too."

I'm appalled, really, that she's threatened by the idea that Charlie and I could win some contest just because of our novelty factor. And that she said "one of you gay people."

"I'm all for romance," I say, unable to think up anything witty or wise or caustic.

She lifts her head and smiles. "Okay. Just so we understand. I mean, technically, the King and Queen can only be boy-girl anyway, but it's better to ward off trouble before it happens. See you at the dance."

When she's gone, I see that she's drawn a big pink heart on my cast, her name elaborately sketched inside it, and below it the words Triple Crown.

It takes me ten minutes to paint over it with Wite-Out, but it's worth the noxious fumes and every stroke of the tiny brush.

It takes me another half hour to write an article called "Homophobia at the Goodwin Valentine's Day Dance? How homosexual couples are made to feel unwelcome."

❖

Understand this: I don't finish the article. Halfway through, I decide that it's stupid and groundless and that I let Farrin annoy me needlessly. Let her have her Triple Crown, which sounds like the emptiest goal ever. I delete the file, go to my afternoon classes, gratefully accept a ride to the train station from one of Charlie's housemates, and spend the whole evening studying for my algebra test. I've got the highest grade in class and I want to keep it.

Charlie texts me at eleven thirty at night. *Did u write article says Goodwin homophobic?*

I can't call him. He'll get a demerit if the resident assistants hear him on the phone during quiet hours. Quickly I type back, *no no no deleted stupid rant why?*

He responds back with *paul found it on computer.*

His roommate, Paul the Snoop, writes the *Gazette*'s sports column. Apparently he has a habit of going through the trash folders on the shared computer. He found my draft, printed it out, brought it back to Goodwin, and showed it around. Now Tom Porter is mad at me, which means he's mad at Charlie in an auxiliary fashion, which means Charlie's mad at me, too.

This is so not good.

I want to take the train back to school, find Paul, and beat the snot out of him. But the trains don't run this late and I can't leave the Spawn alone, anyway. Charlie sends his last text at midnight and after that falls silent. I don't sleep much.

Nobody meets me at the train station the next morning, which isn't much of a surprise. It's a good thing that most of the snow's melted and my arms have gotten pretty strong. Halfway to the campus I see Charlie walking my way, looking as tired as I feel.

"I wasn't going to come meet you," he announces, "but then I thought we'd find your frozen corpse face-down in a pile of snow and I'd be haunted by guilt forever."

"Thank goodness for guilt," I say. "It was just some stupid paragraphs and no one was supposed to see them."

He shakes his head. "Talk while you walk. Otherwise we'll be late for the algebra test."

So I tell him about Farrin's visit, and the Triple Crown silliness, and the big pink heart on my cast. By the time we get to campus Charlie's giggling at the thought of us being King and Queen, or King and King, or Queen and Queen, of the Valentine's Dance.

"It's not so far fetched!" I protest. "We're a cute couple."

"Yes, but I don't think they make a crown big enough for your big dumb head," he says.

So Charlie forgives me, but that doesn't mean either of us are in good graces with Tom Porter and his friends. Apparently they take it seriously when someone accuses them of baseless homophobia. But it wasn't something they were ever supposed to see. It was just dumb ranting, and I deleted it. It's not my fault Paul went spying. That's probably a violation of the honor code.

"Still," Charlie says, after algebra is over and we're on our way to politics. The oak-and-mahogany corridor is full of noise as students pass between classes. "You have to apologize."

This is not what I want to hear. "But what if it's true?" I ask him. "Farrin said that by the rules, only a boy and girl can be King and Queen."

"There's no rules," Charlie says, exasperated. "It's just a dumb social event. Anyone who attends gets to vote on the King and Queen."

"Has this school ever crowned a gay couple for anything?" I ask.

You can see where this is going, right? The Irish are a stubborn people. They had to survive English occupation and rotten potatoes and prejudice in the New World. The more I think about it, the more I wonder if my original idea was right. Maybe Goodwin House is just following the footsteps of Endicott Academy as a whole.

Charlie steers me toward a padded bench and makes me sit

down. "Listen to me. There are hundreds of high schools here in Massachusetts, and maybe a handful of them have ever had a gay couple as homecoming King or Queen, or whatever. Systemic prejudice sucks, but this isn't about that. This is about how you never want to apologize for anything, but you need to apologize for this."

"Fine," I say tightly. "I'm sorry."

He rolls his eyes. "Not to me."

"I'll apologize to Tom Porter," I grind out. "Happy?"

Charlie pats my knee. "You have to apologize to the whole house."

"What? No!" Because that really is going too far, and Charlie knows it. Why should I apologize to a bunch of rich kids who probably are homophobic anyway? Everyone knows they don't tell you what they really think. They're too polite for that. Too well bred. Tom wanted Charlie to arrange the dance because he really does think that all gay boys are good at arranging flowers and hanging disco balls and designing pink and gold invitations.

From outside, the first of the nine a.m. bells start to ring. The hallway crowd immediately thins out as everyone races to be in their seats by the last bell. I don't move, and neither does Charlie.

In his most patient voice, Charlie says, "You know you have to."

"I don't have to do anything," I protest. Classic Irish stubbornness.

"Fine." He stands up. "Don't call me until you regain your sanity."

And that's how we break up.

❖

For three days I cling to my pride. Then it's Friday night, and Mom's working late again, and the Spawn won't stop fighting. John stole Joe's candy. Joe stole John's soda. Jeremy hit Joe in the arm. John hit Jeremy on the head. Seth is hungry and wants cereal, but we're out of milk and Mom didn't leave any money for me to send John to the corner store. Meanwhile, at Goodwin House they're probably toasting their own wealth with hot apple toddies and chatting about their fantastic future lives as the titans of America and—when did I turn into such a jerk?

By the time Mom comes home I'm slumped on the sofa, a pillow over my head. The Spawn are either exhausted themselves and asleep or have escaped out their bedroom window. I don't care either way.

She leans over me and nudges the pillow aside. "How's my oldest son?"

"I'm very stupid," I tell her.

"I doubt that." She smells like antiseptic and her uniform has unidentifiable stains on it, but she's still lovely. "What did you do to Charlie?"

"It's what I didn't do. And it's not just Charlie."

"What didn't you do?"

"Apologize."

Mom hides a yawn behind her hand. "So apologize. Charlie's a sweetheart. I'm sure he'll forgive you. Now I'm going to bed, and I suggest you do the same. You're so much more handsome when you don't have tea bags hanging under your eyes."

"I'm not handsome," I tell her, because we both know it's true. I don't have looks and I don't have money. What do I have? Stubbornness and a broken relationship with my best friend in the world.

She tilts her head and studies my face. "You're handsome to me, oldest son."

That's why I love my mother.

After she goes to bed I text Charlie: *okay yur right and I'm stupid.*

Ten minutes later he sends back: *Come to brunch on Sunday.*

❖

Goodwin House is an old brick mansion, two stories high with dormers and chimneys, and the front yard is covered with snow. The green hedges are carefully trimmed and the fir trees are dusted in white. It's the perfect cover for a Christmas card. The entry hall has an impeccably waxed hardwood floor, brass hooks for coats, and a solid oak bench for boots. Nobody is sitting at the small desk where guests normally sign in. The house smells like cinnamon and honey, and it's blessedly warm after the frigid air outside.

It's also a madhouse. Running footsteps thump from up above as if someone let loose a herd of elephants. Doors slam, re-open, slam again. Three different songs are playing from speakers. Thirty boys live here, ranging from eighth grade to twelfth grade, and the ones in the common room are sprawled out in jeans, sweatshirts, and T-shirts.

Like a total dork, I wore my uniform today. I thought brunch was a formal affair.

"Oh, Matthew!" That's Mrs. Winthrop, an apron tied over her sweater and skirt. She takes my coat and hangs it up. "Did you walk? I would have picked you up."

"It's okay. My mom drove me down."

"Come on back. We're in the mews."

The mews is the old carriage house attached to the house. It's got white wainscoting and wide plank floors and a dining-room table that seats twenty people. The upperclassman of the house are already sitting down, drinking their coffee or orange juice. To my relief, they're wearing their uniforms. Charlie sees me and his face lights up, but he doesn't rise from his chair.

Mrs. Winthrop says, cheerfully, "Pancakes will be arriving in ten minutes. Make your peace by then."

Tom Porter is sitting at the head of the table. He doesn't look especially happy that I've come, but he says, "O'Malley. You wanted to say something?"

I have a speech prepared. It's on index cards. I practiced it in front of Mom on the way down, and she liked it. But I'm suddenly nervous, and my hand shakes a little, and the letters get blurry.

"I wanted to apologize," I say, ignoring the cards and trying to look at all of them at once. Porter and Slater and Paul the Snoop and Charlie and everyone else. No one seems especially encouraging, but I keep going anyway. "I mean, I do apologize. I wrote something that was stupid and not based in fact. I knew it was dumb, and I tried to get rid of it. Sometimes you think something's gone but it's not. I shouldn't have done it."

And that's it. Because I really can't repeat what Farrin said. That would just annoy her boyfriend. And I can't blame Paul the Snoop, because this isn't about him.

"Nothing else?" Tom asks, staring straight into me.

I hesitate. "Well, I'd like to say I'd look fabulous in a tiara, but that's not true."

Steven Slater laughs. "You're such a dickhead, O'Malley."

Tom doesn't smile, but he does relax. "Sit down and shut up."

Charlie pulls out the empty chair beside him, Mrs. Winthrop delivers a huge tray of blueberry pancakes, and that's it. Apology accepted.

❖

Except, okay, the systemic prejudice thing really bothers me. If you go online and search for how many schools have voted in a gay couple for prom or other honors, you'll see it's not a lot. As in, less than the fingers on my right hand. Some schools have even explicitly banned gay couples from being nominated, citing "tradition."

So much for social progress.

"It's going to come," Charlie promises me as we dance cheek to cheek at Goodwin's Valentine dance. The common room has been cleared out of furniture, the lights are down low, and Charlie's decorations are gorgeous. The party is a raging success. The music is slow enough to keep my newly healed-up ankle from protesting. Charlie continues, "Maybe when we're seniors we'll win."

"You're the optimist in this relationship," I tell him.

"You're a secret optimist and you know it."

Sure, okay. If he says so. Maybe one day Goodwin will crown two boys and no one will bat an eye. Meanwhile, in my not-so-humble opinion, Charlie is the handsomest guy in the whole room. We both rented black tuxedos, which wasn't cheap but is definitely worth it. I feel awkward in mine, but he's like a movie star, all grace and charm.

"I've got a gift for you," he says, his breath hot against my ear. "Let me show you."

We sneak off to a closet under the back stairs that Charlie found a few weeks ago. "Mine first," I whisper. There, in the dim light with the music nearby, I give him a tiny gold locket with our pictures inside. It's not much, but he grins like I gave him a diamond. Then he unfastens his pants and slides the black fabric just past his right hip.

There's a tattoo there. Our initials, small but clear. It's all healed up, which means he must have done it a while ago.

"You're too young to get a tattoo!" I complain. Meanwhile

I'm amazed. He thinks that much of us that he's stenciled us on his body forever. Little black letters with small swirls, the most romantic thing I've ever seen.

He climbs into my lap. "Shut up and kiss me."

Being a day student means you don't get all the advantages of living on campus, but you don't have to share the bathrooms with dozens of other kids, either. It means you get to go to Sunday brunches and Wednesday night study sessions and then go home to help your mom out with your rotten little brothers. It means that you can make out with your boyfriend on Valentine's Day and realize that the most important connections are the ones you make one-on-one, heart to heart.

All I want is Charlie. And right now, right here, under the stairs, with music in the air and our mouths tight together, I've got him. We've got each other.

DANIELLE PIGNATARO was on bowling teams for many years but never came in first place. She has an MFA in Writing for Children and Young Adults from the Vermont College of Fine Arts and an MST from Pace University. She lives in Brooklyn, New York, where she writes and teaches seventh graders English language arts and American history.

Her favorite moment of queer pride recently was when a former student, who is transitioning MTF, wrote to her and said, "u begin to feel powerful and strong, to be who u always wanted to be." Kudos to Simone Tamara Roselmond, a confident, beautiful, amazing young person.

GUTTER BALL
DANIELLE PIGNATARO

Believe me when I tell you this: Everybody saw it happen. Well, okay, not everybody. But everybody who was there that day. Which wasn't really many, I guess, since not many people hang out at Maple Lanes during the Friday afternoon high school league time. But whoever was there, whoever stuck around right afterwards when I was packing up my ball and shoes and wrist brace—those people, they saw.

Just when I had placed my marbleized pink, personalized bowling ball, which I got in fourth grade, into my bowling bag, Donna D'Amico—queen of crunchy hair and manicured nails—pushed into me from behind and said, "Fucking dyke. Just wait."

And she didn't just say it, she said it loud. So loud, in fact, that I swear for one long moment there wasn't a sound to be heard in all of the bowling alley. Pins ceased to crash, ball returns failed to swish, and not one person dared cheer or jeer for a teammate. And I knew, right then, that it was on.

I don't usually tell stories. I'm more the "keep to myself" type of girl. But this is a story about struggle and hope and just keeping your big mouth shut. A story everyone can learn from. Sort of.

I mean, what the hell? Donna generally left me alone. We

went to the same school, but we weren't friends. She didn't usually participate in any of the "Gay Bash Angela" antics at Our Lady of Promise Catholic High School, but she wasn't particularly nice to me. On that day, the day she decided to start with me, our team—me, Abby, Colleen, and Jesse—had just kicked her lame team's collective ass by an insane number of pins for the second time that season.

Apparently we were the only team they couldn't beat, which meant one thing: "Just wait" meant "Just wait for the championship," which was the following week. Our team, Mind in the Gutter (awesome name), and her team, the Banana Splits (double lame-o name), were going head-to-head for the Teen League Championship Trophy, which may not seem like a big deal to you, but trust me, it's about as big as it gets for me considering my favorite band, the Septics, just broke up, and my girlfriend decided to make out with her best friend. Make that ex-girlfriend.

So that day, after Donna verbally hate-crimed me in the bowling alley, making our bowling game more of a "Gays Can Win" campaign, I was waiting at the bus stop with my team, watching a pigeon drink from a grimy gutter puddle and discussing revenge tactics. And just for the record, I'm the only gay one. My teammates are gay supporters, so we were coming up with ways to support the cause.

Except for calling her a bitch and winning the championship, we were pretty much stumped for ideas on how to get back at Donna. I didn't want to bring it into school, and I'm generally not a vindictive person, but I knew that Donna had to get her comeuppance somehow. I just wasn't sure how.

While standing in the fading, fall light, Abby suggested we break into Donna's locker at Maple Lanes and steal her ball, a fugly, neon yellow thing left over from 1989. I immediately vetoed that one since I wanted her to be able to bowl for the championship, wanted her to bring her best, wanted to shoot her down fair and square. Jesse thought we should just let it go. But she's like that. She just lets things go. Colleen thought we should find her when she was alone and do some physical damage. I had never been in a fight in my life; I wasn't about to start because I wasn't sure I could kick her ass (or even know how to) when it came down to it. What if I broke an arm or sprained my wrist? My bowling career could be ruined.

Yeah, they all had ideas, but they all went to public school. It wasn't like they'd be there if Donna decided to take the first strike. I was left to come up with my own plan.

❖

I spent the weekend preparing myself for the hostility I imagined I would face on Monday. I practiced my scowl, my middle finger, and my nose-in-the-air ignore. I mapped the fastest way to get from class to class with minimal trips to my locker throughout the day. I even decided to skip the cafeteria that week and made a list of stuff for my mom to pick up at the grocery store for lunches. I'd eat in the library, which was fine with me since the cafeteria smelled like warm bird droppings anyway.

I wasn't taking any chances. Some of the students and teachers (the older nuns, obviously) don't like me at school because they just don't like different, but my parents pay the same tuition as everyone else, so there is really nothing the teachers can do. I became an expert at avoidance.

Monday came, and I trudged to school. First stop—my locker—was painless. I loaded up my army-surplus backpack, smiled at the picture of Earl Anthony, the greatest bowler of our time (and left-handed, like me), and was on my way. In fact, it seemed as if all of my preparation was for nothing because my day went smoothly. Until I got to my locker before homeroom in the afternoon.

There was a note that had been folded tightly and stuffed through the vent:

Watch you're back you bald headed bicth!

Bicth?

I stared at it for a few seconds and looked around. No one was watching me. I corrected the spelling and punctuation and taped it on the outside of my locker. I mean, if you're going to write a threatening note, at least make sure it's grammatically correct. Nothing makes my scalp burn more than a poorly phrased sentence.

❖

The next morning, the note was off my locker door, and there was a new note inside.

Your gonna get you're ass kicked!

Again I corrected it and taped it to my locker door, along with a note of my own:

Donna D'Amico doesn't know the difference between your and you're.

By third period, word was out. Donna and I were at a War of Words, and clearly I was winning. People I had never spoken to before were telling me how funny my sign was and how true it was. I caught sight of Donna once or twice that day, and she was looking pretty bad. Her normally crunchy hair looked puffy, her mascara had clearly been running, she had broken a nail, and her friends were surrounding her like it was a movie or something, patting her on the shoulder and petting her head like she was a hurt kitten. Oh, please! She started this.

The thing about all-girls Catholic schools is that they're all girls. And girls love gossip. By the end of the day on Tuesday, I heard through the grapevine that someone heard the dean say that notes on lockers "would not be tolerated." Jesus.

❖

As the day of the big game approached, things became both more hostile and more hysterical. On Wednesday, *LEZBO* was written across my locker in blue chisel-tip permanent marker, and I got called to the dean's office.

Sister Rosemary led me into her office, which reeked of old-lady potpourri, and told me to sit across from her desk. Before I had a chance to say anything, the soft lines of her aged face hardened as she set her jaw and began a lecture that was both condescending and confusing.

"Dear, here at OLPCHS, we respect diversity. We also encourage personal expression. However, we feel you have taken that to the extreme."

I tried to interrupt, but she wasn't having it.

"You see," she said, "society goes one way." She moved her arthritic pointer and middle fingers like two legs hobbling to the left. "And you go the other way." She made those finger-legs walk to the right.

I tried to keep a straight face. It took all of my willpower. I nodded at her.

"What I'm trying to say, Angela, is that in this world people have different opinions, and you have to be open to those opinions. Understand?"

"No," I said, because I had absolutely no idea what she was talking about. She was dancing around what she wanted to say, and I wished she'd just get to the point.

"Well, dear, you can't just shout your business from the rooftops. Someone's going to get offended. It's not appropriate to write a word like that on the outside of your locker in bright blue marker. Plus, it's vandalism."

She started to say something else, but I cut her off. "Sorry to interrupt you, Sister Rosemary, but just to get things straight, I didn't shout anything from the rooftops. I don't have to. I'm me, and people see me, and people know who I am." What I was trying to get at was that my practically shaved head, short nails, combat boots, and thumb ring pretty much sealed the deal for people. There's no guessing when you look at me.

I continued my defense. "In fact, I believe I have been the victim of a hate crime." I ran my hand over my cropped locks—or lack of locks—for emphasis.

Sister Rosemary just sat there for a second and looked at me. I thought she might have fallen asleep with her eyes open when she finally spoke. "Dear, who in this school would do such a thing?"

"I can name a few people. I've also gotten two horribly written threatening notes over the past two days, and I think they're from Donna D'Amico." Maybe she'd get in trouble and not be allowed to bowl. Probably not. That wasn't what I wanted anyway.

"I can't believe anyone in this school would do such a thing." She pushed up her oversized glasses and gave me a look that let me know she really believed herself.

"Um, Sister Rosemary, not to state the obvious or anything,

but I just told you somebody in this school *did* do such a thing, and I'm pretty sure I know who it is. Unless you think homophobes are breaking in through a side door during the middle of the day. We can call the police and have the trespassing looked into if you'd like."

"Now, now, dear, that's not necessary," she said, buttoning the top button of her cardigan and standing up. "I'm sure we can address this vandalism here in school. I'll have to ask Donna about this. I'll have the custodian clean your locker. You can go to class now, dear."

❖

As I walked to class through the brown-tiled hallway, I wasn't very hopeful about anyone doing anything about it. I was glad that meeting was over, but I knew that was the only thing that was over. I handed Ms. Barandi my late pass as I walked into math class and sat down. The second I opened up my textbook, a note landed on top of it. I looked around but couldn't identify any possible culprits.

I have to admit, I was a little scared to open that note. I mean, it could have been another poorly written threat. And nothing is more frightening than misspelled words and punctuation errors.

As it turned out, there was nothing to be afraid of because every word was spelled correctly. She had even put a period at the end of the sentence.

Meet me at the alley at four.

I had planned to go to the bowling alley that afternoon anyway, so it's not like I was going out of my way or anything to meet her. Plus, my teammates would be there, so if I needed backup, I had it. I'm not sure how Donna knew I practiced on

Wednesdays, but I'm not surprised she did. After all, I was clearly her biggest rival. She must have been scoping me out.

We tried to time it perfectly so we could all arrive together, so Abby, Colleen, and Jesse were on the bus already, on the way to the bowling alley, when I got on at my stop in front of school. Donna had a car, and my guess was that she was in it and on her way to the alley at the same time. I imagined she would position herself in such a way that she could see me arrive but I couldn't see her so that she would have the upper hand.

We entered the alley at exactly 3:40 p.m., got our lane for practice, and proceeded to our lockers to get our gear. I made a big show of *not* looking around as we sat at our lane. I laced up my new Etonic bowling shoes (Lava leather!). After the last game, my parents had finally agreed to buy me my very own pair of bowling shoes for the championship. No longer did I have to hold my breath against the "smell of a thousand feet" of alley shoes!

Then I toweled my ball to make sure there was no oil left over from the game that weekend. I took a few warm-up shots before we officially began the game, and that was when I felt her eyes on me.

It was no surprise when I turned around and Donna D'Amico was standing at our lane. It was exactly 4:00 p.m.

"Angela," she said above the din of collapsing pins, "we need to talk."

I stood there, transfixed, for one dramatic movie moment. In my peripheral vision I could see Abby holding Colleen's arm in a precautionary act of fight avoidance. Jesse shrugged, picked her ball up from the return, and threw a practice shot. The sound of her head-on strike awoke me from my trance, and without a word, I climbed the three steps out of the bowlers' area and stood in front of Donna.

Like a dusty duel at noon, we faced off on the mauve-carpeted concourse. An audience of three watched us from the lane below.

"What?" I said. Let's face it; I didn't have to be nice. She certainly wasn't.

"Angela, you have to stop writing things about me at school." Her threat came out as a desperate, nasal whine, and I nearly choked on my own spit as I let out a snort of disbelief.

"Seriously, everyone thinks I can't spell or punctuate now," she said.

"You can't."

Donna didn't think that was as funny as I did. She silently pleaded by staring at me with this look of intense sadness. Gone was the arrogant look of a bitchy teenager. I almost felt a pinch of empathy. Almost.

"Sorry, Donna, but you started it."

"Listen, Angela, I want to kick your ass at bowling. I know I can, too. But what happens in the alley shouldn't be mentioned at school."

"You put a note in my locker. You brought it to school. You made the scene. Deal with it." I turned to go back to practice.

"But it's not like people don't know you're a dyke, Angela. I don't see what the big deal is."

I turned back. "Excuse me?"

"We all know you're gay. Saying it out loud doesn't change anything."

You know that phrase about blood boiling? I never understood it until that moment.

"No, it doesn't," I said. "But using it to threaten and insult me does."

"I wasn't trying to insult you, I was just stating a fact." She was back to her nose-in-the-air face, and I wasn't going to deal with it.

"Donna, the only reason I'm not slapping you right now is because I don't want to get disqualified from the championship." And because I don't actually know how to fight, but she didn't need to know that.

She looked disappointed. Then it hit me like a Mack truck on a deserted highway. "Wait. You want me to hit you in the bowling alley, don't you?"

She turned to go. I was right.

"Not so confident, are you?" My voice got louder. "Doesn't seem like it!"

She didn't turn back. I was yelling now. Behind me, Jesse tried shushing me.

"Donna, go home and practice your homophones. You're going to need something to fall back on when your bowling career doesn't pan out. Homophobe!" I yelled, though I'm pretty sure everyone thought I said "homophone" given my previous sentences.

❖

After a fantastic practice (and I mean that; we rocked!), we hung around at the food court and ate curly fries. Abby, with her long bangs dangling in front of her look of concentration, was stretching a fry straight to see how long it actually was. Jesse was texting her boyfriend with one hand and dipping cheese fries into ketchup with the other. Colleen sat down next to me. Her chipped black nail polish definitely needed a new coat. She still wore the Egyptian Goddess oil she had been wearing since middle school, and the scent was a comfort as she put her arm around my shoulder.

"You did well, Ange. I don't know how you held yourself

back. There would have been a full-blown smackdown if she had spoken to me like that."

"Yeah, well, Coll, unlike you, I actually want to be able to bowl on Saturday."

She slugged my arm and stood up. "I want to bowl. If you won't let me smack that pill, then I *have* to help our team win. Should we go?"

"Sure."

We trekked to the bus stop and began the journey home. For me, it was the journey toward the championship and my chance to prove to Donna that I could come out on top regardless of her failed intimidation and slurs.

School on Thursday went without a hitch, and by the time I had my LGBTQ teen group at the center that night, I almost didn't mention what had happened with Donna.

But I did, which at first I thought might have been a mistake because the group became so angry that within the hour they had made signs and arranged to meet at the bowling alley for the big game. They thought I needed some queer support to cheer me on. I was slightly mortified at the thought of such a spectacle.

Dixie, who's MTF, said that even if I lost the championship, Donna needed to know that Queer people exist and aren't going anywhere. She actually said, "Queer with a capital Q." She said that Donna needs to realize that the world is wonderful because everyone is different. Different strokes. Melting Pot. And a bunch of other clichés. I gave her a look that I hoped conveyed my doubt, but I didn't want to rain on their parade, or burst their collective bubble, or steal their thunder, so I didn't try to stop them.

I just thought that Donna was dumb. And I generally avoid words that classify people's intelligence. But Donna just didn't get it. Not only could she not spell or punctuate, but she was clueless when it came to tact. If she truly believed that everything she said in the bowling alley was okay to say out loud, then she just didn't know how to keep her thoughts to herself.

Dixie caught up with me after the meeting, placing her hand on my arm as I was about to leave. She had spent part of the evening making everyone feel how soft her hair was—she had taken her weave out, dyed her hair fuchsia (which looked *a-mazing* against her dark skin), and had it cut in an awesome faux hawk. It suited her well, and she knew it.

"Got a sec?" she asked.

"Sure. I just have to be home by nine thirty or my mom will freak since it's a school night, and I have to take the bus," I said.

"I could maybe drive you?"

Um, okay. "Um, okay."

After getting in the car, we sat there in silence for the first few minutes. We were friends but only through group. Even outings were group outings. I wasn't sure what to say to Dixie since we had never been alone before. Luckily, she was the first to speak.

"So, I noticed you don't seem too hot about us coming to the game," she began, "but I think you should reconsider." Dixie had moved from Barbados when she was nine but kept a little of her accent. Alone with her, I could really hear it. I liked it.

"I just don't think a spectacle will have an effect on her."

We'd stopped at a red light. She turned to look me in the eye. "Is it that, or do you not want to be part of a spectacle?"

I guess she had me there. Did I really want the entire group there, in front of everyone? It wasn't that I was embarrassed; I wasn't. But did I really want to expose us to even more discrimination? At the group, we were a unit of support. As a group, in public, we make ourselves much more vulnerable.

Dixie saw right through me. "Listen, Angela, I know what

you're thinking: a big group of homos all at one place at the same time. Perfect target."

"You're right," I said. "I don't want to give Donna and her friends the opportunity to bash me even more. I'm alone at school."

"I know," Dixie said, "but you have to realize that as long as we exist, they exist, and we have to fight back in the ways we know how. Making ourselves more visible is one of those ways. And in a group, we're stronger. She'll realize you are not alone. Because you aren't."

"I guess you're right."

"I am right, Angela," she said, pointing at me with a long chartreuse-painted nail. "You're part of our group. We want to be there for you. We want to be strong for you. Screw that skank and her posse of tramps." She touched my arm again in support.

It felt *very* supportive. I didn't pull it away.

I'm pretty sure I never told Dixie where I lived, but soon we were pulling up outside my house.

"Thanks for the ride," I said. "I'll see you Saturday, then."

"You bet," she said.

I got out of the car. She watched me until I made it to the front door. I turned around and waved. She was right; I didn't just say that to appease her. Donna should know that I'm not alone. Because I'm not.

This was going to be the gayest championship Maple Lanes had ever seen.

❖

And it was. They had set up some risers and chairs on the concourse, just like it was a real PBA tournament. My parents and my teammates' parents were sitting the closest to us, and behind them was a sea of rainbow T-shirts along with handmade signs. Well, maybe not a sea. More like a pond. Their enthusiasm overshadowed the usual pre-game hush. And it *was* exciting.

The signs were a scream, too. *Throw Your Homophobia in the Gutter!* Another was *Spare Me the Gay Slurs!* A third read *We're Here, So Split if You Don't Like It.* Obviously these queers were really into puns.

Strike Down Homophobia was my favorite.

Dixie wore a turquoise shirt and matching eye shadow, both of which totally complemented her fuchsia hair and lipstick. Her sign read, *Angela Doesn't Like Balls, but She Sure Can Throw One!*

"Highly inappropriate," I told her. She put it down and picked up her "just in case" sign. *Pin Your Hate on Yourself!*

"Much better."

My teammates cracked up when they arrived and saw the spectacle. Our parents looked a little freaked out but pretended to be comfortable for the sake of pretending to be comfortable. Donna arrived wearing sunglasses and a hat. I pointed her out to Dixie, and my crowd of supporters (okay, there were *maybe* ten queers total) began to jeer when she approached the lane.

Abby, Colleen, and Jesse were smooth. They didn't even glance at Donna or her teammates. In our pre-game ritual, we buttoned our black bowling jerseys over our T-shirts (I wore my Earl Anthony T-shirt for good luck) and laced up our shoes. And when the game was about to begin, my team was all business. Donna's team, on the other hand, needed a beatdown. They kept talking loudly to each other about the crowd, the game, us.

"What's with the freaks?" Donna asked her teammate Alessandra.

"I know, right? Isn't the Pride Parade in June?" Valerie responded.

They were only about ten feet away from us, so we knew they wanted us to hear them.

"You ready to kick some ass?" Alessandra asked.

"Totally," Donna, Valerie, and Kaia, their fourth member, responded.

They did some lame "all for one" hands-in-a-circle type of inspirational move to pump themselves up. I looked over at Dixie and rolled my eyes.

"You, go, Angela!" she yelled from her seat and laughed.

"Who's that weirdo?" Kaia asked.

"None of your business," I responded before anyone else could.

Donna emerged from behind her, a glint of hate in her gray eyes, and just as she shouted over the crowd, "You better watch it, Angela, because by the end of this game, you and your herd of oddball homos are going to be crying and wishing you were normal," the lights dimmed, and the owner of the bowling alley, Phil Trattoria, stepped down onto the lane. The crowd hushed so that everyone heard Donna's weak threat. Awk-ward. I shot a look over to my parents, who looked mortified. Even Dixie's jaw had dropped to the floor.

Donna held her head up high. "What?" she addressed the crowd.

Phil made a face, but he basically ignored her and got the game started. When he announced our team, the crowd was clearly with us. The dearth of applause (except from their parents) for the feeble Banana Splits was a definite statement.

And the game began.

I'll spare you the frame-by-frame of this match, but I will tell you this: I can't say we weren't worried. Donna hit bedposts in the eighth frame, and it was such pure magic even I was impressed. Valerie threw a turkey in the middle of the game and had me holding my breath until the next frame for fear she'd throw a four-bagger. Luckily, she didn't.

My team didn't do too badly, either. Jesse knocked a few

baby splits in a row and then sent all ten pins into the pit in a movement that could only be described as pure poetry. Abby, who had clipped her bangs back for the match, was set to get a Dutch 200—alternating strikes and spares the entire game. Colleen was her usual, steady self (much unlike her non-bowling self), completely at peace with the game and doing very well. And me, I was sweating bullets the entire time. I had to dry my hands over the fan and on my towel constantly. My ball didn't like the oil pattern of the lanes, and I felt like it was rolling very slowly every time I threw it. I mean, my count was fine. All of our counts were fine. Even theirs.

As you might guess—because you can definitely guess how this story is going to end—we approached the tenth frame pretty much even, except they were up by twelve pins. As all bowlers know, that's pretty insignificant because anything can happen in frame ten. Anything.

I approached my last frame with a positive outlook. I didn't lose my cool or get disqualified. Colleen didn't try to smack anyone. Even if we didn't win...well, I wasn't going to think about that just yet.

My approach to the foul line on my first throw took on a cinematic quality. I knew it wasn't quiet around me, but in my head, all was silent. My peripheral vision faded, and for those few steps, it was me and the pins. Me and the pins.

And then it happened. I lost my concentration. My groove. I heard, above all the other voices, Donna's. "Get a gutter ball, dyke."

In that fraction of a second, my heart started pounding, my hand started sweating, and on the release, I practically dropped the ball. As it fell from my hand onto the lane and bounced three times, it curved sharply. I thought it *was* going into the gutter, but it didn't. It rode the edge of the lane all the way to the ten pin, knocked it down, and kept going.

Damn.

There was a collective sigh of disappointment from the crowd. There was no way I could bounce back from this. No way. The game was almost over, and there were nine pins waiting for me and then one more throw if I made the spare. That wasn't going to be enough, not if they hit pins every throw. Which I was sure they would.

When my ball returned, I picked it up off the rack and walked to the start point. There was no way I was going to blow this, so instead of separating myself from everything—which clearly hadn't worked on the last throw—I let the ambience of the alley surround me: the fries and frozen pizzas from the snack counter, the old shoes and the lane oil, the liquid bandage and the beanbag chalk on my hands as I held the ball close to my shoulder and prepared to throw it. This was all part of the game, of the experience. The lighting was always slightly dim. My fellow bowlers murmured, with the occasional shout of joy or distress. The squeak of cheap bowling shoes on well-sealed wood, the bounce of poorly released balls, the tumble of a slow strike, where each pin fell individually. And my favorite sound—all ten pins simultaneously being swept away into the pit.

I took it all in; I let it take me in. As always, I counted down my steps as I moved down the runway towards the lane. A smooth approach.

Five, four, three, two, one.

Fuck.

A yank shot. I released the ball late, and it stayed in the air for what seemed like forever before hitting the lane. Which meant it would be slower than I had planned. Which meant it probably wouldn't—

Yes! I swept all nine pins on the next shot and then threw a strike to end my game. Totally unexpected given the loft throw! 205. Not a personal high, but not bad. Not bad at all.

We alternated players, with Valerie up next, then Abby, then Kaia, then Jesse, then Alessandra, and then Colleen. By the time those frames were over they had all managed to throw some combination of strikes and spares to keep us mostly even. It was pretty much up to Donna at this point. I tried not to calculate ahead. We often avoided this because it was more fun to see the final score pop up on the screen, but this was serious, and I had to be prepared. If my calculations were correct, she needed a three-bagger to bring her team ahead of ours.

Three strikes in a row.

I wasn't sure she had ever done it, and I didn't know if she had it in her this late in the game.

I almost want to end this story right here—not tell you whether or not Donna pulled it off, not make a statement about the bad luck that could befall a homophobic person, not gloat in the glory that was our win, but I will.

Because there's really only one way this story can end. Who wants the bad guy to win? No one, which is good because she didn't. She blew the last frame, missing the strike.

We won by four pins. The LGBT group waved their signs and cried like babies. The crowd cheered wildly. Dixie hopped onto the lane and kissed me on the lips (weird!).

Donna turned her back and wouldn't even look at us. Her teammates surrounded her, and they all hugged. For a brief moment, my heart was almost touched. But then it wasn't.

My teammates and I hugged and laughed and danced silly dances to no music. Phil came out onto the lane and gave us our trophy. Our parents snapped pictures, and someone from the local newspaper asked us for quotes. We made plans to go home and meet later at the diner for burgers and fries to celebrate.

❖

After the championship, I saw Donna at school every day, but she barely looked at me. I'm not really sure what happened to the Banana Splits. When the new league season started, they weren't on the roster. I guess they split.

But before all that, before my night of glory ended, there was one more interaction with Donna. When the crowd thinned, I headed to my locker to pack up my gear. Donna was standing a few lockers away, at the same locker she had had for all the years that we had been playing against each other. She was putting away her stuff, and she didn't look up when I entered the aisle. I expected some type of resolution, the kind you expect when you hear a story like this—some apology, some lesson learned, some kind of takeaway, some message.

But there was none of that. Donna slammed her locker shut and looked up at me. Wiping the running mascara from her cheeks, she blinked a few times. I opened my mouth to say something—I'm not sure what—and she held out her hand in a "talk to the hand" way. She wiped her eyes again, pushed past me, and disappeared along the concourse.

I'm pretty sure she whispered "Dyke" as she passed me by.

Bicth.

ALEX JEFFERS lives in New England with two grumpy cats (not as grumpy as he is) named after canonical English novelists. He listens to pop music from Turkey, Israel, and the Iranian diaspora, sometimes to Baroque opera seria, while he writes stories, edits and proofreads other writers' stories, or designs their books. His own books are three: *Safe as Houses*, a full-length gay novel of the eighties and early nineties; *Do You Remember Tulum?*, a short novel in the form of a gay love letter, dated April 1988 though most of the story takes place in the seventies; and *The New People*, a short science-fiction novel about one gay future, which Sandra McDonald (see her story in this book!) called "a lyrical, intricate story of passion and regret that hooks your heart and never stops tugging." One day soon, Lethe Press will publish a book of Alex's fantastical tales.

Back in the mists of prehistory, I was my high school soccer team's only fan. I got it into my head they'd have more if they advertised. So! In all my faggy artistic naïveté, I painted a poster. A portrait of our star striker banging in a pretty goal.

He'd been a good friend of mine until the day I accidentally broke his arm. Maybe years later he didn't even remember, but he'd grown up into an obnoxious jock. And of course he knew by now I was a homo.

I put my poster up.

He tore it down. Didn't want my icky contagion touching his world. (Or maybe he just thought it a bad likeness. No hard feelings, James!) (Really, there are hard feelings.)

But the thing is, when the next home match came around, I was once again the only supporter in the stands to watch us lose, again. Afterward, *every other* member of the team came over to thank me for being there and cheering, apologize for losing, and tell me James was a shithead. They all knew I was a fag, too. But what they cared about was that I was a fan.

So this story is for them. And for all the gay boys and girls on soccer teams around the country. But it's not for James. Sorry, guy.

CAPTAIN OF THE WORLD
ALEX JEFFERS

I'm wrestling with the trunk of my old beater Jetta, trying not to break the key in the rusted-out lock, when I see something wrong with the Turkish flag sticker on the back window. For a second I can't figure it out because I'm not really looking, it just looks like black dirt smeared on the red field below the white crescent and star. But it's not dirt. Dirty but not dirt. Somebody's taken a black Sharpie to it, neat, really small, all caps: *WATCH YOUR BACK RAGHEAD.*

My heart goes bang-bang. This is really not something I can deal with right now. I've got a game on in half an hour, got to get kitted up and warmed up and on the pitch. Got to be calm. The team depends on me, I'm the captain. Captain can't be trembling with fury over something beyond the touchline, outside the match.

Half of me's angry, just amazingly PO'd at the stupidity of it and the cowardice of not confronting me for real. How much guts does it take to insult somebody when they're not there—it's like those evil comment trolls on every newspaper's website, only even more chickenshit. Just as ignorant as those trolls, too, calling me a *raghead*. I'm Turkish, a fezhead. Three-quarters of the Muslims in the world aren't Arabs. But my other half's all panicky scared because 1) I have to get a razor blade under the sticker and slap a new one on before Baba sees it. He'll blow his head off for sure. Desecration of the national flag is seriously bad even if it's not really his flag anymore, not since he swore the U.S. citizenship oath last year.

And 2) I'm looking around the parking lot for suspicious characters. I *know* there's morons at this school, students, teachers, staff, who're certain me and my little sister have got to be terrorists in training, but nothing like this ever happened before. So maybe a total stranger, somebody from another school.

Whatever, whoever. Lots of bad stuff since "Ground Zero Mosque" got into the news. Lots of ugly. Even in this little town. One of the local preachers posted a crazy hateful sermon on his website and the next day our suburban-strip-mall mosque had a brick through its window and death threats on the voicemail. It's even worse than right after 9/11, the hatred, my mother says. Makes no sense. Back then, Baba got an American flag painted on the restaurant's front window beside the Turkish one. Maybe that worked, or maybe Turks just weren't as scary as Arabs and Afghans. Or maybe I was just a little kid ten years ago and didn't notice the dirty looks and under-the-breath insults. Plus the president then was whiter than white and Jesuser than Jesus, not a terrifying black man with an Arab middle name and a long-dead Muslim daddy he barely ever knew.

Not like my sister and me know *our* Muslim baba.

All the time I'm still fighting with the trunk lid. Finally it bangs open. I throw in my book bag, grab my kit bag, and I'm off at a run toward the athletic center. Shit just has to wait 'cause our rivals from St. Joe sure won't.

I'm in the locker room, trying to come down from hyperventilation. I've got my shirt off before I even open the locker. The clock says I've still got time but the nobody-else-is-still-here says I don't. The metal door slams wide but the noise isn't what makes me jump.

"Dammit, Burak, Coach is about to have a coronary."

I didn't hear the clatter of Blake's cleats on the tile. I whip around but he's actually grinning.

"Sorry," I blurt. "Two minutes." One shoe off.

"Captain Perfect's never late. What happened?"

Other shoe. Belt buckle, button, zipper. Blake's like the one I *could* tell, the only one (maybe Lale, my sister), but not now. Bad idea to get him as riled up as me. I push my pants and shorts down so he has to look away. "Stuff. Later. Tell Coach I'm on my way. One and a half minutes."

Only he doesn't go and he doesn't look away, so I do, and that's when I see the thing on the floor of my locker that makes my heart go bang-bang again.

"What stuff?"

It's a white envelope, like for a birthday card only my birthday's in July and why would somebody push a birthday card through the vent in the locker door instead of handing it to me? *Somebody:* I don't have a good excuse for recognizing the big blue block capitals spelling *B-U-R-A-K*. Big macho Raki the Turk, captain of the soccer team, shouldn't know the handwriting of the weenie water-polo player he's got a crush on—but I do.

"Stuff." I feel like Blake's got to be staring at my naked ass. I feel like just one more thing is all it'll take to make me cry. "Not now. Get out of here."

"Yessir!" Blake says like I'm a marine sergeant and he's a private, and I hear his cleats clatter away. And I take a breath.

Jockstrap on. For some reason, *oh, I dunno*, I have a real hard time stuffing the hard cup into its pocket and it's really freaking more uncomfortable than usual. Paul. Dammit, Paul. It's just an amazingly bad time for you to be giving me a stiffie when you're not even here. Regulation undershirt. Shorts. Shirt. Strap on the shin guards, pull on the knee socks. Paul's water-polo kit's got to be like five hundred times easier to put on. Even though the little cap with the plastic things over his ears makes him look like a

SyFy space alien, nobody who's not crazy or the uptightest fuck ever would deny the whole ensemble's five hundred times sexier than me in all my gear. Ass on the bench to tie on my shoes. But if Paul threw wood in his suit, everybody in the world would know.

Which would not be good. If it was me making him throw it. If anybody knew that. If *I* knew that. Because it's so incomprehensibly stupid that I don't. That we talk about everything in the world, Paul and me, except me crushing like crazy on him and him, I'm pretty damn terrified sure, on me.

No way I'm going to open his card now.

I throw the empty kit bag into the locker on top of it, my street clothes after, smash the door shut, grab up my gloves. It's like three and half minutes instead of two. I run.

Coach doesn't say anything about me barging in late. Blake gives me a look but doesn't say anything. *Nobody* says anything, they just keep on with their drills and stretches and mini-sprints along the touchline. So I try to melt in and maybe it works.

Just a quick gander at the bleachers. Soccer's a bigger draw than you'd expect. More people than you'd see around the pool for one of Paul's games, anyway. Maybe—probably—maybe he's up there but I can't pick him out right away. Just as well. *Cannot* think about the thing in my locker yet. Whatever it is.

I see my sister. Lale sees me and gives me a big grin and a big wave. She's not alone, got a couple of girlfriends with her, so that's good. I don't know how she isn't bitter that she's fifteen but our father won't allow her to wear lip gloss like her friends, or wear a sleeveless top or cut her wavy black hair. The single fat braid down her back makes her look like an antique porcelain doll. I wave back but seeing her makes me remember that little talk we had last summer and that makes my heart bang, so I swallow and turn away, pretending to stretch.

"You're gay," she said like it wasn't anything. "You should come out."

Yeah, right. (How'd she know? How *the fuck* did she know?) Wouldn't Baba just raise his voice in thanksgiving to God if he ever found out. Gay son: five hundred times worse than a daughter who wants to chop off her hair.

"Just at school," she said with that irritating all-knowing-adolescent look. "It's the twenty-first century, Burak. Everybody knows somebody gay. You don't have to be afraid of your peers."

The same way I don't have to worry about my peers thinking I'm a raghead terrorist? Besides, the only other kids I care about besides her (I sure didn't mention Paul) are my teammates. Athletes aren't known for open-mindedness.

"You might be surprised," she said, and I said, real fierce, "I can't afford to be surprised. Baba's not going to let me go away to college without a full-ride soccer scholarship, I can't mess this up. So just— Please, Lale. It's the only way. Don't tell anybody, please."

Bang-bang.

Stop. Thinking. Stretch those hamstrings.

Maybe it works. Brain keeps racing but pulse goes down to where it should be.

Then we, the home side, trot onto the pitch to line up for the good-sportsman handshakes. St. Joe's captain doesn't want to shake my hand. He barely hesitates and his fixed smile doesn't change, but I'm not imagining it. All right, then. Something different to think about. Something that'll help me focus instead of distracting me. When his limp hand slides out of mine I think at him, *I'm your worst nightmare*—he's a midfielder, their playmaker, so he's got to get through me—and then because I'm last in line he moves on and here's one of his teammates. None of them seem to have the same problem so I'm wondering while they all file past, keeping up my own grin and gripping one hand after another, until the other keeper Geary Winograd's squeezing my fingers real hard. "Geary," I say, clamping down, and he says, "Burak."

We don't really know each other but you play the same position, you keep an eye out. "Good luck," I tell him. "You'll need it."

He just widens his eyes like he's remembering the state of our offense last year, and that's fine.

Then St. Joe reserve keeper's glaring at me like I killed his mother or just trying to psych me out. Pathetic. Won't even make it onto the pitch unless Geary does something really stupid. So I smile real bright like I could be bothered to know the kid's name—really, I don't—and that ritual's over. The other captain, glowering, and I stand over the ref for the coin toss while the rest of both sides take their positions. I win the start and the ref waves us away.

I pull the bulky gloves out of my waistband with one hand, adjust my cup with the other. It's not the same uncomfortable as before. As I head toward our goal I've got my eyes open, making sure everybody's where they're supposed to be. Riley at right back gives me a confident little nod when I pass, says, "We'll keep 'em away from you, Cap, no worries. You won't have to work at all." Which would be hilarious if he wasn't as big and mean as me and quicker on his feet.

"Oh, man," I whine, "I'll get so bored!"

On his way over, Blake cackles. He's even bigger than me. Not usually as mean, though. Like we do at the start of every game we slap hands (my glove makes a stupidly loud noise against his bare palm), he says "Peace be with you" in Arabic and I say "And with you peace" in Turkish. Which, if you think about it, is kind of dopey since soccer's gentlemanly warfare.

Then I'm in the mouth of our net. I jump up to smack the crossbar with my right glove and blurt "İnşallah!" *If God wills.* Not that God's got anything riding on a high school soccer match. Out on the pitch, I know St. Joe Catholics are crossing themselves or kissing their silver crucifixes before they stuff them back under their shirts. Maybe ours, too. Same deal. (Blake maybe says *inşallah*, too.) And then I turn, in position, half hunkered over with my gloves on my knees. In his goal at the other end of the field, Geary's like my mirror image, waiting for the ref to blow his whistle.

The match starts. My mind splits, like always. Half of me's watching the ball bang around the pitch, gauging St. Joe's weaknesses and strengths. A quarter keeps an eye on my guys, watching for missteps and what to praise at the half. And a quarter starts poking at the look in the eyes of St. Joe's number 10 when he didn't want to shake my hand. Vaughan, that's his name. I probably know his first name, it's not the first time we're on the same pitch, but it doesn't come. Last year he wasn't captain. (I was.) Wasn't number 10 either. I wonder if he just inherited the number or if he earned it. The old number 10 was good. Got past me three times in two years, though one goal got disallowed for offside. But Vince Maskrey graduated and went off to college, and now here's Vaughan who's got no reason I know to hate me but does.

Andy (our number 10, probable next captain when I graduate) and Gage and Dennis are taking the ball down the field. It's a beautiful thing to watch, short, precise passes and almost telepathic teamwork. When a St. Joe defender pops up to harass one, the ball's already at the feet of another, twinkling. In the bleachers somebody starts yelling. And then, I don't quite see it, a man goes down. Gage. Whistle blows. Vaughan backs away with his hands up—*I didn't touch him*—and the ref agrees because he only awards a free kick.

Fast restart. Andy's wide open but Gage screws it trying to hit Dennis because Dennis has a better view on goal. Also two St. Joe defenders right on top of him. Naturally he can't get his head under the ball. And here it comes toward me, Vaughan right behind it.

He's fast. I'll give him that. Good ball control. He knows or guesses that Riley's weaker than Blake. The ball jinks and Vaughan dances right around Riley to get his foot on it again, one of those trick moves you laugh at because it shouldn't work. I'm coming off my line, too intent to laugh. In the corner of my eye, Blake's dashing this way when he should be trying to force the offside trap. Strategy's not always Blake's strong suit. My other defenders and midfielders coming up. A crowd in St. Joe's white shirts. But there's no time. It's just Vaughan and me with the ball between us, like he wants it, and one of us is going to be the hero.

There's no time but somehow there's time for Vaughan to line up his shot. He's not even watching the ball. Got eyes in his toes. The eyes in his head stay fixed on me, hateful, and as his right foot aims and shoots I think he says something. One ear hears "Raghead!" Wait. Wait. Was he—? But the other ear hears "Faggot!"

I'm already in the air. That word throws me. I know in my hands I'm not going to catch the ball to smother it. My fists bunch up together and I punch it clear. Never the best tactic, you can't control the flight. I twist in the air and my shoulder hits the ground hard but I'm up again before the ball lands outside the touchline for a St. Joe throw-in.

In the bleachers, our self-declared ultras make a chant of my name. Not my name—the nickname they call me: "Raki! Raki! Raki!" I think I hear Paul yell "Burak!" but I know I'm imagining it. He might be yelling and it might be my name because he knows I don't like *Raki* so much but I wouldn't be able to hear him. Rakı (no dot on the *i* in Turkish) is booze, horrible Turkish booze that tastes like licorice only worse—I tasted it once. My father serves it in the restaurant. Sometimes he brings a bottle home and when he's hungover the next day swears all over again never to break God's commandment against alcohol ever again. Baba keeps that resolution about as long as you'd expect.

Ball's back in play and I don't know if I tense up again or if I never had a chance to untense. Vaughan shot his wad or he's spooked by that clumsy, spectacular save—he passes the ball to one of his forwards and stays back with the midfield. Savage and efficient and really thoughtful not to foul the St. Joe striker, Blake strips him of the ball and taps it across the turf to Riley, who holds it for a couple of yards, then flights it beautifully half the length of the pitch right to Dennis, who chests it down and knocks it over to Andy.

While back here in my own goalmouth I can breathe again. And think. A glance up at the board—only nine minutes elapsed. I'm not happy with my save. Catching and then getting the ball to one of my guys, I could have opened up a faster counter. Should have. Half a glance into the stands, and I half think I see Paul. He wouldn't know it was a bad save. All he'd care about is it was a save and I made it. Paul doesn't really understand the fine points of soccer, like I don't really understand water polo, so we're even there.

Of course what I'm really thinking about is what I heard that made me almost botch the save completely. What Vaughan said.

Or did he? He was outside the box. Anything he said loud enough for me to hear the ref should have heard, too. The conference started cracking down on abusive language a couple years ago. *Raghead, faggot,* either would be a yellow-card offense.

And if the ref somehow didn't hear—

"What did he call you?"

Blake heard. We're in for it now.

All innocent while my guts churn, I say, "What?"

Blake's hulking out five yards away watching for the action to come back our way. That's not the standard defensive tension winding him up. He glances over his shoulder at me. "The little guy. When he shot."

Thing is, Vaughan and his teammates probably don't know there's two Muslims on our side. Me—everybody in the conference knows Raki the Turk. But Blake never makes any real noise about his beliefs, not so St. Joe would hear about it. Hasn't got around to changing his name though he swears, soon as he turns eighteen, I'll have to start calling him Faruq. In Arabic it means *one who distinguishes right from wrong.* Ignorant people who confuse everyday Muslims with terrorists enrage him. He knows about terrorists. His mom's brother was a Manhattan firefighter who died at Ground Zero when we were just kids. Somehow (don't ask me) that was what started Blake on the road from Irish-Catholic altar boy. By the time I met him in ninth grade he was a lot more knowledgeable and passionate about his chosen faith than I'll ever be. I mean, some of the rules and expectations chafe really hard, and there's one in particular I know I'm going to break one of these days, over and over and with real joy.

"How should I know? I was stopping the shot, not listening to him."

"*What did he call you,* Burak?"

And I know I've got to stop this. Captain's job. Can't have my best defender wound up and distracted.

"Drop it, Faruq!" Blake flinches when I use his real name. "If the ref didn't hear anything, it never happened. You've got a game to play."

I was too loud. Riley looks over, interested. "Eyes on the ball!" I snap at them.

They don't want to. Blake especially, hunching up his shoulders. But an order's an order.

I look at the board again. That only took a minute and a half. Down at Geary's end of the pitch, Andy has the ball just outside the box. Dennis is *inside* the box, and onside, and open. The ball rolls to his feet and he takes the shot without hesitation. Time slows. It's too high. No, it's going in... No. Desperate, Geary gets just a finger under it to deflect it over the bar. We'll get a corner.

❖

At the still scoreless half, when I'm soaking my tonsils with Gatorade for a minute and scanning the bleachers for Paul, I see Blake coming at me all thundery, with Riley (whose family's holy-roller born again so he like *knows* Blake and me are going to a worse hell than the worst Catholic) as back up. *Run away,* somebody in my head says.

"Blake told me," Riley says in a voice that rings with righteousness. "We can't let him, them, get away with that."

"With *what* exactly? I didn't see any yellow cards flashing. If I see 'em flashing at either of you for doing something stupid—"

Blake pounces. "So he did say something that shoulda been booked."

Blundered right into that. "Maybe he did." *Raghead. Faggot.* "Like I said, I was too busy stopping the shot to be sure." *Faggot. Raghead.* "Maybe he'll do it again in the ref's hearing. Until then it's over and it didn't happen. We've got a match to win. I need to be able to depend on you two."

Shaking his head, unresigned, Riley says, "Captain speaking?"

I give them both the captain's eye. "Captain *thisclose* to telling Coach to sub you out right fast."

Wouldn't you know, Coach calls me over right on cue. Not about that, and I'm not gonna bring it up. Not about how clumsy my save was either. Bet I'll get that tomorrow, in private. In public there's a united front to keep up. We talk strategy and (it's still amazing) he listens to me and we use up five of the remaining seven minutes of half-time. When that's over, I've got a minute and a half to guzzle more Gatorade and try to search the stands without being obvious. I pick out Lale again right away but push my eyes right past.

I've been assuming Blake heard *raghead* because I don't know what he'd do about *faggot*. The insult part, qua insult, yeah, it'd make him mad. I'm his friend, his captain. But if he knew I *am* a faggot... If anybody on the team knew. If anybody knew besides my sister and me and Paul.

If Paul even knows. It's not like I've said anything.

I know he knows we're not just friends. Sometimes I know that. Sometimes I worry he's just amused that Raki the Turk has a dopey man-crush on him and he's waiting, kind of interested, to see what happens when I figure it out. If I'll recoil like a straight guy should.

No, he's got to know. Any crush between us is mutual, reciprocal.

I should tell him. I need to tell him. Need to tell somebody. Lale's right, damn her.

There he is—there's the boy I want so bad to kiss, who keeps me awake at night remembering how he looks in his little water-polo suit, imagining what he's got inside it, pretending it's that I'm touching instead of me. He doesn't see me—he's got his phone out, thumbing the keys, eyes on the screen. All alone. None of his friends like to watch soccer. I'm kind of afraid to ask if he does. I mean, I started watching water polo before I knew I had a crush on him but there was an ulterior motive: fit guys, almost naked, carousing in the pool.

Whistle blows. My cup's too small again. I sprint to my new goal and jump to slap the new crossbar, knock away any bad luck Geary might've left for me.

❖

Four minutes into the second half, Gage draws a penalty in the box and I feel a real wince of sympathy and pity for Geary. Penalty shots are the worst. He misreads Gage and the ball curves neatly into the net while Geary's leaping the other way.

Attack after attack from St. Joe once they're down but my boys foil almost all of them—Blake gets booked for a tackle that didn't look so bad to me, but I wasn't as close as the ref. I worry Coach will take him off but that doesn't happen. The first three saves I have to make are easy enough, neat and efficient, not like the first.

Now here's Vaughan again, him and another midfielder shuttling the ball down this way while the striker, trying to set something up, can't evade Riley, close as his shadow. Then, crazy, the other St. Joe midfielder goes down, not a foul, nobody within five feet of him. (Somebody's going to hear about that come end of the match.)

So it's just Vaughan again, Vaughan and me. His eyes are ugly.

What's freaky is it's *now* I see how hot the guy is, this precise microsecond when he wants me dead and I'd be just as happy if he was at the other end of the pitch or out with an injury. Not

Paul hot. Nobody's as hot as Paul. But if Vaughan and I were someplace else, someplace really alone, and he was coming at me with that expression in his eyes, the challenge I'd kind of really want to tackle is changing it from savage hatred to savage lust. And see what happens. Fuck. What the hell's wrong with me?

"Can't let you do that," Blake growls, coming in for the tackle.

I don't see it! The whistle blows. Vaughan's down, yelling. Blake scrambles back to his feet with his hands up and jogs a few steps back while the ref glares at him and in ultra-slo-mo shows the second yellow card, then the red.

It's not possible. Blake's never that stupid. I blink. Blake's just shaking his head in disbelief. Ignoring him, the ref writes in his little book. Off to the side, Riley shouts, "That was never a foul!" but the ref gives him just one glance and he shuts up. Vaughan bounces to his feet, grinning like Christmas, and now he's the ugliest person who ever lived, boner-kill on two legs. I wouldn't touch him with his own hands.

Accepting the unfairness like a sportsman, Blake looks at me once, apologetic, and turns to shuffle off the pitch.

"Buh-bye, faggot," says Vaughan.

I hear him. Blake hears him—a whole-body wince makes him shrink a half inch though he doesn't give Vaughan the satisfaction of looking back. Riley hears him—starts to raise one hand and shout, "Yellow—" Everybody in the world hears Vaughan except the ref, who glares a *you're next* warning at Riley and goes back to figuring out where to place the ball for the restart.

Next thing I know the ball slams real hard into my hands and I start to go down to smother it just as something a lot bigger and angrier than a ball bangs into me with a sound like ribs cracking and everything goes sprawling onto the turf while the whistle bleats like a distant ambulance. I keep hold of the ball.

When I look up, Vaughan's groaning on the floor two feet from me and I don't care if he's really hurt. I hope he is. "Fuck!" he snarls. "Fucking raghead cocksucker faggot bastard shit!"

"That's *enough*!"

I can't even process it. Did I say that? I'm getting to my feet—everything hurts but I know I'm still solid and I've still got the ball cradled against the bruise on my chest. There's people shoving all around us, my people mostly. Riley. Riley gets an arm under mine to help me up the rest of the way. "Yellow card offense," he says flatly. "Abusive language." He glares at the ref. "You can't ignore it this time."

The ref ignores him. Looking down at groaning Vaughan, he calmly says, "Dangerous foul play," and pulls out the red card, lifts it high.

"*What!*"

Ref's already turned his back, writing in his little book. Some St. Joe guy crouches to help Vaughan up so he can shuffle away after Blake, but he's not having it, spitting with fury. "I was going too fast, I couldn't stop!"

"Don't argue," warns his helper.

And all of a sudden all my anger goes ice cold. "You got it wrong, Vaughan," I say in my captain voice, steady and stern and loud so the ref half turns his head and can't ever claim not to hear me. "My parents were married three years before I was born, so I'm not a bastard. If you were less ignorant you'd know it's Arabs who wear what bigots like you call *rags* on their heads, not proud Muslim Turks like me. I'm also proud to be gay. Not a *faggot*. My friend Blake who you got sent off? Not gay, far as I know, not that I suppose it would bother him much if an insecure little sack of shit like you called him that. Definitely not a faggot. And just

FYI, Blake is a proud Muslim, too. Now, you, stop sniveling and quibbling like a faggot, stand up like a man, and get off the pitch like the referee said." Screw the soccer scholarship if I don't have any respect for myself, if *I* can't be a man. Lale would be proud. Thank God she can't hear me from the bleachers.

Everybody's staring at me like I suddenly went DayGlo pink. (I guess I did.) Everybody except the ref. One of the St. Joe players who I don't know from Adam goes from shock to what looks like rue with half a shrug, half a smile, half a wink, before he turns disgusted and leans to help his teammate wrangle Vaughan to his feet. 'Nother friend of Dorothy on the down-low, must be. I knew I couldn't be the only one in the conference.

"Back to your positions," I bark at everybody in general and hold the ball out for the ref to take. I was in my box when Vaughan fouled me, so it's my privilege to clear but no way I'm going to give this bigoted old man an opportunity to say otherwise. He's already pissed.

Tucking the ball under his arm without a word, he finishes what he was writing, waits for sulky Vaughan to cross the touchline, hands it back with a nod. Not a *you done good* nod, not a *let's get this game going again* nod—an *I've got my eye on you, fag* nod.

Whatever. I'd call him a prick except, you know, I like pricks.

Whistle. Restart.

❖

Both sides down a man. Twenty minutes of play left, plus however much stoppage time. St. Joe is furious but not as mad as my guys, who've got reasons to be mad, and not as intelligently mad. We trample them. Six attempts from play and Geary Winograd, more brilliant than I've ever seen him, can only stop four. He almost catches Andy's header but doesn't quite, commits the wrong way when Gage fakes him with a pass across the box, and can't get out of the wrong corner fast enough to gather Dennis's strike.

So, yeah. Three-nil. We're still undefeated. My sheet's still clean. Everybody knows I'm a homo. As I head downfield to praise my boys I'm feeling really deflated, like we just got cleaned up. But I know what my job is, so there's slaps on the shoulder for everybody and big bear hugs for our scorers. It's weird none of them shy away. I don't even notice Geary until Andy pushes me off and trots away.

Geary's holding his gloves in one hand. He slaps them against the empty palm of the other. "Good game, Burak," he says.

"Not really."

"No." He's wearing the captain's armband Vaughan had to give up when he was sent off, I notice. "No, you're right. Look, Burak, on behalf of my teammates and St. Joe's, I want to apologize. Vaughan's a dick. He's about our best player—"

"You're better."

"Yeah, but I'm in goal so I can't, you know, score goals. Anyway, look—I'm going to tell you this. In the parking lot, when we got here, he saw a Jetta with a Turkish flag on the back window. Yours?"

"Yeah. I figured it had to be him. Ignorant bastard."

"He's an asshole. He's not fit to lick your shoes *or* Blake's, and he's going to hear about it. Okay?"

I nod. It doesn't mean anything. "Okay. My advice? You should keep that." I point at his armband. "Unlike Vaughan, Geary, you're a grown-up. Also, today, you outclassed me in goal."

Big incredulous grin. "You mean it?"

"Yeah, you were really something." Captain of the world, that's me.

"I gave up three."

"You didn't *give up* anything. I couldn't have stopped any of those if they came at me." (That's probably a lie. Gage's penalty shot, I might've missed that.)

Still smiling, he shakes his head. "So, um—"

You're really gay? he's going to ask. *I heard that right?*

"So, see you around?"

I swallow. "Yeah."

We shake hands like gentlemen. He walks away. I don't know what I'm feeling. I stand where I am for another minute, hollow. Then I hear, tiny from a distance, "Burak!" and I look up into the empty stands.

Empty except for Paul. Fucker waves his phone over his head and points at me, then toward the athletic center where *my* phone's in my locker. Unreasonable happiness paralyzes me for a moment until he shrugs when I don't make a move, and then I'm hollow again when he makes his, heading toward the exit. I mean, it's going to be all over school by tomorrow: Raki the Turk's gay! I came out to my teammates, I came out to the school and St. Joe and the whole world, but it should have been Paul first.

Now he's gone.

"Burak!"

I know it's not Paul before I look up, before Riley adds, "Cap!" He's all showered and dressed already, hair still wet.

"Hey, Rile." Still captain, I start toward him. I need a shower too.

"Burak, you need to know—" He stops when I draw level, looking confused and unhappy. "The Bible says— Ah, you know it already, what the Bible says. But—but that doesn't change anything, so that's what you need to know. I respect and admire you, Cap. Everybody's a sinner, I'm a sinner, sometimes we choose our sins and sometimes we don't have a choice. I respect you and I'll always be your friend, that's what you need to know."

"Riley." It was hard for him—he couldn't look me in the eye while he said it. "I appreciate that more than you can know. We're going to disagree about things, that's inevitable, but we're both big boys who can see past the disagreements, right? So thanks. And the respect is mutual."

He's blushing when he looks up. He wants to say more, I know it, tell me just how I can stop being a sinner—but he *is* a big boy now, I'm not giving him a different choice, so he just nods and mutters, "Gotta go. See you tomorrow." I bet he'll pray for me. Which is icky but also kind of sweet.

When I get to the locker room it's a relief not to see anybody. I strip down, dropping my kit all anywhere (mostly on the bench), grab a towel, head for the showers. I'm too deflated to appreciate the hot water. In my head, I recite the salat prayers over and over. I don't really know what the Arabic verses mean, not literally, only the Turkish and English paraphrases, so it's just holy noise that usually puts me almost into a trance like a yogi's mantra.

But not this time.

What a shit day. Still have to figure out how to get the flag Vaughan vandalized off my car and replaced before Baba sees it. Baba. My father's going to hear about the other thing, somehow, unless I work up the courage to tell him first. For exactly one minute I let myself hate my father. My strict old-fashioned *you're a Turk before you're an American and don't forget it* Baba who wouldn't answer to Dad if I was brave enough to try. One minute.

Tomorrow. I'll tell him tomorrow. Come out to him. Maybe. After I get some more advice from my sister.

Back at my locker, I bundle soiled kit into the kit bag before I start to dress, and when I set the bag aside I see the white envelope on the locker floor. I pick it up like it's white-hot. *BURAK* in Paul's handwriting. What if he hates me for telling the world before I told him? I can't face that. I can't. I'm going to cry. Holding it like it was the heaviest thing ever, I sit down and just stare at it. A drop of water from my hair falls but I'm not sure if that's what smears the ink or if it's tears smearing my vision.

"What's that?"

"Fuck!" I'm up with my back against the wall of lockers before I know how to breathe. I have to grab at my towel to stop it falling off my hips. "Shit, Blake, give a guy some warning!"

"Oh, captain, glorious captain!" he says. He's not looking as broken up about being sent off as he should, clean and dressed, while I'm basically naked and almost blubbering. "I heard about your speech. That was amazingly brave."

"It needed to be said," I mutter, fumbling to get Paul's envelope back into the locker behind me. "Faruq—" Because he's my best friend and he should have heard it directly and calmly from me, not secondhand—"I'm sorry I never told you. That I'm gay."

"Not like it was a big surprise, dude," my friend says easily, knocking the earth off its axis. "I knew it already. Good for you finally saying it, though. You didn't think it meant anything? Anything bad."

I can't say a word.

"Hey? Burak?" He sits down on the bench. "I mean, you've got a boyfriend, right?"

I cough. "I do?"

"You sure look at Paul like he's your boyfriend. And him at you. Isn't he?" He looks up. "Are you going to cry?"

My friend gets up to take me in his arms and let me sob violently, horribly on his shoulder. "Hey, now," he says while I try to strangle the breath out of him, "hey, Raki. Cap. What made you think a little thing like that could make me stop caring about you? I love you, man. I'm your biggest fan."

"What about—" I can't get it out. "What about God?"

"What?" Now I've succeeded in offending him. He lifts my head up so he can look in my eyes. "*My* God—your God, everybody's God doesn't want me hating you because of who you are any more than He wants me to hate Christians or Jews or Hindus because of how they see Him. It's what you *do*, it's how you treat other people, when you hurt them. Go murder little babies and rape innocent kids, then we'll talk. Don't ask me to hate you, Raki, 'cause it's not gonna happen."

A while later, when I can't cry anymore, Blake says, "You all right, Cap? I've kinda got to get home. Plus, you know, if anybody sees us like this, you without any clothes on, Paul would be real jealous, I bet, because I'm way better looking than him."

So he lets me go and I pull myself together like the captain has to and mumble, "In your dreams you are." I pull the towel tighter, glowering at the floor. "Anyway, he's not my boyfriend. Not yet." I look up. Blake's smiling. Not a grin, just a smile. "Maybe tomorrow." İnşallah—if God wills. "Get out of here."

"Peace be with you," he says in Arabic, "my friend."

"And with you peace," I reply in Turkish.

"Oh, I'm all the time peaceful," he says in English, and walks away.

❖

BURAK. My name. In Turkey it's mainly just a name for boys now, but in Arabic it's the name of a species of magical beast. It was the burak that carried the Messenger of God on the night journey, when he flew from the Ka'aba in Mecca to Al-Aqsa in Jerusalem and then into the heavens to consult with the

earlier prophets and speak to God. When I open the envelope
finally, I find that Paul's painted my name in brilliant watercolors
on a 4x6 card.

The burak's *bigger than a donkey but smaller than a mule,*
according to the stories, and its stride stretches from horizon to
horizon. I've seen other paintings before. It has slender, cloven-
hoofed antelope legs and a long tail like a cheetah's swerving
behind as it paces across a meadow of flowers under a starry sky.
It has wings at its shoulders with feathers of every color in the
rainbow, and a human neck and head. In the Persian and Mughal
miniatures, the head looks like a woman's or a pretty, girlish
boy's, but on my burak Paul's painted my head. It's beautiful.
I'm beautiful.

That's all, the painting, no written message, just his signature.
I can picture him waiting for the paint to dry, then flipping it over
and staring at the blank white back. "If he can't figure it out—"
Paul says, smiling a little sadly, and I go hard under my towel.
Paul's beautiful.

He knows. He already knows. He knows I know.

I reach for my phone.

L. A. FIELDS is the author of *Maladaptation*. Her short fiction has been featured in *Wilde Stories 2009*, *Best Gay Romance 2010*, and the Bram Stoker Award–winning *Unspeakable Horror: From the Shadows of the Closet*. She has a BA in English from New College of Florida, and lives in Chicago, Illinois.

For National Coming Out Day my sophomore year of high school, I made a sign out of cardboard, computer paper, and string to hang around my neck. It said: "If you're GAY, today's the day!" I listened to Heather Small's "Proud" to get pumped up that morning, wore my sign on the bus ride, and walked across the huge open-air courtyard of my school (which is the initial setting for "The Proximity of Seniors"). The administration had me take the sign off before the first bell even rang, but they also granted me permission to start a Gay/Straight Alliance, and the few sightings of me made it around school by word of mouth before the end of the day. I was actually extremely relieved to take it off—it's hard to be that visible, as anyone who has come out well knows—but I was glad I had the nerve to do it at all. Years later people have contacted me to tell me how much they admired my bravery, even though I was shaking the whole time. Every act of pride makes a difference.

THE PROXIMITY OF SENIORS
L. A. FIELDS

Three boys circled Brandon. He didn't know their names; they weren't in his classes and might not even be in his grade, but they weren't here to introduce themselves. They were spouting little *bons mots* of hate, and not just jabs, but complicated pileups of profanity and innuendo. Brandon was pretty sure one of them had just asked him if he'd like to suck a fat rat's dick. What did that even *mean*? Was it a fat rat with a dick or a rat that had a fat dick? Literal rat or figurative?

Why couldn't they just leave him alone?

Brandon received a small shove from someone standing behind him, and then another that made him stumble forward a step. Brandon started worrying about chipping his teeth on the paving stones in the school's courtyard. He had *just* gotten out of braces, he was not looking forward to more dental work, but it didn't appear to concern his tormentors as they shoved him farther and farther forward into a crowd of kids that morphed around him like water. They formed an impromptu fight circle with a neat perimeter. Looking at the thickness of the student population out for lunch, it would take even their most formidable administrator half a minute to get through the rabble. Plenty of time for Brandon to get beat up.

Brandon's eyes started darting for weak spots in the wall of teenagers—just like playing Red Rover as a kid—where was the easiest place to break through if he got a chance to run? He found a likely spot with a cluster of freshman girls in possession. They might get a little flattened if he were to really blast through them, but screw them for staying to watch in the first place. Brandon started to let his perception range out from the escape route, trying to track and predict the movement of the three boys who were still pushing him. He stopped hearing their insults long ago; he'd heard it all before anyway.

Suddenly the group of girls Brandon had his eye on parted. A miracle! Brandon knew he wouldn't get a better opportunity and readied to hurl himself at the very spot, but before the message to launch reached his feet, there she was.

Emma Carroway. She was the kind of girl whose scrunchie always matched her outfit. She wore makeup, but only to emphasize what her mother already gave her. She had pretty ornaments pinned to her sweaters, sparkling unironically. She was the kind of girl his mother wished he would bring home, but he'd never bring home any kind of girl, and everyone knew why.

She was out of breath, and the smoothness was gone from her hair; had she run all the way across the courtyard, shouldering aside the rabble of underclassmen just to get to him? And why would Emma Carroway, arguably one of the most popular girls in school, even bother?

She had her cell phone out, bravely, since it would be strictly confiscated for the rest of the school year if a teacher even saw it, but she had it held high and was pressing numbers with an unseeing thumb.

"I have the police on speed dial," she announced, glaring around at the boys who had been harassing Brandon. "Seriously, get away from him."

His bullies kind of snorted, and the biggest talker told her, "We haven't done anything, sweetheart."

"Um, I witnessed a physical assault, *buttercakes*. And I'd be perfectly happy to tell the cops all about it."

"Whatever," the jerk said, rolling his eyes and walking away. His friends followed him, ducklings after their mother, and suddenly it was all over. That kind of defusion left Brandon in astonishment. He couldn't have said anything to get out from under those other boys, not if he had talked all day and his uncle was the president. You couldn't teach that kind of presence and authority she had, that kind of command; she was amazing.

"Are you okay?" Emma asked him.

"Yeah," Brandon said as the crowd around him dispersed. No blood, no entertainment today.

Emma tucked her cell phone away somewhere deep inside her sweater (your bag could be searched, but not your body without serious suspicion; everyone had a hiding place), and she came over to help straighten Brandon up.

"Thank you," Brandon told her earnestly, "but why did you do it?" He didn't understand why anyone would risk themselves for someone lower on the social ladder.

"Well, obviously no one else was going to help," Emma said, glaring around at her coterie, who slunk off frowning, at last leaving Emma and Brandon alone.

He didn't know what else to say to her, or why she was still standing with him and not leaving with her friends. He had been peripherally aware of her for all four years of high school, but she could not have been farther from him socially. They were both in advanced classes, and they were always jockeying for valedictorian in the scholastic ranking, but Emma was a teacher's darling, the lead in the school play, the one they took pictures of for the newsletters home to parents. Brandon was smart because of a concentrated effort on his part; lunch periods spent in the library, weekends at home alone. But Emma was social and extracurricular and still nipping his heels in grades. She made it all look so easy.

"So," she said to Brandon, tactfully masking the awkward silence between them. "What did those boys want?"

Brandon shrugged. "I guess they wanted to make sure that I knew that they knew that everyone knew I was gay."

"Oh! I didn't know that," Emma said, effortlessly following his meaning.

"Well, it's true," Brandon said. He found it hard to believe anyone could be unaware of his sexuality. Not that he advertised it, quite the opposite, actually. Brandon had literally studied how the other boys dressed, how they talked, how they moved, all for the sake of wanting to blend in. Being gay wasn't a choice, but being obvious certainly was. He had last year's haircut just like everybody else. He was wearing the same jeans. And yet somehow boys he didn't even know…knew. It was like they could smell it on him. "Sorry if it makes you uncomfortable."

Emma arched an eyebrow at him, took him by the arm like they were walking into prom, and led him out to the front of the school. Brandon didn't think they were allowed out there during lunch, but Emma walked them right to one of the benches and sat them down. They must have looked like they were waiting to be picked up early. For some reason, none of the passing adults stopped to ask them if this was so. It must have been Emma's presence again, projecting some sort of confidence that protected her from suspicion. She was an actress, after all, Brandon remembered. It was probably a skill she had developed.

"You shouldn't be sorry to be who you are, no matter how much it bothers someone else. I'm never sorry."

"Sorry for being what?" Brand asked. "Too perfect?"

"No," Emma told him primly. "I'm a lesbian."

"Really? But you're so…" Brandon trailed off, gesturing at her outfit, mostly. She looked like a birthday card, she looked like the 1950s, she looked so wholesome and cheerful and sweet. It wasn't as if all that was mutually exclusive with being gay, but it did seem uneven to Brandon. Probably she wasn't out yet and this was her disguise.

"I know I'm so. I'm *so* many things, but I'm a lesbian, too. It happens," she said, smiling at Brandon.

"I guess it does," Brandon agreed. "Well, I won't tell anyone."

"Oh dude, tell everyone, maybe from you they'll believe it. I swear when I say I have a girlfriend, people look at me like I don't realize what I'm saying. It's not like how my grandma has girlfriends for canasta."

Brandon was speechless again, not just because Emma Carroway had just called him "dude," but because he couldn't believe she could be so blasé about coming out when it was an almost daily struggle for him to be honest. Brandon knew, statistically speaking, that he couldn't possibly be the only gay guy at East Arrow, but most likely those other boys knew the same truths he did: that lying was easier, and hiding was safer, and that these were just as true at home as in school.

"Um…what about your parents?"

"My dad thinks it's a phase, and my mom told me that I'm too pretty to be a lesbian. I think it might confuse her that I like skirts and heels still."

"Well, yeah, clearly you're not official if you haven't been issued your uniform and haircut yet."

"Right?" Emma laughed.

There was a lull in their conversation as Emma got her lunch out of her bag and wordlessly offered him half her sandwich. The sound in the trees came to sit with them, and Brandon noticed, in the silence of being finally left unhassled, just how loud the cicadas were. It was a peaceful noise, like the sound of a lawnmower running in the distance, and thinking about that, Brandon could suddenly smell the hot Florida grass in the patches of landscape all around them, the smell of every summer of his childhood. It was nice to sit under the shade of East Arrow High's carefully kept live oak and feel that summer was really approaching again. Brandon looked forward to nothing but the summer now, since in spite of the heat it would mean graduation and a release from this place. It was already beastly hot during the day anyway and it was only February. They'd hardly had a winter at all. Brandon might as well be hot and free.

"My parents don't even bother with excuses," Brandon blurted. He realized he'd been wanting to let this out for a while, but had no one to say it to. "They just flat-out pretend I never said anything to them." At school visibility was the problem, but at home it was almost the opposite. He wanted to feel safe enough to talk to his parents, and though he *could* speak, no one was willing to listen. He could talk about how svelte the swim team looked this year, but he might as well be the cat meowing for all the reaction he'd get. If they don't like what they hear, they pretend to be deaf. It's like being a ghost in a house full of scientists. He felt so…disappointed in them. He wondered if maybe they felt the same way, but he was too afraid of the answer to ask.

"I told them I was gay on my birthday last year," Brandon continued to Emma, "and my mom still asks if there are any cute girls at school. She even asked about you once, since I guess she knows your mother from working at the bank."

Emma rolled her eyes sympathetically.

"Sorry," she said, moving on to eating apple slices from a baggie.

"I thought you didn't apologize," Brandon teased her. Certainly she could handle a little ribbing, since she seemed so at ease. Brandon wondered what the difference was between them. Was she more confident because she was a girl? Did she have more faith in her parents? Or did she just pretend better than him? Whatever it was, Brandon was a little envious, but he couldn't really hold it against her. Heck, maybe it would rub off on him.

"For *me*," Emma clarified. "I'm not sorry for *me*. I do apologize for my mother."

Brandon laughed and dug his soda out of his backpack. It was warm but fizzy, and he shared it with Emma in thanks for half of her sandwich. This was the easiest lunch he'd had in four years at this school. Even the very first day had been a nightmare of confusion and uncertainty, and someone had tripped him, he thought accidentally, though now Brandon wondered if he hadn't been targeted right away. It had been a relentless campaign of subtle psychological harassment ever since. But this was finally nice. It certainly took long enough.

"So, do you have a girlfriend?" Brandon asked.

"I do! I met her at theater camp." She pulled out a boxy wallet that—for the love of sanity—also matched her outfit, and unclasped it to show him a picture. There was a plain girl in a T-shirt, no makeup on and with her hair brushed straight and unadorned. She looked a lot more average than Emma, except that she had very distinct freckles, and the picture was clearly taken while she was laughing at something.

"Cute, I guess," Brandon told her. "Are you two in love or whatever?"

"Probably not. We had a heck of a time at camp, but…" She shrugged a little wistfully. "Nothing can last forever."

"I'm sorry," Brandon said again. "That's too bad."

"I don't think so," Emma said optimistically. "I think it's for the best. Everything means more when you know it's got to end, and besides, wishing it were different doesn't change a thing. Me and her, we don't even live in the same state. I'll probably never see her again unless we go to the same college."

"Is that the plan?" Brandon asked.

"Nope!" Emma said brightly. "She's going for a business degree, and I'm afraid I can't be persuaded out of theater. We're only applying to one school in common, and it's a reach for us both. Our relationship was sort of ill fated from the beginning."

"Like Romeo and Juliet?" Brandon asked. He only knew about so many plays, and they'd just read it in English.

"Like all of them," Emma said, shaking her head sagely. "So do you have a boyfriend?"

"No, not here, how could I?" Brandon said with defeat. He thought he sounded like a real sad sack, but what could he do about it? He felt like all his best years were going to waste while everyone else had experiences and memories that would last them forever.

Emma nodded. "Next year, then. College! I can't wait."

"Won't it just be more of the same?" Brandon asked. "Frat guys and tests and the same old crap. I figured I'd do my time at a commuter school, try to get through most of it online. I'm ready to live my life already."

Emma goggled at him. "But that's what I'm talking about, living! Do you have any idea how many colleges there are? They aren't all the same! I've got half art schools for my applications. No sports teams there, some of them have no fraternities, and some even have no *grades*. You aren't thinking of all the possibilities. With your scores, seeing as they're almost as good as mine," Emma teased, "you could probably go anywhere. Think about it."

And Brandon did.

❖

Emma's graduation party was one of the best nights of his life. Some aunt had given Emma a bottle of wine and they sneaked off from the group (since it was mostly her cousins) to drink the whole thing and pretend it made them way more buzzed than it actually did. There were white lights wrapping her porch, and they piled into the hammock together, which should have sold them both out as being sober, but it's where they got the most maudlin anyway.

"I'm going to miss you so much!" he'd told her. "I can't believe it took us so long to find each other and we hardly had any time at all."

"I know, but do you have any idea how long we're going to live? Life expectancy is pushing a *century*. We'll have time."

"I have something for you," Brandon suddenly burst out. It occurred to him because he felt the thing stabbing him in the head; Brandon had hung a charm on his earring—a little gold-plated sparrow since Sparrow was his mother's maiden name. He took his time getting it off, it was so small and he didn't want it lost. But Emma wouldn't lose it once she had a hold of it, not as careful as she was, and not as much as they meant to each other.

"I love it! I told you I thought it was so pretty." (She really must have loved it, too, because her postcards from college often had the bird doodled on them instead of her name, a mark of significance for her).

"I want to give you something, too!" she'd declared excitedly, and she pulled the ribbon out of her hair and tied it around his wrist like a knight's favor. "There; a remembrance of me." He tried not to roll his eyes about someone older than six wearing a ribbon in her hair, and he gave her a difficult hammock hug in thanks.

❖

It would be almost four years after graduation before he'd see Emma again, and at first he didn't recognize her. Not because her appearance had changed so drastically (actually Brandon was the one who had gone through an outward metamorphosis in college, experimenting with his hair, with thrift store outfits, with piercings, with how various guys looked on his arm), but something had been added to her. She still moved with that same light confidence as ever, but now she was wearing a lab coat. At first he thought it was a costume, but this was Christmas, not Halloween, and they were celebrating her early acquisition of her bachelor's degree (the show-off). But then he remembered: actress. Duh. She had probably just come from a rehearsal.

College had taken them to opposite ends of the country, Emma to New England and Brandon to California. They didn't know much about each other's day-to-day activities, but they were never totally out of touch. They sent goofy postcards mostly, with jokes or riddles or drawings if it was something too delicate to say. Brandon remembered struggling greatly to draw the loss of his virginity in a way that would be tasteful, but at last simply wrote *did it—very proud* on a suggestive postcard of a deli shop. They kept up their connection, no matter how distant or tenuous.

Emma had helped him pick out the perfect schools to apply to, she had edited his entrance essay through more than ten drafts, and Brandon felt like she was a big part of the reason that he was now only one semester away from his degree in art history. He admired her, and wanted to keep up. He'd even applied to a few programs for next year, in fashion and interior design. She had changed his life by being a cheerleader at a time when he was such a drag, and he found out soon enough that she had changed hers, too.

"Hey, girly," he said when she finally found him, after cutting a fancy cake and shaking a lot of hands. They met under an overhang of blue and white crepe paper streamers like a forest of hanging strands. Emma had to part her way through to reach him.

"You look like you're in a band! Are you in a band?" Emma cooed as she hugged him.

"No, I'm just really cool," Brandon said with pride. He certainly had a lot more going for him now than he used to. "What's with the doctor jacket?" he asked her. Brandon flipped the lapels. On one was a mortarboard pin and on the other was his sparrow on a safety pin. They smiled secretly over it, but said nothing. Emma answered his question instead.

"My dad insisted I wear it. He's so proud to have a scientist for a daughter."

"What?" Brandon asked. "What happened to theater?"

"I fell in love with chemistry," she said to him rakishly, and then giggled. "There's more drama in the lab than you might think."

It got quiet between them, and not because they were out of things to say, for they had years of information to exchange. But all the same, there was just a sure, comfortable feeling that they'd have the time to get it all out, that they didn't need to rush. That was another thing Emma had taught him: the value of time.

"Stick around for a while, yeah?" Emma asked. "I have an adult beverage I want to discuss with you."

"Yes." Brandon grinned. "I'll wait."

To occupy his time, Brandon mingled for a while. Emma's

friends had never been his friends, but he wasn't intimidated by them anymore. After all, who were they? Hometown people, gonna live and die right down the street from their parents. Brandon's parents had frozen him out even more now that he was far away. They paid for school, thankfully, but it was like they were sending him to sleepaway camp so they could get on with their own lives. Brandon let them have it; he'd found that he didn't particularly want what they had to give anymore.

Eventually Brandon got bored with everyone else and wandered off with a smirk. It was soooo good to find that these people bored him now. They used to be such a big deal in such a small place. Brandon felt worldly, he felt superior. He left them to their brain meltingly boring small talk and made his way through to the empty part of the house.

He made his way to Emma's old bedroom, which he remembered well enough from those few months of friendship in high school. It looked just as he remembered, like a gumdrop fairy princess lived there. Most girls would have grown out of the décor, but Emma had always liked her bows and canopy and off-white princess furniture, and Brandon could never awaken any desire in her to update the look, no matter how often he criticized it. Brandon stepped inside and turned on her shimmering bead-shaded lamp to get a good look at the horror he remembered.

Brandon would go insane in a room like this. He never stopped shaping his surroundings or clarifying his style. Catching a glimpse of himself in Emma's vanity mirror, he certainly looked out of place. He had dressed up a little fancier than usual for Emma's party, but his suit jacket had patches sewn onto it to emphasize the shape of the cut, and small artful modifications like buttons he'd replaced with a hook and beer tab each, and a series of carefully preserved slits on the back. And yet outside of the jacket Brandon considered his look to be understated. Hair parted preppy on the side in a retro comb, just leaving the ends artfully frayed. And of course his ears, nose, and eyebrow glimmered with jewelry. It was a long way from how he had looked in high school. He wasn't trying to be invisible anymore.

Brandon kicked off his shoes and stretched out on Emma's bed to wait out the party. He found her headphones and went listening through some of her music for a while, eyes shut, toes twitching in his socks. He was time-tripping really hard just being back in this room. The timelessness of Emma's things, the air-conditioning that smelled like home wherever he went since no other state used it like Florida, even in the so-called winter. And not just the smell of it; he could feel the artificial blast, he could hear it humming. Brandon didn't know how long he'd been reminiscing when he finally opened his eyes again.

Emma stood over him patiently. Her lab coat was gone and she was wearing a more muted, mature version of her old skirt-and-sweater combo. No more kindergarten colors, now a beige and cream. And she was holding something that went well with it: an expensive bottle of scotch.

Brandon made room for her and they started to share back and forth. In Emma's other hand were two tumblers, one of which she gave to him. Brandon took one of the earbuds and tucked it into her tiny ear so that they were in the same place mentally, four years ago. They started talking there.

As they traded stories, the liquor seeped into their words, blurring their speech around the edges, running it all together. They started with school; how art, why science. They moved on to roommates; mine was crazy, mine was worse. Next, naturally, was romance. Brandon had actually started with his roommate (didn't find out the guy was manic and OCD until later), then he made his way through the queer activists on campus, then moved on to guys who would try anything before graduation, and he even got some action off a TA in the end. Emma on the other hand had apparently done her damage in one group of friends. No one-night stands on her end, just a game of musical chairs between girls who already knew each other way too well. It sounded to Brandon like a nightmare of hair-pulling.

"It pretty much was," Emma said, her voice thick with a slur. "I'll probably never speak to half of them again. You know, I learned in sociology"—she stretched and pursed her lips trying to get the word out right—"that the biggest factor in finding love is *proximity*. Who you're physically closest to. I might as well not even start looking until I settle down somewhere. Who knows? Maybe I'll die a bachelor."

"A bachelor of science," Brandon said. It was definite proof that Emma was drunk when she spluttered a laugh instead of groaning at his bad pun.

"Oh man, I almost don't want to go for my Ph.D. now, that's awesome."

"Do you know where you're going next year?" Brandon asked.

"I'm going to Duke," Emma said, taking a swig. "University."

Brandon whistled low. Amazing. He never could whistle sober.

Emma sighed profoundly. Her eyes were greener with a watery sort of excitement. Three and a half years at college had taught him what that meant; Emma was on the cusp of either laughter or tears. He might have predicted which way she'd go.

"I know!" Emma exclaimed. "Let's go *outside*. C'mon, remember? Like last time?" She peeked out her window through the blinds and started to giggle. "Ooh, the stars are out!"

Brandon chuckled loosely as she grabbed his arm and he followed behind her, his body feeling like a puddle around his bones. They walked through the living room where her mother was cleaning up. The guests were all gone, and Brandon could hear Emma's father in the kitchen doing dishes. He tried to look respectable for Mrs. Carroway, but he and Emma couldn't stop giggling when she asked them if they had a nice time at the party.

"It was really nice, thanks, Mom," Emma said, blowing her mother a kiss. Probably her balance was way too off to walk over and give her a hug if the way she leaned on Brandon was any indication.

"Yeah," Brandon said. "It was so great to finally see Emma again. Thank you very much for having me."

"Of course, Brandon. You know you're always welcome. You and Emma go way back." Mrs. Carroway smiled with satisfaction when she said it, and Brandon wondered if he heard a lilt in her tone, like maybe she was hoping for something heterosexual to happen here. Poor Emma; she might have a lot going for her, but she'd never be able to stop dealing with this.

"Don't get your hopes up, Mom," Emma said with a weary sigh. This was the kind of thing that could ruin a good buzz. Brandon wasn't going to let that happen.

"Not so fast, Emma. You aren't thinking of all the possibilities—why, if we got married, that'd be the first gay marriage in the state."

Emma snorted and nearly dropped to the ground. It looked to Brandon as if that ladylike behavior really was just an act. Here was the real Emma underneath, a chortling dork you could really hang out with.

Brandon nodded to Mrs. Carroway and half carried Emma outside. They were on the porch again, and not only were there Christmas lights flashing red and green, but the stars were out in brilliant white just like the lights four years ago. The hammock was gone, but in its place was a porch swing her parents had recently acquired. Though it was easier to mount, they almost went spilling right back out of it. Their elegance was without them.

"So what about you?" Emma asked as they rocked pleasantly outside, half the bottle still sloshing around in her hands. She lay back and threw her legs across Brandon's lap. "Where do you go next?"

"Well," Brandon began carefully. "I've applied to a few places for my master's, might get in, might not, might not be able to afford it either way, but..." Brandon hesitated to say it; it felt serious, like saying "I do." "Probably I'll try to go wherever Dylan goes."

Not in a delusional way, not like Brandon thought this was the one and only true love forever, but he could honestly say he'd experienced enough to be optimistic. He might not know exactly what he wanted, but Brandon did know what he hated, and Dylan didn't have any of his deal-breakers. Brandon hadn't expected to find common ground with a computer programmer, and he never thought he'd find glasses and chicken legs so sexy, but something about Dylan saved him from being a complete stereotype. There was a nerdy but sharp humor in his eyes, and he was totally unrestrained in bed, and he had this soft hair that was long enough for Brandon to really run his fingers through... Brandon just felt a growing suspicion that he might really be in love with Dylan. This could be the start of something so long and solid they'd call it forever. Some things just last like that, like him and Emma.

Emma stayed quiet while Brandon got lost in thought. She was silent for so long that Brandon thought she had fallen asleep, but he could always count on her not to give up on him. After a bit she sighed heavily and murmured, "Tell me about him."

And Brandon did.

Lucas J.W. Johnson is a freelance writer from Vancouver, where he received his BFA in Creative Writing with Honours from the University of British Columbia. His first published short story, in 2009, was about queer werewolves, and LGBT themes and characters suffuse much of his work. Lucas has published short fiction and stageplay, and has had articles appear in the *Ubyssey* student newspaper, the *Globe & Mail*, and the *Lambda Literary* website. While not working on queer YA speculative fiction novels, Lucas creates transmedia projects under his business Silverstring Media. He can be found online blogging about writing and queer issues at lucasjwjohnson.com and on Twitter under the username @FloerianTheBard.

When I first came out to my parents in high school, they were always supportive, but it took my dad a while to really embrace it. At first he'd ask those typical questions like, "Are you sure?" (as if I hadn't spent months agonizing over it all), and for a long time we just didn't talk explicitly about it. He'd be hesitant to tell extended family, or wouldn't want to bring it up in certain company, having rather just avoided the issue than caused any conflict.

But over time, he's changed. He works in upper management corporate America now, and on National Coming Out Day in 2010, his office had a presentation by the in-company LGBT organization. As a result of that presentation, my dad volunteered to make himself a visible Ally, putting the symbol of a pink triangle within a green circle right on his office door, signifying it as a safe space for LGBT coworkers.

He's come a long way, and I'm so proud of him for doing that, for taking pride in his son and stepping forward to actively promote that pride, rather than a simple silent acceptance.

SUBTLE POISON
LUCAS J.W. JOHNSON

We were all a little drunk when Alex told us that, despite previous evidence, he was a boy. It was Tuesday, second period—so, not unusual. The drunkenness, not the coming out (which had only happened once before, when I told them I was gay during a night of relatively tame Truth or Dare). From experience, we all knew that by around second period the previous night's drunk would wear off, so it seemed a logical time to start again. And since Mr. Barowski's chemistry lectures were about as enlightening as the average Fox News segment, and far less entertaining (but in the same painful way), we spent the hour sitting in the bleachers at the empty baseball diamond.

"Oh thank God," Amy said. She flicked an uncooperative wave of red hair away from her face, her dimples showing briefly as she passed me the wine bottle (we thought it classier to drink wine straight from a bottle rather than vodka straight from a bottle; it's the little things, you know?). "There I was afraid I'd have to start asserting my position as Alpha Female."

Alex smiled a bit. "Nope. You're the only girl around." He sat beside me, looking so small—barely over five feet tall—in loose pants and a black Tegan and Sara T-shirt, with close-cropped hair.

"So, what, you're transgender?" Jay asked. "Like, for real?"

"For real," Alex said. "It just—I started considering it, and everything started to make sense. I just wasn't born with the right equipment."

I hugged his shoulder, then passed him the bottle. "Welcome to the acronym."

"Thanks, Stef." He gave me a genuine smile.

"It's an initialism," Jay said. "Not an acronym." But he smiled. Jay was tall and lanky and didn't smile much, but when he did, it lit up his whole angular face.

"If you're a boy, are you attracted to girls after all?" Amy asked. Alex had always been a tomboy, and a lot of people assumed a lesbian.

Alex shook his head. "That hasn't changed—still attracted to boys."

"So you're gay," I said.

"I'm kind of fond of the term 'transfag' to describe myself," he said, with the hint of a smile.

"Transfag," Jay said. "I like it."

"Oh, you're not allowed to say it," I said with my best poker face. "You're straight. That's offensive."

"Fuck." Jay finished off the dregs from the bottle.

Alex grinned.

We heard the bell ring, dumped the empty bottle, and got up to head to third period. As we did, Jay deadpanned, "Wait, if I think you're hot, does that make me gay?"

I glanced at his tall, lanky body out of the corner of my eye. I wished.

"Still girl parts," Alex said. "For now. Your straightness is secure."

Alex and I headed to our side-by-side lockers as students poured into the hallways like a flash flood, flowing against one another in a frantic attempt to get to their next class.

"Hey, Lexi." The voice of Tom Leery, part-time rugby

player, full-time asshole assaulted our ears. He was addressing Alex. "This faggot your new girlfriend?"

I smiled at him. "You're just jealous I fucked your dad last night instead of you."

He shoved me, hard, into my open locker door before merging back into the flood of bodies.

All right, so I probably asked for that. But I do stupid things when I'm drunk. I righted myself, nursed a bruised back, and grinned at Alex. "Leery amazes me with the amount of ignorance he can pack into one sentence."

He gave me a wan smile back as we turned to go to our separate classes.

❖

When I got home from school, both my parents were still at work. My mom worked the desk at an old folks' home in town; my dad suffered through two janitorial jobs. I had dinner cooking by the time my mom got home. I'd also sobered up.

"Dad's working another double," Mom said as she peered at the bubbling pasta sauce. I had to lean over the sink as she did. Our kitchen was that small.

"I guess we'll have leftovers, then."

"With the amount your brother seems to be able to scarf down, who knows?" Mom smiled at me.

I didn't actually have a brother. I was an only child, but my parents had always thought—when I was younger—that they'd have another kid, but they'd never been able to afford it. So it had become a bit of a family joke, this ongoing narrative about my nonexistent brother. Not a great joke, but we found it funny anyway, in that way families have of developing humor over years until it is no longer recognizable as humor to anyone but them.

"How was school?"

"Tom Leery got ripped apart by drug-sniffing dogs. Steroid-laced blood all over the gym. Or did I just dream that?"

"So, the usual."

"Yep. Work?"

"Another layoff scare. I wish I was a nurse, I'd be guaranteed a position." She adjusted the heat on the stove, as if I wasn't carefully monitoring it. "I saw a girl there today visiting her grandfather, she reminded me of your friend Alexis. Is she gay yet?"

I blinked. "If by that you mean, has she come out as a lesbian, then no. Actually"—I started serving out the pasta—"Alex is a transboy. Just told us today."

"Transboy? Like, a cross-dresser?" She sprinkled cheese on the pasta—too much on mine, as usual.

"Like, he's a boy in a girl's body."

We sat down in the living room, which doubled as dining room. "So she *is* attracted to girls."

I sighed. "No, actually, he's attracted to boys still, always has been."

"So she looks like a girl, is attracted to boys, but says she's a boy?" She snorted.

I frowned, slurping some wayward sauce from the side of my bowl. "What's that supposed to mean?"

She shrugged. "It just seems—unnecessary."

I let it pass. Mom had been having a tough time—we all had, I guess. My parents had more debt than income, and with touchy subjects like my post-secondary education on the horizon the last thing I wanted was to create a fresh argument.

After dinner, I drove over to Amy's to do homework. Jay and Alex were there already. Not because we all studied better together. But Amy *did* have a brother—a generous one who was eighteen and had a fake ID.

❖

Weeks passed without much of note. It was getting toward the end of the school year, so it was increasingly easy to be distracted by the sun when we should have been in class. But as long as we passed, grades weren't important until senior year.

Alex seemed a bit more comfortable when around just us, since we knew. But we also didn't talk about it much. He wasn't out to anyone else yet, which meant he was still passing as a girl in class.

Amy and I both worked at the local pizza place, and our usual ramblings between spitting on the pizzas of annoying customers turned to pronouns.

"I mean, I just don't know what to call her. Him. You know?" Amy said. "What's the proper thing to say?"

I shrugged. "I guess it depends. I mean, it should be 'him,' all the time. But he's not out to a lot of people, and calling him that in front of other people would be, like, outing him." I didn't want to ever unintentionally out someone. I knew I was gay by the time I turned thirteen, but it took me until last year to really be out and proud about it. If someone had outed me before then, I would have killed them—then died of shame.

"So we have to use different pronouns depending on the situation?"

I nodded. "Seems like the best thing to do."

"I'm afraid I'll fuck it up. Alex doesn't make it very easy for us, does she?"

"Yeah, because I'm sure his first concern with coming out as a transboy is how hard it is for *us*."

"Oh. Right," Amy said. "Yeah. Sorry."

Apologizing to me as if I represented all of Struggling Queerdom. But I took it.

The next day, I met up with Alex before first period. His eyes were red, and the bags under them big enough to pack a trip to Europe, his normally calculatedly unkempt hair was a lot less calculated in its unkemptness, and I swore he'd worn the same T-shirt the day before. (I couldn't be sure, though—my memory of the previous day was Response Hazy, Try Again Later.)

"You look like hell," I said.

"Good morning to you, too."

"Seriously, you okay? It looks like you didn't sleep."

"Rough night," Alex said. "Can we talk, later?"

"Of course. Jay's tonight, remember?"

"Yeah. Okay."

If I weren't still a bit drunk, I might have noticed the quiet desperation in his eyes, too.

Tom Leery walked past us with a drive-by "Hey, faggot."

"Morning, douche-nozzle," I said.

The four of us had been friends since the start of high school, or thereabouts. The summer of that year, my parents and I had just moved into the area, finally finding a landlord that would have us after years of moving from place to place, dodging rent payments and bills. I met Amy when I saw her sneaking a pull from a mickey of Jack Daniel's, and asked for some. A week later, Jay—who was labeled that kid who was brilliant but didn't apply himself—joined us. Then we took Alex in when we saw him—her at the time—skipping the same math class, out in the parking lot.

We drank because none of us felt like we had anything else. When you can't relate to or really communicate with anyone else, you turn inward—and find yourself empty. Except for your own thoughts, which you seek to obliterate. Or force into some state that can coexist with the rest of the world. Or at least *deal* with the rest of the world. Thus, booze.

We each had our own reasons. I'd been forced to move around so much through school that I never knew anyone. The dawning realization that I was gay on top of that made it very hard to relate to anyone around me in this small town—even my parents, who were so busy trying desperately to get their lives in order for my sake that they all too often neglected me entirely. I'd always only had myself, and I didn't know how to deal with life any other way.

Amy had four siblings and a single-parent father who struggled with them all. Even with an older brother, she'd been forced to grow up far too fast to help take care of them all. And I think she believed no one was looking after her.

Jay *was* brilliant, he just thought on a level above anyone else—but it made it excruciatingly difficult for him to relate to other people. He wasn't challenged enough in his environment, wasn't pushed, and so he turned instead to trying to shut his mind down.

And Alex—Alex was an only child like me, but his parents were well-off. And they were hyper-religious. And they were complete assholes. He needed escape, and—well, I guess we had learned why Alex hadn't been able to talk with anyone else, hadn't been able to relate to anyone else.

None of us had anyone we could relate to. None of us had anyone else that got us, that we could communicate with, that we could share our burdens with. So together, we turned to alcohol, to distract us or push our concerns away. Except—I'm not sure Alex ever drank as much as we did. Of all of us, maybe he handled his burden of silence best of all, just finding a space he could figure himself out.

The problem was, even though we spent every day together, we didn't communicate with *each other*, either. Not really. Not the kind of communication we each needed.

We were at Jay's that night, listening to music, ostensibly doing homework, and passing around cheap wine that slowly stained our lips purple. I had already forgotten that Alex had wanted to talk. My energy at the moment was focused on Jay, as he talked about the anti-Muslim messages inherent in the Halo franchise. Not that I cared much for the content of what he was saying—just his ability to put that kind of analysis into something, that intelligence. And the way he had to keep flicking the hair out of his eyes. I was turned on at so many levels.

Amy caught my eye and suppressed a grin. Apparently I was staring again.

When Jay had fallen into a lull, Alex finally spoke. "I told my parents."

We looked at him.

"Well, my mom. Who told my dad."

"And?" I asked.

He gave me a look that said I should know the answer.

"That bad?" Amy asked.

"Worse," Alex said. He might have said more, but Amy spoke first, grabbing the bottle.

"Well, your parents are assholes."

"It's true," I said. "Remember when they wouldn't even let me come over to work on that *Great Gatsby* project, once they found out I was gay?"

"They threw a fit when you *cut your hair short*," Jay said. "Talk about living in the Dark Ages."

"Or when they forced you to wear a dress to that wedding?" Amy added. "I'd *never* seen you in a dress before."

The general suckage of Alex's parents was a common topic of discussion. It elicited the smallest of smiles from Alex. "True," he said. "Still."

I nodded. "It's tough, I know. I'm sorry." It was a dumb thing to say. I honestly didn't know what it was like to be rejected by your parents for who you are; mine had always been supportive— or at least, as supportive as they could be, given that they weren't around a lot.

"At least you got away from them tonight," Amy said.

"Yeah," Alex said. "But—"

"Ah, just fuck 'em," I said.

"Fuck 'em," Amy agreed.

Jay took the bottle from Alex. "I can drink to that." And he did.

❖

A few weeks later, Alex started to quietly talk to his teachers, ask them to call him Alex, to use the male pronoun. Most seemed to humor him, at the very least. He was still coming to school looking rough—like he hadn't slept much, sometimes like he'd barely washed, barely eaten. Maybe they just took pity on him.

Students had a harder time adapting.

It was fourth-period biology, and I had excused myself to the washroom for a swig of something out of my locker. Alex had been skipping biology all week—we were studying cancerous cells and he said he'd done a project on it last year so he didn't need to be there. I wondered why he'd given such a lame excuse to skip class when we usually did it just for the hell of it anyway, but as I was about to open my locker I heard his scream from the facility I was supposed to be visiting.

I pushed open the door into that haven of graffiti that the janitors could never keep up with—where I'd often laughed at such juvenile etchings as *Mr. Sanders is a faggot*, and *Stef Cameron sucks Mrs. Rutherford's cock*, next to a huge drawing of said purportedly hermaphroditic penis—to find an attack much more severe.

Tom Leery had Alex up against the row of sinks, bent over backward as ceramic dug into his lower back. "The fuck are you doing in *here*, 'Alex'?" Alex struggled and kicked, but Leery loomed like an ox next to tiny Alex. "I'm pretty sure this"—he reached up and locked one meaty hand over Alex's left breast— "means you're in the wrong room, dyke."

"Get the fuck away from him," I shouted while grabbing Leery by his shoulder and hauling him back. I'm not a big guy, but anger—and alcohol—give me strength. "He's no dyke—he's a bigger man than you'll ever be."

This earned me a fist in the face.

Alex took the opportunity to bolt, but when he opened the door, he found himself face-to-face with Vice Principal Sanders. Graffiti notwithstanding, I was pretty confident he wasn't a faggot.

"All of you, to the office," the towering force of authority said. *"Now."* No one messed with Sanders, not in person.

We were asked to explain ourselves. Tom said Alex had provoked him. Alex quietly said he'd been attacked. I said I was trying to defend Alex.

"Thomas," Sanders said, "your actions were unacceptable. We do not tolerate violence against any of our students. You're suspended for three days."

Tom grumbled, and I thought this wasn't quite enough punishment, but Sanders wasn't done.

"But, Alexis, there are rules about washroom use for good reason. I hate to say it, but you've invited this kind of response with this rebellious phase you've initiated. I'm also giving you a three-day suspension."

"*What?*" I said.

Alex was looking at the floor, silent.

"Stefan, thank you, you should return to class."

Never mind my imminent black eye. "That's bullshit," I said, "Alex was just sexually assaulted—"

"And Thomas is suffering the consequences—"

"Bullshit. This is literally criminal."

"Stefan, return to class *immediately*—"

I know when to shut up. I did so. Turned on my heel. Stalked out into the main office. When I'm sober, I would never, ever, *ever* consider doing something as ridiculous as peeing in the school office. But I do really stupid things when I'm drunk.

I'm amazed I wasn't suspended longer.

It was a while before the scandal from that calmed down, but as the weeks passed and the end of the school year loomed before us, things got back to about as normal as they could. We perpetuated our inability to connect by poisoning ourselves. Alex continued to present as male but was quieter about it, less demanding that others use the right terms; mostly this just left people confused. I continued to silently, achingly lust after Jay and provoke Tom Leery. Tom continued to call me a faggot and Alex alternately a dyke or a tranny or a hermaphrodite.

End of term also meant prom, and though we weren't seniors, for us there was still the after-party—and the people who hosted those kinds of events, in this case a popular senior named Chris, knew we had access to booze, so we all got invites.

By end of term I'd also been fired from the pizza place—apparently someone complained to my manager after I swapped their veggie meat with real meat out of drunken spite—so my alcohol fund had dried up. The night of the party I headed to the kitchen to take some of my parents' booze. (It occurs to me now how fucked up that was—that I worked just to buy alcohol, that I was fired for drinking alcohol, that I resorted to stealing alcohol to deal with it. I don't think the others were ever as desperate as me. I hope they weren't.)

My dad was in the living room watching TV on the couch as I passed by. "Party?" he asked, stopping me.

"Yeah, I told you. Prom."

"Right. Friends of yours?"

"Yeah, Amy and Jay and Alex will be there. You've met them." My dad didn't like having people to our house—I think he didn't want people to see how shabbily we lived—but I know they'd met at some point or another. "Actually, I don't think you've seen Alex since he started transitioning."

"Alex?" my dad said. "You mean, like, Alexis? I remember her."

"Yeah, but he just goes by Alex now. He's transgender."

"But she's a girl."

"Well, he was born with girl parts. But he identifies as a boy."

"So she's a he."

"Well, no, he's a he."

"But he has girl parts."

"Yes, but—oh forget it," I said. I loved my dad—both my parents—but he wasn't an educated man. He'd never finished high school, had been working blue-collar jobs since, had never had money, and sometimes his lack of insight bothered me. I knew he was trying to understand… It was just frustrating that we could never really communicate.

At least he was better than Alex's parents. I thought it telling that Alex never revealed how they were handling his transitioning.

I went to the kitchen and shoved the bottle of wine into my bag before Dad noticed, and headed for the front door.

"You taking your brother with you?" he called out.

"Nope, you're stuck with him for the night."

I could tell he was a bit upset with me, like I was purposefully keeping him from understanding. And I felt a bit frustrated that he didn't try hard enough to understand my life.

Chris's house was big enough for an entire grade's worth of kids to cram into with booze and food and the latest suburban drugs. I found Alex standing underneath a tree in the front yard. I guess he'd been waiting for me.

He looked better than he had in a long time—cleaned up a bit, anyway, though he still had dark circles underneath his eyes. He smelled like chlorine.

"Hey," I said. "You smell like chlorine."

"Yeah. I was at the public pool."

"No showers at home?" I joked.

He didn't laugh. "Had to use the girl's change room." He reached out for my wine bottle.

I passed it to him. "Well, you do what you have to do, right?"

He took a swig of wine.

Alcohol doing what it does to one's memory, there are only two other things I remember from that night.

The first was bursting into a bathroom to vomit into the toilet and finding myself sharing the tiny space with a similarly drunk-off-his-ass Jay.

"Heeeyyyyyy," he said, sitting on the floor, his head leaning against a towel rack.

"Hey," I said, wiping my mouth and plopping down on the floor across from him. The size of the room meant our legs overlapped. The two of us weren't often alone together. "How ya feeling?"

"Splendid." He looked at me, then at the ceiling. "Well, no, a little lonely." His head lolled, then he tried focusing on me again. "All these people. Prom. Dates and such."

I nodded, but didn't say anything, whether because I just liked to hear him talk or because I was too drunk to form a coherent sentence more than once every five minutes. I knew what he meant, though—you could practically smell the hormones in the air.

"God, I'm horny," he said. "Y'know?"

The proximity of my leg to his crotch suddenly became apparent to me, and his words were about all the invitation I needed in that state. Like I say, we'd rarely hung out just the two of us. I had no idea if he knew the feelings I had for him—I'd only ever confided them to Amy.

I moved my leg so it was now against his crotch, and rubbed a little. Jay let out a tiny groan, his gaze returning to the ceiling. I rubbed a bit more.

I wish I'd been in a state to remember it better. I ended up giving him what I thought to be a pretty decent hand job. I know *I* enjoyed it, anyway.

We stumbled out of the bathroom a few minutes later as someone pounded on the door in need of the toilet. Everyone was apparently too drunk to take note of us emerging at the same time.

Which brings me to the other thing I remember of that night. We went into the living room, where the biggest crowd was, to find Tom Leery being a belligerent asshole. Normal, yes, but he was being a belligerent asshole to Alex again, and that upset me.

"So, what, you think cutting your hair and wearing a T-shirt too big for you makes you a boy?" he said. "That just makes you a dyke." This generated laughs from the crowd.

Alex looked so tiny there in front of Tom. I could tell he was scared—no doubt, after what had happened in the school bathroom.

"Hey," I said, making my way toward them over the bodies sprawled on the floor. "The fuck is wrong with you?"

"Oh look, it's *Stephanie*. What, is she your boyfriend, Stef? Coming to protect her?"

While part of my brain tried to parse the contradiction of the phrase "is she your boyfriend," and part of my brain considered that Alex *was* the only other gay boy in the room, in his way, my mouth had plans of its own.

"No, but God you are hot when you're a bigot. Do *you* want to be my boyfriend? I could fuck you—"

He shoved me away before I could finish the sentence, but I grabbed his arm as he did, leaned forward, and tried to kiss him instead.

Did I mention that I do stupid things when I'm drunk? The last thing I remember was his fist coming at my face.

The bruises I wore the next morning suggested it hadn't stopped with one fist.

The week after prom was the week of exams, when everyone in the school holed up at home, or formed study groups, or, well, didn't really change their routine at all. We'd sometimes "study at Amy's" as usual, but when it came to exams, we actually wanted to do decently well, so more often we kept to ourselves.

The night before our English exam, my phone rang. Alex. A surprise since the number displayed wasn't his cell.

"Stef, I need your help." He sounded miles away.

"I'm sure the exam will be fine, you're good at English."

"No, it's—I need you to come pick me up."

"Um, okay. Where are you?"

"The police station."

"What?" I asked. "Are you okay?"

"I'm fine—just—come get me, please?" At which point he hung up before I could ask anything else.

I rushed to the station. Well, it took me a while to find the station. I'd never been there before. I wasn't that much of a drunk yet.

Alex met me in the custody of an officer at the front desk.

"What's going on?" I asked.

"Is this your sister?" the cop asked.

I looked at Alex. His eyes just said, *please.*

"Yeah. What happened?"

"We picked her up sleeping on a park bench."

I looked at Alex again, but was going to get no answers from him with the cop standing there.

"She says you'll take her home. Can you fill out these forms?"

"Of course," I said.

The forms asked me for my own identification, as well as Alex's. After another glance at him, I put "female" for gender. They asked me for ID, and I explained our different last names by saying Alex used our mom's maiden name. The cop looked like he didn't believe a word we told him (I suppose our dates of birth would have given us away) but let us go anyway.

"Why the hell were you sleeping on a park bench?" I asked as we climbed into the car.

He didn't answer immediately.

"Alex, what's going on?"

"My parents kicked me out, okay?" he said.

I stopped trying to start the car and looked at him.

He choked out a sob, and covered his face with his arm.

"When?" I asked, quietly.

"A month ago," he said. "When I told them."

"A *month* ago?" When he started coming to school looking tired, bedraggled. The unkempt clothes, the pool… "Where have you been staying?"

"There's a shelter downtown. There, mostly." He was trying to calm down, sniffing back the tears. "It was full tonight. It's been full sometimes."

"Jesus, why didn't you tell us?"

He just shook his head. "I dunno. I couldn't."

"Fuck. They kicked you out? For being transgender?"

"They said God had given them a daughter, and if I couldn't accept what He had made me—" He choked again, took a deep breath, and finished. "They said they'd rather have no child than the wrong one."

"Fuck. Fuck," I said. "That's—if God made you anything, he made you what you are, you *have* accepted—that's the whole— *fuck!*"

Alex was silent.

"Jesus. Your parents are monsters, Alex. They're assholes. You can't let that—" I stopped, because what I was about to say was ridiculous, and I knew it. Of course it would get to him. They were his *parents*.

"Look, I can sneak you into my room tonight," I said, "but you know how my parents are about having people over." They were weird about it, like I said. Which was usually fine with me—I didn't want them to see how much I drank with my friends. I think they would have been disappointed.

"Yeah," Alex said. "I can go back to the shelter tomorrow. Thanks."

I felt like crap. But I didn't know what else I could do.

Exams passed, and we didn't see much more of each other, but when the year was over, we all got together at Amy's for an end-of-school binge. There were truly epic quantities of alcohol in her room, and the four of us started in on it without much thought to anything else.

I think we passed most of the night with the same kind of conversation we always had, the kind that never actually said much. We played games, we complained about school and our families, we watched stupid videos on YouTube, and generally lost track of time and ourselves.

I'm sure Alex's parents came up again as Jay railed against religion and Amy railed against bad parenting. But I don't think either of them even knew Alex had been kicked out. Maybe I should have told them.

Looking back, I think Alex had been unusually quiet all night. Like perhaps he was trying to get our attention through his distance. But it ended up meaning that at three a.m., in the deepest depths of drunkenness, I suddenly noticed his absence from the room and had no idea how long he'd been gone.

I lurched to the bathroom, thinking he might be there—and there's where I found him.

Not bent over the toilet, but sitting on the floor, a knife in front of him, blood flowing down his thin arms as he looked up at me, terror in his eyes.

What happened next is a blur, flashes of images. Kicking the knife away. Grabbing a towel to bind his arms. Sopping up the blood. A stream of words coming out of my mouth, pseudo-comforting nonsense. His eyes on me the whole time, silence on his tongue.

When you can't really communicate with anyone outside your own head, you turn further inward, you become self-destructive. When alcohol couldn't block out his pain, when even that nectar that loosens tongues and makes friends of strangers couldn't get us to really pay attention to him, to really *listen* to what he was saying in his silence, he turned even further inward—and there found only darkness.

The cuts weren't deep. Bound, he wasn't in any real danger. I told him I was getting Amy, getting medication, getting an ambulance. I stood, and left him sitting on the floor.

I went back in Amy's room, but Alex's name froze on my lips when I saw Amy and Jay writhing together on the bed. "What the *fuck*," I said instead.

They groggily untangled.

Amy stood. "What?"

"How the hell could you?"

"The fuck is wrong?" she said. Jay looked drunkenly confused.

"You *know* what the fuck is wrong," I said. "You know I—" I stopped.

"Like him? Yeah, but guess what, Stef? He's straight. Okay? Deal."

I felt like an ice pick had been driven through my chest. Some part of my foggy mind knew that it was ridiculous, but I felt betrayed. I felt…undone.

Alex had been driven from my mind by something infinitely less important.

I ran from the room, from the house. It was three a.m., I had enough alcohol in me to pickle a cucumber farm, and I got into my car. I do stupid things when I'm drunk.

The next thing I remember is miraculously waking up in my own bed. Shivering, sweating, sicker than I had been in a long time. Only then did I remember Alex. And then I threw up.

I didn't get out of bed all day. I moved in that feverish dreamworld of half sleep, seeing again Alex's terror-filled eyes, the blood, imagining that he'd killed himself, that Amy and Jay had killed him, that he'd killed me.

It took me until the next day to call him, but I got no answer. I called Amy and Jay, but couldn't reach them either.

I called Alex again the next day. And the next. Finally I got a text from him that just said *Stop*. I breathed a *Thank God*. He was alive, at least.

❖

I didn't see any of them again for a month.

I'd see Amy or Jay pop up online sometimes, but they didn't initiate conversation, and I had nothing to say. When their online relationship statuses went from *single* to *in a relationship*, I blocked them both.

I stopped drinking, too. At first I couldn't stand the smell of booze, then I just couldn't afford it, then I began to see what it had done to me. I was an alcoholic, and a dangerous one. Without Amy and Jay around to encourage it, I could stay away from it. I didn't want them in my life anymore.

I took the car a lot, would go driving out into the country. I just let my mind wander—I'd enter a kind of meditation, driving for hours. It was a better way of not thinking than blacking out from drink.

In mid-July, I got an event invitation to a party at Chris's place. I imagined that party. I imagined a bunch of our friends getting together, drinking, getting high, having fun.

I ached to go. I ached to join them. I declined the invitation. Rewatched a whole season of *Queer as Folk* that night instead.

I must have done something in that month, but I couldn't tell you what it was. Everything was kind of a blur, the same pattern every day, an existence without change, without movement.

I thought about Alex a lot. I thought about what he had to go through, the journey that was ostensibly just like the one I'd gone through when I came out, and yet was so completely different. Transphobia is a subtler thing than the casual homophobia I put up with daily. Name-calling I can ignore. But when ignorance erodes your very identity, when the world is a constant challenge of who you are…

When Tom Leery said, "This faggot your new girlfriend?" he was just calling me names, but he was utterly disregarding everything that Alex was as a person.

When you have to lie on a simple police document to avoid questions, when using the bathroom that should be yours risks sexual assault, when people like my parents, who for God's sake have a gay son, can't even wrap their heads around a boy trapped in a girl's body, don't understand that sex, gender, and orientation are completely different things.

When even the closest thing you have to a friend is someone who can't be bothered to try to get them to really understand.

This was what he had to deal with. It wasn't his parents that were the worst—as horrible as they were. It was everyone and everything around him, a constant push of ignorance pressing in on all sides like being deep underwater, always at risk of drowning.

Then, at the end of July, I got the text from Alex.

My mom died this morning. I need you.

❖

My parents drove us to the hospital. In halting, soft words Alex explained that his mom had been battling ovarian cancer for years, that she'd been hospitalized last week, and that Alex had been calling the hospital for updates every day.

His mom, on her deathbed, did not want him present.

"But now—I just need to *see* her," he said.

"Why didn't you tell us she had cancer?" I asked.

He looked at me. He looked so tired, so...small. He'd been staying at the shelter all summer, working there for his keep and a guaranteed bed. He hadn't seen Amy or Jay since that night, either. We didn't speak of that night.

"I needed you guys to hate them for what they were," he said. Then he looked out the window again. "Because no matter how much I wanted to, I couldn't."

When we arrived at the hospital, the nurse at the front desk looked over some files.

"I'm sorry, sir," she said to Alex—he did look like he could pass for a boy; I wondered if he was in any state to take joy in that simple pronoun—"but Ms. Hall has no children listed under accepted visitors."

Alex sank away from the desk.

"She *had* a daughter," a voice said from nearby. We turned to see Alex's father in a rumpled suit watching us. His gray face was an unemotional mask, but his eyes smoldered.

"Dad—"

His father stopped him. "She *had* a daughter. But apparently, that daughter is dead now. All she wanted during her last week in this life was to have her daughter back."

"Dad—"

"To have the daughter God gave her."

"God gave her a son!" Alex yelled.

"We have no son," his father shot back. Then he turned and walked away.

Alex just about leapt after him, but I grabbed him and pulled him to me, wrapping my arms around him. He clung to my shirt and sobbed into my shoulder.

"I'm sorry," I said, and I hoped he understood the weight behind it. "I'm so sorry."

I don't know how long we stood there, in the hospital foyer. Eventually, his tears began to slow. Then I felt a hand on my shoulder, and looked at my dad.

And my dad said, "Alex, if you would like, you can come and live with us."

I looked at my dad, and wondered. I wondered what *he* had seen these past months. Maybe he had understood more than I gave him credit for.

It took a moment, but Alex looked up, and sniffed. "Mr. Cameron, I couldn't—"

My mom touched Alex's arm. "Of course you can. Besides— we've always wanted Stef to have a brother."

There it was, in that one word.

Alex sniffed, and nodded.

Things were tough for us, there's no doubt. There had been so much poison in our lives, there still was. In the days ahead, things might still be rough. But I knew we had the antidote now.

WILL LUDWIGSEN is a 2011 graduate of the University of Southern Maine's Stonecoast MFA program. When he isn't writing fantasy-tinged fiction for *Alfred Hitchcock's Mystery Magazine, Weird Tales, Asimov's Science Fiction*, and *Strange Horizons* among many other places, he writes fantasy-tinged nonfiction as a technical writer. He lives in Jacksonville, Florida, with his partner Aimee Payne, a greyhound named Graham, and a cat named Oscar (after Oscar Wilde).

So a few years back, a friend of mine and I are tilling up the front yard to put down sod. It's an early spring morning in Florida, and two men stroll past the house. They pause to admire the work we're doing and say hello. Their names are Craig and Greg, and I introduce myself and motion over to "my buddy there, Scott."

They narrow their eyes and say, "You mean buddies like we are?"

And standing there, a little dazed from working all morning and only barely keeping up with the social niceties, I say, "Yeah, sure."

As the conversation continues with increased enthusiasm, trading stories about restaurants and bars and art galleries in the neighborhood, it slowly dawns on me that I may have—accidentally—falsely admitted to being gay. As the conversation builds up steam, though, it gets harder and harder to mention; there's no way to slip that in without sounding dumb, insensitive, or embarrassed worst of all.

See, what's funny is that as I'm listening, I'm finding myself strangely honored to be mistaken for gay. Almost every gay person I know is extraordinarily perceptive, nuanced, and interpersonally aware, perhaps born out of years of treading carefully among people who decidedly aren't. I've shared more with my gay friends than with many of the others, and at that moment, I was proud to be thought the kind of person who could be trusted with something so fundamentally personal.

I haven't seen them around the neighborhood since, though I've promised myself that I'll tell them this anecdote if I do so we can all get a laugh out of it. I hope they'll still want to be my friends.

So "Forever Is Composed of Nows" is dedicated not only to all of you but to Craig and Greg, who took a chance coming out to strangers and honored me by mistaking me for someone as brave as they are.

FOREVER IS COMPOSED OF NOWS
WILL LUDWIGSEN

Carlos was more a writer than a scientist throughout high school and college, but one of the ideas of physics always struck him as deeply and intuitively true: Time is nothing more than the movement of the universe, and every moment of your life, good and bad, is really just a moment in space, some tiny spot in an orbit that's six hundred million miles long.

He always liked to imagine that you could go to the exact same places but at different times, reach out with all your heart and feeling, and share something with your ghost. That's why Carlos sometimes visited the house where he grew up, now abandoned, to tell himself that his father wouldn't live forever. That's why he sometimes stood on the Bluffs where the first boy he ever liked shoved him from his bike, to tell himself that he would be loved. And that's why, twenty years after graduating from Lincoln Bluffs High School, he arranged to speak to an English class there about his newest book, sneaking away afterward to the boys' bathroom where he'd lost four teeth.

Two decades hadn't improved it at all. It was filthy and horrifying even when he was a kid, filled then and now with the reek of cigarettes and lunch farts. Every pale green tiled surface seemed smeared with a moldy film. The heavy black seats had been slammed down by a thousand other teenagers. The industrial steel mirrors had seen another generation's bleeding acne and fuzzy mustaches. The fluorescent tubes still flickered and hummed.

The overflow drain in the center of the floor, too, remained—the one into which his teeth had fallen. He'd heard them more than saw them on the day he lost them, his eyes clotted with blood, and they'd rattled somewhere deep inside the school like pebbles in a rain stick. Carlos, twenty years older now and rich, still glanced over his shoulder before stooping beside that drain. He squinted with one eye, but of course the teeth were long gone.

He had new ones now, made from materials no one had ever heard of in 1990, and no one but him could tell the difference.

Carlos stood and pushed open the door of the stall farthest to the right, the one with the wide door for a wheelchair. That's where he'd taken Eric that afternoon, squeezing inside with their coats and book bags before bolting the latch. That's where he'd come out to his best friend.

"What's up, man?" Eric had asked. He'd had thick, wavy blond hair that Carlos loved and slightly envied, plus a slender neck that had a way of tilting Eric's head with an expression of total attention, total interest. Together, they'd talked about everything, except the obvious.

Carlos had practiced it, he had, but he couldn't remember the script. That was probably just as well because it had never sounded quite right even in the privacy of his own bedroom mirror. It wasn't something to be practiced, anyway, but something to be blurted.

So he did.

"Eric, you need to know that I love you," he'd said. Ugh. That's not what he wanted to say at all, so formal and prissy. His heart had almost leapt out with the words, perhaps to take them back and try again. It almost did again now that he remembered them.

This was the point in the script where Eric was supposed to

open his eyes wide, tear up, and confess what he felt, too. But he didn't. He only looked thoughtful, as he often did, perhaps considering it all as some kind of puzzle to be worked.

They'd stood there in silence, jammed into the stall, looking from each other's eyes to each other's lips. Eric opened his mouth to say something but closed it again, and instead he put his hands on Carlos's shoulders.

"Carlos, you need to know that—"

A fist thundered against the door, followed by four others. On the other side came the cackling laughter of Marcus Zenner and his idiot buddies. How they'd gotten into the bathroom so quietly, he couldn't figure; it wasn't like them, all punching and belching their way through school. But they'd overheard. God, they'd overheard. And now, Eric and Carlos were trapped.

"You gonna kiss?" purred Marcus, squinting through the gap between the door and the hinges. "You gonna go down?"

Before they could answer or deny, the boys buffeted the walls of the stall like animals flushing out prey. Eric and Carlos pressed closer and closer from the edges. Carlos kept watching Eric for any sign that he was still on his side, that he was still his friend even if everything else had gone wrong. Even if he didn't love Carlos back.

Now, two decades later, Carlos put his hand to the door of that stall. He closed his eyes, held his breath, and shared himself with the past. Shared his strength. His hope.

Eric had reached for the bolt and Carlos's breath caught. The latch snapped loudly home.

"You know I love you, too," said Eric. Then he kicked the door open.

It swung fast and true, right into Marcus Zenner's forehead. He sprawled backward over the sinks, blood already streaking down his face. It was the best first shot Carlos had ever seen, and he enjoyed it even when the others circled in, their fists coming again and again like pistons. He enjoyed it even when they'd kicked his legs out from under him, when someone planted a class ring into his jaw, when—yes—his teeth tumbled down the pipes.

He and Eric gave what they could in return. It wasn't an epic battle but one scrappy and dirty with kicks and scratches. They hadn't won, quite, but they hadn't lost either. It took Dean Kleiner, Vice Principal Moulton, and half the baseball team to pull them all apart, and they'd gotten a month of detention for it. Funny how Marcus Zenner and his cronies didn't say much to them ever again, though God knew a hundred others would take their place over the years.

Carlos leaned into the stall door. His younger self and his older one passed each other through. From himself, he took strength. To himself, he gave hope.

"We win," he whispered. "Eventually."

Somewhere, someplace, he answered, "I know."

Carlos pulled his hand back. He looked around the bathroom one last time, took in one last breath of the awful scent of urinal pucks and antibacterial soap, and nodded. He had a speech to give, students to encourage, and then a flight back home to Eric.

DIA PANNES divides her time between searching for valuable antique books and writing short stories. Neither activity pays particularly well, but both take up a great deal of time, and that's really all one can ask of a vocation. With her trusty pickup truck, fat Irish setter, and poor sense of direction, life is always an adventure for Dia. "Spark of Change" is Dia's first short story; she is currently working on a novel.

I was twenty-four years old before I ever saw a Pride Event. There I was, in Albany, New York, totally lost. Turned the corner and *Whammo!* Gay pride parade, full steam ahead, music and guys marching and the most amazing group of lesbian bikers I'd ever seen. I'd heard of stuff like this, of course, and seen it on TV, but to all of a sudden have it be there, an entire community, real and in my face and so welcoming—it was a life-changing moment.

I just joined the parade. I don't even know how to explain it. One moment I was watching the parade and the next moment, there I was, marching along. These were my people. I belonged. The parade went on for a couple of blocks, but I was meeting people and getting introduced to people, and my mind was absolutely blown.

I also totally missed my bus. Was it worth it? Absolutely. Since then I've learned the gay community is like any community: we have our problems. But to know that there are other people in this world who are like me? I'd miss a million buses for that.

THE SPARK OF CHANGE
DIA PANNES

If you ever find yourself in a situation where you have to put out a fire and you happen to have a fire extinguisher, remember PASS: *pull* the pin; *aim* the hose at the base of the fire, and *slowly sweep* the foam over the flames. The foam will choke out the flames, and before you know it, the fire will be out.

All that's left then is the cleanup and the explaining.

Trust me on this one. My dad is the assistant rescue chief with the Randsville Volunteer Fire Department. "I don't want this place burning down, you know?" he'd say. "Can't have a firefighter's house go up in smoke!" Growing up, I had every Sparky the Fire Dog coloring book and was the only girl who brought a real chief's helmet to show and tell. I'm the only seventeen-year-old I know with a silver Child Finder sticker stuck to their bedroom window.

But Dad left a few details out of my education. You can be an absolute artist of fancy foam work and it's not going to do you a whole lot of good when the side of the garage is caught up in flames taller than you've ever seen. He also never mentioned the heat a fire gives off, how it punches into you like a bulldozer, trying to knock you off of your feet. He left out the bit about how the waves roll and dance, wide scarlet flags twisting toward you, gold fingertips trying to grab, pull in, and consume everything they touch.

I learned all that myself, responding to a fire on Grange Road. What was I doing there, armed with a kitchen fire extinguisher, trying to do alone what the Randsville Fire Department managed with a crew of eight and two trucks?

That's a long story.

❖

Five days ago, Dad and I were sitting there, eating dinner. It's just me and him now; my older brother Aaron lives with his girlfriend and Mom moved out when I was a tween.

Dad had gotten subs on the way home from work. Ham and cheese for him, turkey for me. A bag of chips and a couple of sodas and we were in good shape—at least until his pager went off.

Here's the thing. Being in the fire department means wearing a pager 24/7. Fire can't tell time. Fire doesn't care if it's two in the afternoon or two in the morning. When it starts, you go take care of it, as fast as you possibly can. Dad's always available. It doesn't matter if he's sleeping, if he's working on the car, if he's trying to watch the football game—if that pager goes off, he gets up and goes. We even have a backup pager in the house, atop the refrigerator. Dad doesn't want to ever miss a call. I've seen my dad get up and go to fire calls in the middle of blizzards.

So when the pager went off, I knew what to expect. Dad would grab his turnout gear, tear on out of the house, jump in his truck, and speed away, blue light flashing, to save the day. But I wasn't ready for him to listen to the call, pause, and then sit back in his chair. He took a big old bite out of his sandwich while dispatch repeated itself:

"Randsville Fire Department, Randsville EMS. You have reports of a structure fire, smoke visible, the Gibbs residence, 659 Grange Road."

"Dad! Didn't you hear that?"

It'd been a while since Dad had a haircut. His brown hair went fringing out all over the place when he nodded. "I heard. Up on the Grange Road. That's that schoolteacher of yours and that girlfriend of hers, living way up there."

"Ms. Gibbs?" I had Ms. Gibbs for seventh-period study hall. She wasn't really my teacher; she taught French and I take Spanish, but I saw her every day. "Why aren't you going?"

"A man can't respond to a fire on his own," Dad said.

"What?"

"Nobody's going to that fire, and I ain't going to go alone." He tipped his head toward where the pager sat, kitty corner on the top of the refrigerator. "Wait. You'll see."

We sat there, Dad eating, me staring at my plate, then him, then the clock on the wall, while dispatch toned out Randsville every few minutes.

"Nobody's responding."

"I told you." Dad had finished his sub. He crumpled the wrapper into a ball, thick fingers squeezing it until it almost disappeared. "Nobody's going to. Not from Randsville, anyway. I don't think they're even going to acknowledge the call."

Dispatch seemed to hear Dad, somehow, because their next calls were for mutual aid from nearby departments. Nearby, of course, is a relative term. It's many miles from our station to the next one, and miles from our station to the Grange road.

All I could think of was Ms. Gibbs, with her house on fire, waiting for someone to come. Waiting and waiting and waiting. Fire moves fast. It doesn't take long for an entire house to go up in smoke. Dad had taken me to controlled burns, and I'd heard all the stories: ten minutes, twenty minutes tops, and you're looking at a total loss. Everything gone, nothing worth saving.

What would happen if Ms. Gibbs was still in the house? What about her girlfriend? They owned two chocolate Labs, named Tigger and Bongo, that always came along when Ms. Gibbs coached softball. Did they make it away from the flames? From the smoke?

It made me want to puke. My stomach was turning over and over. Acid was splashing up my throat. My whole mouth tasted sour. "You can't just sit here. You have to go!"

"I don't have to do shit," he snapped back. "I'm a volunteer. We're all volunteers. Nobody pays me to go to a scene."

"What are you talking about?" I was really confused then. What did this have to do with money?

"Fighting fires is dangerous, Rimi. You know that." Dad shrugged. "You can get hurt. You can get killed. It's not a game."

"Of course I know that."

"And it's a volunteer department. We sign up for it. But none of us signed up to risk our lives for people who live like that. Not open like that, the way they do, right out in your face, like there's nothing wrong with what they're doing."

"But letting somebody's house burn down? Letting them die in a fire? That's all right?"

"I'm sure they're going to be fine."

"How do you know that? How can you possibly say that?"

Dad shrugged. He stared at the television, as if he didn't notice it was off. Maybe his reflection was fascinating. He couldn't tear his eyes away from it. "They knew what type of community this was when they bought that property. There's no surprises about this. Your teachers knew what they were getting into, moving up here."

"Because they're gay." The words hurt to say.

Dad nodded. "People like that should stick to their own. New York. San Francisco. The cities. Where they already have their own community, and they can look out for each other."

"So if Ms. Gibbs was black, you'd still sit here and let her house burn down? We don't have no black people up here."

"That's different."

"How is that different?"

"People can't help being black."

"And they can help being gay?"

Dad covered his face with his hand, pinching his nose between his fingers and thumb, squeezing his eyes shut. "It's complicated. You wouldn't understand."

"Why don't you try me?" That's what Dad always said whenever I told him he wouldn't get it. That's always his answer. When I wanted to drop AP Math, when I wanted Aaron's friend Steve to stop coming around—I always have to try him. My word's never enough. I have to have a reason.

He sighed. "I don't know if people can help being gay or not. Some say yes, some say no. I don't really worry about it myself since I'm not."

I nodded. "I'm with you so far." That's what he would have said, if he was me and I was him.

"But either way. Whether they can help it or not, they don't need to be flaunting it. Pushing it in everyone's faces. They know people don't agree with it. No reason to be out there showing it to everyone." Dad shook his head. "It's like they want to make everyone agree with their lifestyle choices." He traced air quotes in the air with his fingertips, mocking the last words. "And this is what happens."

"When do you see Ms. Gibbs?" I asked. "She doesn't go to church with us."

"No, I guess she doesn't." Dad laughed, kind of. It wasn't like anything was funny, though.

"So do you see her at the grocery store?"

Dad shook his head.

"Does she come by the shop?" I couldn't picture the French teacher having a whole lot of call for small engine repair and parts, but stranger things have happened.

"No. Course not."

"And she doesn't hang out at Stuckey's." Dad hung out at Stuckey's. The entire department did. Every Saturday night, you could find Randsville's entire fire department drinking beer and eating greasy hot wings at Stuckey's. It was tradition.

Stuckey's is where Dad would go after a fire, too, or a real bad wreck. The entire department would wind up there. They called it "debriefing." Two years ago, when Bobby Hyatt's dad wrapped his pickup around a tree and did himself in, they were at Stuckey's for three days straight.

"No." Dad took in a deep breath. He looked at me like I was up to something. "I can't say I've ever seen her there. Or her girlfriend."

"So when Ms. Gibbs is flaunting her lifestyle on you, when does she do that?" I kept my eyes on my sandwich then. "Exactly?"

When I looked up, Dad was getting red in the face. "I didn't say she was flaunting it in front of me. To me. But it bothers other people." He shrugged. "We've got to have each other's back."

"And what are they doing that bothers other people so bad?"

"They don't like having someone like that in the school." Dad's face lit up, like a dog who dug up a bone he forgot about burying. "And that girlfriend of hers always comes around when there's a softball game."

"Ms. Gibbs is the coach!"

"Still."

"Mrs. T never missed a single ball game when Aaron was playing." Coach Teague's wife was a regular institution at Randsville baseball games. She had a bright orange folding chair that she'd set up next to the bleachers, and she'd spend nine innings there, cheering hits and screaming about bad calls.

"That's different."

"So because Ms. Gibbs's girlfriend does the same exact thing that Mrs. T does, all the time, you're going to let her house burn down?"

"Rimi…"

"And not even because it bothers you, because you don't go to no softball games."

"You don't play softball."

I went to plenty of games, though. Not 'cause I care about softball, but I sure do like looking at Emily Masterson. A senior, she owned first base. Some afternoons I'd lean forward and just stare at the way sweat formed at the back of her neck just below where she bobby-pinned up her hair beneath a dirty cap. I shrugged off the mental image; this really wasn't the time to let my mind wander in *that* direction. "But because she's going to games you don't go to, and this doesn't bother you, but it bothers other people, you're going to let her house burn down."

"A man can't fight a fire by himself."

I sat back against the back of my chair, just astonished. Flat-out astonished. I'd heard some unbelievable stuff in my time, but I never expected to hear it coming from my dad.

"Everyone else is doing it, right?" It was my turn for the air quotes, even though they didn't really fit. "Since everyone else is being hateful, it's okay for you to do it, too."

"Careful, girl."

"What is that you say all the time? About everyone else jumping off the bridge?"

"I told you you wouldn't *understand*." Dad wasn't yelling, but it was pretty close.

"You know what I understand, Dad?" I got up from the table and pushed my chair in. I did that real slowly and carefully, making sure the legs didn't scrape across the floor or hit too hard. That'd give Dad something to yell about, and then I'd never get to say my piece.

He cocked his head. "What?"

"I understand that someday I'm going to have trouble in my life. Maybe not now, but someday I will. Big trouble. And now it turns out that if people don't approve of my lifestyle, help's not coming." My dad's eyes are just like mine, wide and brown and ferocious. They opened a little bit wider when I said that, but I was so mad I didn't care. I just stared right back at him. I wanted to see that he heard me. "And that you're okay with that. As long as everyone else is doing it."

"What are you saying?"

I didn't want to tell him this way. He should have known, should have *known me* better. "What do you think I'm saying?"

One of us was going to have to look away at some point, and I was determined it wasn't going to be me. I'm always the person to give in, to say okay, to be the peacemaker. I'd rather have everyone get along than get what I want. I'm that way with Dad. With my friends. With everybody. But not this time. This time I stared my dad down.

"Jesus Christ, Miriam."

I shrugged. Everything had been said, and nothing had been said, and there were no words left.

"I am…we are…we are not having this conversation." Dad wasn't nearly so careful with his chair. It went out behind him, into the wall, almost, but not quite, hard enough to put another dent in the sheetrock. "I am not. Not with you."

"So you're going to the fire? You're going to do the right thing?" He'd spent a lifetime saying these words to me, and here

I was saying them right back to him. You'd think it would feel better than it did. "Never no mind what everyone else says and do what you're supposed to be doing?"

Dad stared at me then, a long, long time. His eyes were bright and shiny, and his mouth was all pressed shut, tight, like he was working at keeping the words in there. Looking down at his hands, I could see they were twitching, fingers curling toward his palms, almost fists, but with his thumbs out, loose. If you're gonna hit someone, you tuck your thumbs in tight against the side of your fist. Keeps 'em from getting broken.

My daddy taught me that. Taught me how to take care of myself in this world. Taught me how to look to see who knew how to take care of themselves. He said a girl needs that in this world, especially when she's got a brother, so she doesn't get surprised.

He saw me looking at his hands. I saw his eyes look at mine, and then down at his hands. His fingers went all straight, shocked rigid like he'd grabbed hold of the electric fence, and then he looked back at me.

Dad didn't say nothing then. I thought he would, maybe, but he didn't. Not a word. Just looked at me for forever, and then he turned away. Put his back right toward me and walked out of the kitchen, through the living room, and into his bedroom.

When he shut the door, I thought I was going to throw up. My whole body was shaking. I was cold and wobbly from the inside out.

He didn't come out of his room again. I sat there in the kitchen, waiting and watching, trying to will my stomach to calm down and stop doing somersaults.

All this time went by, and there I was, watching his door stay shut while dispatch called out pumper trucks from three surrounding companies—two to the scene, one on standby.

The tones sounded again and again. The pager was relentless, high sharp notes stabbing through our house every time dispatch announced that more manpower was needed to respond to the scene of Randsville's working structure fire.

Four times that happened. Four times, Dad's door stayed closed.

I waited, and waited, and waited. Maybe if I'd waited longer, the right call would have come through, something that would have shaken Dad up enough that he remembered who he was, what he was about.

But I waited until the eleven o'clock news—with its report of a major fire on the Grange Road, one that needed four companies to battle it—switched over to Letterman and from there to an infomercial promising rock-hard abs in thirty days and then I guess I fell asleep.

When I woke up Saturday morning, Dad was gone. Judging by the muddy tracks in our driveway and the still-warm coffeepot, he hadn't been gone long.

Monday morning, Ms. Gibbs wasn't in school. She was all right, we were told, but her partner Tracey was shaken up pretty badly. She'd spent the weekend in the hospital, and Ms. Gibbs was bringing her home today.

Well, not home, exactly. I'm not sure where Ms. Gibbs was going to take Tracey, but it wasn't going to be back to their house. Someone had brought in a copy of the paper, with its front-page picture of Ms. Gibb's house. We were passing it around in Social Studies class, talking about what kind of fund-raiser could be done to help them out, because it was clear that their house was completely wrecked. The roof was totally gone. Some of the walls were standing, charred columns surrounding steaming piles of their history.

Tigger and Bongo were in the picture, too. I never saw a dog look heartbroken before, but those dogs surely did. When it was my turn to look at the picture, all I could do was stare at them sitting there.

"Rimi? You crying?" Stephanie Tyrell had turned around in her seat to get the picture from me.

I shook my head and shoved the paper at her. "No, I'm fine." The last thing I needed today was any drama, and Stephanie was all about the drama. Nothing makes that girl happier than to have someone to talk about. It takes her half a minute to spread shit to the entire school, and that's when she's not even trying. I so did not want to wind up on her radar. "I forgot my allergy medicine."

I don't have allergies. I wasn't fine, either. I stared at Stephanie's back, but all I was seeing was Tigger and Bongo. The newspaper said the dogs had spotted the fire first, barking like crazy to let Ms. Gibbs know something was up. They'd saved their people's lives, which is way more than my dad did.

I didn't want to think about it, how the whole family could have burned up while my dad was hanging out in his room. They could have died. Would that have even bothered him? I wasn't sure it would. I thought about it a lot that day, and that night. Dad took his sweet time getting home from work. Normally he would get in around five thirty, six o'clock—but that night, it was almost eight before he pulled in.

I made sure the newspaper was lying on the kitchen table, just waiting for him. He'd be sure to see it when it came time to make dinner. I was in my room, watching some stupid videos on YouTube and waiting on him.

He came through the house slow, like he'd had the hardest

of hard days. I could hear each step, his boots coming down on the floor heavy. It took the better part of five minutes for him to make it from the front door to the kitchen. Believe me, our house is not that big.

With my door open, I could, if I turned around, see the kitchen table. I knew from listening that he was standing there, but I wasn't about to turn around and look for sure. He had to see the paper. It was the only thing on the table.

He stood there a long time. "Babe?" Dad finally said. "I've had a long day. I'm going to bed. There's money on the table, if you want to call for a pizza."

"All right." I wanted to say a million things, but that's all that would come out. I didn't turn around. If I looked at him, I'd start crying, and then he'd tell me that everything was all right, and I didn't want that. Everything wasn't all right. Not by a long shot.

❖

Ms. Gibbs came back to school on Tuesday. I saw her on my way back from the cafeteria—normally I blow off lunch, because our cafeteria is gross with a capital *G*, and I like to hang out in the library, but I never did get around to calling for pizza delivery and I was starving.

Just the sight of her made me rethink my entire decision to eat lunch. You wouldn't think a hamburger and fries could make you feel so sick, but all of a sudden I was ready to lose it right there in the hallway.

There was no way I could go face Ms. Gibbs. I just couldn't do it. Every time I thought about sitting there in study hall, looking at her sitting at her desk, my stomach hurt even worse. I leaned up against the lockers and groaned, hugging my stomach.

"Miriam." It was Mr. Wyancotter, the vice principal. "As

much as I appreciate your efforts to hold up our building, you need to get off of those lockers."

Mr. Wyancotter thinks he's funny. He's the only person who thinks so.

"Sorry, Mr. Wyancotter." I stood up straight. "My stomach… well, I wasn't feeling too good."

"Do you need to go to the nurse?" he asked. "You do look a little green."

I shook my head. "I'm sure I'll be fine. The day's almost over anyway."

Mr. Wyancotter nodded. "Then go get yourself to class."

Despite all of my hopes, I managed not to get lost on the way to study hall. Aliens completely failed to abduct me. No Hollywood agent swept into the school, discovered me, and swept me away to make movies. There was no hope for me. I was on a collision course with Ms. Gibbs.

Luckily I made it into class before the bell rang.

Ms. Gibbs looked like she always looks: short blond hair, a blue turtleneck sweater under a black cardigan, black pants. On the desk in front of her was the usual pile of folders and papers. It looked like she had a ton of work to do.

With any luck, she wouldn't notice me at all. She'd be all occupied with her grading and whatnot, and I could be totally inconspicuous. I sank down into my seat and opened my chemistry book, staring right at the pages. Looking studious was the best defense. A teacher would never bother a student who was working so hard to improve themselves, right?

It was a good idea, but I couldn't make my stomach believe it. That hamburger and French fries were kickboxing in my stomach, knocking against each other something fierce.

And then the situation got worse.

"Miriam, would you come up here for a moment?" Ms. Gibbs looked fine, but she sounded funny. Her voice was all hoarse and raspy, like she'd strained her vocal cords shouting too much. Smoke inhalation will do that to you.

"Yes, Ms. Gibbs?"

I was standing at her desk. She looked around to see if anyone was paying attention, but no one was. Well, Teddy the Freak was, but he's always staring at everything. Neither one of us noticed him noticing us.

"I know your father's in the fire department."

I nodded, thinking *Here it comes.* My legs were really wobbly. I wanted to hold on to her desk, to make sure I'd keep myself upright no matter what happened, but it didn't seem like a really good idea. "Yes," I managed to croak. My voice didn't sound much better than hers did.

Ms. Gibbs nodded back, and once it was clear we were in agreement, continued on. "I didn't get a chance to thank everyone…it was a pretty crazy situation that night. But could you let him know that Tracey and I, that we appreciate everything everyone's done?"

She didn't know. She didn't know that Randsville never responded to the call. She didn't know that Dad stayed home, behind his bedroom door, listening to dispatch call out for more manpower, time after time after time. She didn't know that the people she counted on to come never came. She had no idea that her neighbors were more than ready to let her burn.

You'd think that that would have made the entire situation so much better. It should have been a relief. The fact that Dad did nothing could be my secret. His secret. Our secret.

Ms. Gibbs kept on talking. "That's one of the best things about life out here in the country. Neighbors take care of each other."

"Yes, ma'am." All of a sudden I knew I was going to be sick. I don't even know what I said to Ms. Gibbs; I just started running for the bathroom. From there I went to the nurse's office, and from there to home.

❖

Wednesday I stayed home from school. I wasn't sick, exactly, but the whole school had seen me puking, and I needed a day away from everything. Away from school, away from Ms. Gibbs, away from my dad, who made sure I knew there was chicken soup in the cupboard and went off to work.

I think he knew I wasn't sick, but he wasn't about to say nothing to me about it. We still hadn't really talked since the fire, and the longer we didn't talk, the harder it was to say anything at all. He said the necessary stuff but beyond that? Nothing.

Dad gets that way when he's angry. Quiet and still, with nothing to say to nobody. He'll even tell you that himself. He calls it the calm before the storm. The way he was keeping himself to himself, I reckoned we were in for a size-ten hurricane when he decided to start talking to me again. I have to admit that I wasn't looking forward to it much.

That brings us to Wednesday afternoon.

I couldn't believe it when I heard it. I was hanging out, watching a movie, and the scanner went off, toning out for Randsville.

"Randsville Fire Department, Randsville EMS. You have a reported structure fire, the Gibbs residence, 659 Grange Road. Garage fire."

Ms. Gibbs' house was gone. Completely demolished. And now her garage was on fire. Something had to be done. I could hear Ms. Gibbs in my mind, as clear as day, thanking me for Dad's efforts. Talking about how neighbors take care of each other.

Randsville didn't respond the last time this happened. More

than likely they weren't going to come now. Fire calls during the day are the worst for volunteer fire departments. Everyone's at work. Dad, if he was inclined to respond to this call, would have to make the thirty-two-mile drive from work to the station before he could even begin to be helpful.

Ms. Gibbs's garage wasn't going to make it that long.

The nice thing about having your dad be the assistant rescue chief of the fire department is you always have a fire extinguisher in the house. We have two. Dad makes a point out of getting them charged every year. I took the big one off the front porch and took off running.

It took me a bit to drive up to Ms. Gibbs's place, but I was still the first one there. I didn't see anybody at all—but the garage was definitely on fire. There were flames flickering out around the front door, little yellow tongues curling up from the ground.

"Not again." I don't know who I thought I was talking to, but I wasn't about to let Ms. Gibbs's garage burn down, too. The fire extinguisher was heavy—forty, fifty pounds, I bet—and I couldn't really carry it right. So I dragged it up as close as I could get, the canister tracing a line through their gravel driveway.

Then I aimed the hose and pulled the pin.

There's a lot they don't tell you when they teach you how to use a fire extinguisher, that's for sure. Fire is loud. I couldn't see what was going on inside the garage, but I could hear it roaring in there.

It was really frustrating. All the fire I could see was pretty small. The heart of the blaze was clearly behind the door. If I could just get inside, I could stop the fire before it really, really started, before it got to the roof. Once a roof catches fire, it's pretty much game over: if there was any hope for saving the structure, that hope is lost once the shingles start burning.

It was already pretty hot. I couldn't even get close to the

overhead door. The heat was pushing on that something fierce, bowing it out in a pregnant-looking swell.

On the side of the garage, a little farther down, was a door. I sprayed the extinguisher at the flames that were peeking out around it and tried to get up close. It wasn't as hot as the front, although it was plenty hot, and grabbed hold of the door handle.

That was a really bad idea. That door handle was super hot. My hand burned like instantly, and I let loose of it as soon as I touched it. The pain was intense but then I heard a cracking noise, and I forgot about the door for a minute. Fire had burned its way through the front corner of the garage, a big cluster of flames nearly as tall as me.

If I can see it, I can fight it. I moved myself back around to the front corner. It was getting easier to move the fire extinguisher— I'm not sure if it was adrenaline or because I was getting used to the weight, but suddenly it was almost effortless to move the tank and aim the hose and spray the foam.

That's all I had to do in the world. Spray the foam, smother the flames, and wait for mutual aid. If I could keep this fire from getting any more out of control than it already was, someone would come and help me.

It might not be Randsville responding, but someone would come. I just had to hold on.

The flames were as stubborn as I was. Yellow flames turned orange, and orange to red. Every now and then the fire would burn blue or green and I knew that the fire had caught hold of something metal, something electric, something likely far too toxic for me to be breathing in.

The roar got louder and louder. There's no sound like it really; this was motors flat out and heavy-metal concert speakers and jet engines combined, millions of decibels blasting my ears. It was so loud I barely heard the sirens coming.

What I did hear, somehow, despite everything, was the hiss-clink-thud of the extinguisher going dead in my hands. There was no more foam coming. I stared at the red extinguisher, furious. It couldn't not work. Dad made sure of stuff like that. Always. I shook it furiously, trying to urge just one more spray, just a little more foam. I only had to hold on until mutual aid arrived.

And then all of a sudden, someone grabbed hold of me and pulled me backward. I lost hold of the fire extinguisher. Seeing it hit the ground and roll away from me into the flames was the last thing I remember before I found myself face-to-face with my dad.

My very angry dad. My very, very angry dad who was standing there in his turnout gear, black helmet on his head.

"What in the hell are you doing here?" He was yelling and still I could barely hear him above the roar of the flames. The flames had reached the back of the garage. The siding was popping away from the corner, rolling back with metallic shrieks, yawning open to reveal the fire flickering below.

"Fighting a fire!" I shouted right back. My throat hurt. It hurt a lot, so I stopped shouting. I pushed on him, hard, instead. He was wearing his turnout gear, so he probably didn't even feel it. He didn't let go of me, anyway. "I'm taking care of our own!"

Dad didn't say anything then. He just started pulling on me, dragging me away from the fire. And something inside me broke a little bit then, that little piece that says you always have to listen to your dad and that grown-ups always know better than you do, because I wasn't about to let him stop me. I started fighting him like crazy, punching and kicking and screaming as much as I could.

I'm not a small girl. I'm strong. I play fullback on the soccer team in the fall. No one scores on me without working hard for it—nobody. I can hold my own, you know? But my dad didn't even notice anything I did. I hit him square in the face and there was blood all of a sudden, out of his nose, around his eyes, and he just ignored it. He just dragged me over to the ambulance rig and shoved me into one of the EMT's arms.

"Check her out," he growled at them. "Make sure she's all right. Get her out of here."

"No! Where are you going?" I screamed at him. Every word hurt like I was getting stabbed in the neck. "You can't leave now!"

"Fire needs fighting." He raised his glove to his helmet and pulled down his face shield, hiding his face from my view. Then he gave me a nod, and then he was gone. I saw him walking over to the pumper truck, and then the EMT got in my face with an oxygen mask and I didn't see anything anymore.

❖

I wound up in the hospital, sitting in the emergency department. I had smoke inhalation and a second-degree burn on my hand. The doctor at the ER wanted to give me some kind of pain medication to knock me out, but I told him no. "I'm not taking anything until I see my dad." You can't really yell when you've had smoke inhalation, but I made my point. "You can't make me."

"When you change your mind, you let me know." The doctor was already on his way out of the room. "You will change your mind."

"Don't mind him," the nurse said. "We don't get many people who turn down the good drugs." She laughed. "You're really very brave, trying to fight that fire."

"What about my dad?"

She shook her head. "I haven't heard yet. But I'm sure he'll be here soon."

She was right. Dad did make it to the hospital in short order.

He arrived by ambulance, with a broken arm. The back wall of the garage fell in on him. They put him in the bed next to mine, in a little room all made out of curtains. That may have not been the best decision ever. I'm not sure which one of us was more freaked out.

"You could have been killed!" I guess since he's Dad, he gets to yell first. "What the hell were you thinking going up there?"

"I was thinking you all let their house burn down and I wasn't going to let their garage burn up, too." There was a nurse standing just outside the curtained cubby where they'd put us, so I dropped my voice. A little. "Not if I could help it."

"Rimi—"

"Don't tell me I'm wrong. You know it as well as I do."

"We came to the fire, girl. I didn't even know you were there until I got there." He shook his head. "When I come up on scene and saw your car there. Jesus Christ. Don't you know how dangerous that was?"

"I had the fire extinguisher."

"That and a dollar will still get you killed! You don't respond to a fully involved structure fire with a goddamn kitchen fire extinguisher!"

"Way I understood it, Daddy, is that in Randsville you don't respond to fully involved structure fires at all."

"You don't," he shouted. "Your ass should have been in school! That is where you were supposed to be."

"If you're not going to come save them, who will? This is what taking care of our own looks like."

"How is Ms. Gibbs your own?"

"She teaches at my school. She lives in my town. I've played fetch with her dogs!" I wanted to shout back, but my words were getting raspier and raspier. "How is she not my own?"

"I thought you meant...something else." Dad looked at me. "When you said that."

I shook my head. "Can't we have just one problem at a time right now?"

"Is everything all right in here?" The nurse poked her head through the curtains. She looked directly at me. "I can move you to another bed if this one is too...stressful."

I shook my head. "It's all right."

She turned to Dad. "I understand that you're very upset. But this is a hospital, and we need you to tone it down. Now. Your daughter has some serious injuries."

Dad looked at me. "How is your hand?"

"It hurts." The smoke had messed up my throat pretty good. Half the time when I tried to talk, it sounded like I was going to bust out crying. "Hurts like hell."

"I'm sure it does, baby." All of a sudden, there was my dad, standing up and hugging on me, pulling me tight with his good arm. "Next time you plan on doing stupid stuff like this, be careful. You could have at least taken my turnout gear."

I laughed. "Like it's gonna fit."

"The gloves would have." He narrowed his eyes. "You realize that if you'd got that fool door open the fire could have exploded right on out of there? It's called a backdraft. You could have gotten yourself killed."

"I just wanted to save the day."

"I know, kiddo." Dad squeezed me tight. "But what you did was scare the hell out of me."

"Well, you did, too."

"Shit happens." He lifted the cast. "This ain't nothing."

I shook my head. "Not that. I mean, that's no good either. But you scared me before. When their house burned up." I was actually crying now, and the nurse outside wasn't even pretending like she wasn't listening. "You're supposed to be the good guy, Daddy. What happened to saving the day?"

"Ri..."

"You. Always. Save. The. Day." I don't know why I was hitting him, a punch to the gut for every word, my fist pushing into his stomach. I don't know why he wasn't mad—it had to hurt—but he wasn't.

He just held on, and kept holding on, and then he said, "I know. I was wrong, babe. You showed me that."

"Really?"

"It took me a bit. I was listening too much to other people and not enough to you." He let out a deep breath. "Which was stupid."

"I could have told you that."

Dad laughed. "I think you did."

"You didn't listen."

Dad stopped laughing. "No. I didn't. And I didn't do what I should have done." His voice broke a little bit, like he was the one who got a throat full of smoke. "That's not always what I'm best at in this world."

"You came the second time." I didn't want Dad to be sad. I mean, I was mad at him, really, really mad at him, but at the same time, I wanted everything to be okay. I wanted us to be Dad and Rimi, like normal.

Hell, I wanted more than that. I wanted to be able to talk without my throat hurting. I wanted my hand not to hurt. I wanted everyone to do what they were supposed to be doing. I wanted to be able to count on Dad to save the day.

I wanted to not be crying, but I was crying. Tears kept filling up my eyes, no matter how much I blinked them away. They were running over my cheeks, falling onto the stupid gown the nurse made me put on. If I'd had these tears at the scene, I wouldn't have needed the fire extinguisher. I could have put the fire out with tears.

"I can't be leaving it for my little girl to do, now can I?" Dad stepped back for a minute and looked at me. He pulled a sheet up off of the bed and dried my face without even mentioning the fact I was crying. "And you are my little girl, you know. No matter what." He swallowed deeply. "No matter who your own are. I will always love you."

We're not so good at the mushy stuff, Dad and I, so I made a little joke to get him laughing again. "I'm not so little anymore." I reached up and tapped his nose real soft. "I almost broke your nose."

"You're little enough." He smiled. "Little enough to let me take care of the fires, all right?"

"Are you going to go? No matter whose house it is?"

He nodded. "If it'll keep you from going."

My body was shaking, and I felt like I was going to throw up again. Either my life was really too dramatic or there was something seriously wrong with my stomach. There was no reason to be freaking out now, but my body didn't seem to know that. Half of me wanted to run away and the other half just wanted to lay down and cry.

"The adrenaline's worn off," Dad explained. "I feel like that every time, after a call. We all do."

"I'm too little to go to Stuckey's."

Dad laughed, and I could have sworn I heard the nurse laughing too. "Yeah, you are. At least for the next twenty or thirty years."

The hospital said they weren't planning on keeping us long, but that didn't stop people from coming to see us.

I swear that half the Randsville Fire Department drove in for the privilege of seeing us in the hospital rather than our own house. It was weird. They all had plenty to say to Dad, and not a whole lot to say to me.

Most of them couldn't look me in the eye. I made a point of looking at them, though. Sometimes people in this world need to know that you can see what they're about. It's easier to be hateful when you think nobody's looking.

My daddy taught me that.

Ms. Gibbs came by, too. She brought Tracey with her. They'd waited until the department people cleared out before coming to talk to us.

"Miriam." Ms. Gibbs took a deep breath. "That was very brave, what you did. For Tracey and me. But please. Please. Don't ever do it again."

"I promise." I said. "Fighting fires is a lot harder than it looks."

"I know how frightened I was," Tracey said, "when our house was burning." She was taller than Ms. Gibbs, and more solid. She didn't seem like a woman who got frightened easily. "To be willing to run to a fire to save someone else…" She paused and turned to my dad. "You must be very proud."

"I've always been," Dad said. He looked Tracey right in the face. "Rimi is a smart girl. She sees things sometimes that I don't."

Ms. Gibbs nodded, and I guessed she knew Randsville hadn't responded to the first fire. She might not have known that when we were talking in study hall, but she surely knew now. "The younger generation has a different viewpoint."

"On some things," Dad said.

"I didn't know you were planning on being a firefighter," Ms. Gibbs said to me.

"I didn't either. Just kind of happened." I looked up at her. "I'm sorry I couldn't save your garage."

"Screw the garage," she said, and I was shocked, because I didn't know teachers talked like that. "We have insurance,

Miriam. We can always build another garage. We can build another house."

"We'll be doing both," Tracey said.

"What we can't do is get another Miriam. There's no insurance that's going to bring back a bright, strong, determined girl from…well, if something goes wrong. Some problems can't be fixed. So please. You've got to promise me that you're going to be careful." Ms. Gibbs was tearing up. "The world needs every Miriam it can get."

"I will be," I said. "I promise. No more firefighting for me."

I glanced over at Dad. His eyes were shining.

"You hold her to that," Tracey said to him.

"Oh, I plan on it." He nodded. "I'll make sure she doesn't have any reason to think otherwise."

Ms. Gibbs gave him the nod. "We appreciate that." They all shook hands, and Ms. Gibbs and Tracey both hugged me, and then they were gone.

"They seem like decent enough people," Dad said. He let out a big breath and lay back on his pillow, staring at the ceiling. "What a day."

He didn't say good night then, and I don't think Dad really reckoned on sleeping. But soon enough, he was snoring. I didn't mind it. It was the only familiar sound in this place, where everything was beeping and clicking and dinging.

Dad sounded like Dad.

I was lying there listening to him when the nurse came in. "How are you doing, hon?"

"I've been better," I said. "But I shouldn't complain."

"Don't worry about shoulds," she said. "The day you've had, you're entitled to a few complaints."

I looked over at Dad. "It's not the day I had as much as the day I'm gonna." There were still a few beans to spill. Or at least, ones I hoped worth spilling. Emily Masterson hadn't even turned those fine blue eyes of hers in my direction once…and Dad was going to ask questions until he got the answers. Answers I'd give that weren't going to make him particularly happy.

"Don't borrow trouble, honey. Tomorrow will get here either way."

"You sure about that?"

"Pretty much. You see a lot of stuff, working here. And your dad? That man loves you. That'll fix a lot of trouble." She tipped her head toward his bed. "It's pretty much the only thing that does."

JEFFREY RICKER is a writer, editor, and graphic designer. He is a magna cum laude graduate of the University of Missouri School of Journalism, and his writing has appeared or is forthcoming in the literary magazine *Collective Fallout,* the anthologies *Paws and Reflect, Fool for Love: New Gay Fiction, Blood Sacraments,* and *Men of the Mean Streets.* His first novel, *Detours,* is forthcoming from Bold Strokes Books. He lives with his partner, Michael, and two dogs, and is working on his second novel and too many stories to keep track of at once. Follow his blog at jeffreyricker.wordpress.com.

When I was fourteen and in high school, my biggest hope was to make it through the day without attracting too much attention to myself. I knew I was gay, but it would be another four years before I admitted that fact to anyone else, and a number of years after that before I lived my life in a way that I thought did it justice. These days, in the face of greater acceptance—as well as greater adversity—it gives me hope to see a friend's fifteen-year-old transgendered child living with greater self-awareness, strength, and courage than I could have hoped to muster at the same age. She lives her life on her own terms without compromise and without hiding who she is. I hope she's as much of an inspiration to people her own age as she is to people like me, who waited far too long to do the same.

THE TROUBLE WITH BILLY
JEFFREY RICKER

*T*his, Jamie thinks, *is the day when I'm just going to walk in front of the bus instead of getting on it.*

He doesn't, though he's not sure why. Of course, Sarah's on the bus, and he doesn't want her to have to see him splattered all over the road. Even so, turning himself into roadkill would be better than dealing with his oral presentation in English class third period (not to mention having to stare at Mrs. Hathaway's hairy mole, which she apparently refuses to pluck).

He wouldn't have to deal with Billy Stratton, either.

"Did you hear Kate Bush is coming out with a new album this year?" Sarah asks, almost before Jamie lands in the seat next to her. Sarah is obsessed with the singer.

"Please," he says. "It's only been six years since *Aerial*. I bet the next one won't drop until 2014 at the earliest."

Sarah gets a triumphant look on her face, and out comes her smartphone. If there's ever a question about something or an argument that needs settling, she consults Google on her phone, which Jamie calls the Oracle. She shows him a page in the browser.

He squints at the screen and says, "Whatever. Remember when Kate Bush News was saying every two months 'Announcement Imminent'?"

"Well, they were right, weren't they?"

"Eventually, but that's like saying 'it's gonna rain' every day. Sooner or later you'll be right."

"Well, this site was right about Beth Ditto," she says. "And Lady Gaga's new album release date."

"Beth who?" Jamie's never heard of Beth Ditto, and he's kind of over Gaga, at least for now. Kate Bush, though, is the glue cementing his friendship with Sarah. That, and the fact that he and Sarah are both the only children of single fathers, all of them "only" in their own way.

It started in middle school, an eighth-grade dance, when Sarah requested "The Big Sky" off *Hounds of Love* and the DJ actually played it. Jamie was there only because his father had made him go—"You spend too much time in this house by yourself reading," he'd said. Jamie spent most of the evening propping up a table in the corner until that song came on. Her voice was unlike any he'd heard before: high but not airy, as if she weren't breathing air but something even more elemental than that. The next thing he noticed was the girl twirling by herself across the mostly empty floor, her eyes closed—but even so, she moved with a sense that kept her from colliding with anyone else. A few other people danced, and Sarah started bouncing up and down with more sheer joy than Jamie had ever seen in a single person. How could he not get up and join her?

The next day she brought him a mix CD of her favorite Kate Bush songs, which she slipped into his locker along with a note—*I think you need her as much as I do.* Jamie still has the CD and the note. He and Sarah have been inseparable ever since.

"Well," he says, "I'll believe it when I see it." He waves his hand dismissively, only realizing at the end that the gesture is, well, a little *fey.* Someone in the seat behind him giggles, and he knows she's laughing at him, at his hand, at the only pathetic gay in the village. He whips his head around and fixes the guilty party—a freshman, the *nerve*—with a look of such pure venom that the girl's gaze immediately drops to the floor. *Don't mess with me today, missy,* he thinks.

As he turns around he catches Sarah's eye. She raises an eyebrow and purses her lips to show she's impressed. Jamie would like to high-five her, but the nervousness is already taking hold again. They're on the straightaway leading up to school, and there are no turns from here except the one that takes them into the parking lot. And eventually, at some point during the day, he'll run into Billy.

Jamie tells himself he just has to make it through the day, which is the same thing he tells himself every Monday through Friday, until two thirty arrives and he's free for another day, or another weekend. He tries not to think about Monday. Instead he thinks about turning seventeen next month, about being a senior next year, and about going to college and getting out of Athens as soon as possible after that. He's looking at colleges in New York, Chicago, Boston—anywhere but Missouri.

"Penny," Sarah says as the bus pulls into the parking lot. Penny for his thoughts, she means.

"Nothing," he says. There isn't enough time to convey to her the sense of dread that overcomes him every time the bus climbs the hill to the front of the school. *Running up that hill with no problem,* he thinks. *Yeah, right.*

Once they get off the bus, they go to their respective homerooms and won't see each other again until third-period AP English, then lunch. Second period is chemistry, the one class he has that's not honors level—and the one class Billy Stratton shares with him. Jamie can't really explain to Sarah, in the short amount of time they have between the bus and the front door, how getting flattened by the bus still seems like a viable option to him. Life already seems to be doing a pretty good job of it, so why not go for it literally?

He'll never do it, though. He'll keep getting on the bus every day, walking into school, and hoping that today he'll escape Billy Stratton's notice.

❖

He makes it look so easy, Billy thinks, *being yourself.*

From behind the wheel of his Mustang, Billy watches Jamie get off the bus and walk into school, his friend Sarah beside him. He wishes he liked Sarah. She's beautiful in a careless kind of way, as if she doesn't realize it or put any effort into it. But it's not Sarah he looks at, except when she's beside Jamie.

Jamie. He's not much taller than his friend Sarah, and if she's wearing heels, he's even a bit shorter than her. He has nondescript brown hair, though he does this swoop thing with it in the front that makes it look like he's always walking into a breeze. His fair skin looks like it shelters from the sun, that it would burn easily. He flushes red so easily, which contrasts with the green of his eyes.

Sarah says something to him and Jamie laughs, his head tilted back, and for an instant Billy is so consumed with jealousy that he grips the steering wheel so tight he imagines it breaks between his fingers.

Billy's been at school for over half an hour already and needs to hurry up and get inside before the bell, but he's in no rush to get out of the car. For one thing, he hasn't finished his reading homework for English, and knowing his luck that means Mrs. Hathaway will call on him before anyone else. For another, the song on the CD isn't over yet, and it's one of his favorites. He only listens to it in the car or on his iPod, where no one else will hear it, where he won't have to be embarrassed that he's listening to it. He started listening to her when he heard Jamie talking to Sarah about some woman named Kate Bush.

He pulls his textbook out of his backpack, but the reading assignment is almost fifteen pages. It's this Irish guy, James Joyce, and even though he's writing in English, it might as well be in Japanese for all the sense it makes to Billy.

Oh, what's the point? He's falling behind in his classes, and if his grades keep slipping he's going to flunk something. That would mean summer school, which would also mean less time for his job at the garage and, maybe, less time for football practice. It's the last part that worries him most; if he doesn't play starting lineup, there's almost no chance he'll get a football scholarship, and no scholarship means no college.

He returns the book to his backpack and switches off the stereo once "The Sensual World" is over. The next song on the CD is okay, but that one is his favorite. He read somewhere that she was inspired by James Joyce when she wrote it, but if anyone asked him, Kate Bush makes a lot more sense than Joyce could ever hope to.

Not that they *would* ask. He doesn't speak up in English class. Not because he isn't smart—he knows he is, he really does believe that—but he's stretched so thin that he doesn't have time to give any one thing too much attention. Between work, football, wrestling in the off season, and chores at home, there's not much time left for school. His parents have noticed his A-and-B grades have slipped into B-and-C territory. His father worries that he's not going to get into college. Even if he does get in on a football scholarship, he won't be able to stay in if he can't do the work. His stepmother worries that he's overextending himself and she wants him to cut back on something, maybe work—or what about sitting out wrestling this year?

He doesn't want to do that, though.

They haven't noticed what's on the layer beneath those changes, and he hopes he never has to explain. He doesn't know if he can find the words for it, the thing that sits in his gut like some creature. That's why he wants to go away for college, so he doesn't have to try to explain it. But he's not going to get out of Athens if he doesn't bring his grades back up.

Why is it that everywhere he looks, it seems, he sees Jamie? He stands out like a flare, a beacon. Billy needs to stop thinking about Jamie.

❖

Billy somehow makes it through English first period without Mrs. Hathaway calling on him. He tries to follow the discussion for a while, but soon it's pretty clear he won't make sense of it since he didn't finish the reading. Still, sitting in silence with no one taking notice is better than the alternative. Billy hopes his luck will hold out for the rest of the day.

When he gets to chemistry class, his luck goes down in flames with a pop quiz. Of the ten answers he turns in, four are total guesses. He can feel himself circling the drain, as if he's going to descend into a dark place and drown in shit.

Jamie's in the seat in front of him. Billy doesn't realize he's kicking the leg of Jamie's chair until Jamie looks back at him, annoyed. His eyes go briefly wide when he realizes who's sitting behind him, and he looks away quickly, but Billy knows he's gotten to Jamie. On a scoreboard that's only in his head, he makes a little check mark.

When Billy was little, about five or six, there was a girl he liked in his kindergarten class. One day at recess he pushed her off the swings, and the teacher spanked him for it. (This was back when it was acceptable for teachers to spank their students.) When his parents asked him why he pushed her, what she'd done to him, he didn't know, as if any kid knows why they do anything at that point.

Now, though, Billy knows he did it because he liked the girl. He just didn't know how to tell her that.

Finally, Jamie turns around again and whispers, "Knock it off, will you?"

Which of them is more surprised: Jamie, who actually spoke up for himself, or Billy, that Jamie actually said something to him? Briefly, their eyes lock, deer caught in each other's headlights. Billy's the one who blinks first, glances away, and stops kicking the chair. It was getting boring, anyway.

What should he do next? Billy's never sure, though he knows it won't be anything that gets him anywhere. How else is he supposed to relate to Jamie? He can't just talk to him, not with Marc two rows ahead of them. Marc may be a linebacker, but he gossips like a cheerleader. Billy smiles at that. He'll have to remember that one so later he can tell it to…someone. He's not sure who. It's not the sort of thing he can say to most people he knows. They'd think it's too clever, and why is he comparing Marc to a cheerleader, anyway? Does he like the idea of seeing Marc in a miniskirt, shaking his pompoms?

It's not fair, he thinks, though he's not sure what "it" is exactly. Everything. Nothing is fair. His life isn't fair. Specifics don't really matter at this point so much as the blue fire of his sudden and irrational anger, and he kicks the leg of Jamie's chair again, harder and more savagely this time. Suddenly, Jamie's up on his feet and screaming, red-faced, at Billy.

"Stop kicking my chair, you dumbass monkey!" Jamie yells. He also throws his pencil at Billy, which nicks him in the cheek. Billy lifts his hand to his face; he's not bleeding, but he's somewhat dazed.

Mr. McGrath has turned around from the whiteboard, now he's yelling at Jamie. "Mr. Thomas! Up front, now!"

He makes Jamie move to a chair at the front of the class.

As Jamie sits down, the teacher adds, "One more outburst and you're going to Ms. Wood's office."

Billy keeps touching his cheek. He's amazed Jamie actually had the gumption to throw something at him. It doesn't hurt, and he's not sure there's even a mark, but it feels warm, like someone is touching him there. For the rest of the class, Billy can't leave it alone. He wants to forget that Jamie did it out of anger. Would a kiss burn as much?

❖

Sarah can tell Jamie's rattled as soon as he walks into English class. He drops his backpack by the desk next to hers and slumps in the chair. He's never in a great mood after chemistry. She already knows why.

"So, what did he do this time?" she asks.

Jamie shakes his head. "Nothing, really. He just kept kicking the back of my chair. I don't think he even realized it was me sitting in front of him until I looked back to tell him to knock it off."

She takes note of his phrasing. "And did you actually tell him to knock it off?"

"Actually, I called him a dumbass monkey and threw my pencil at him. And almost got sent to the principal's office."

Sarah starts to laugh, but the look of irritation from Jamie silences her. He shuffles through his notebook—he has to give a report this period—and it looks to her like the sheets of paper aren't the only things he's barely holding on to.

"Maybe Mrs. Hathaway will let you do your report tomorrow," she says, but Jamie just shakes his head.

"And if Billy gets it in his mind to do something else tomorrow, do I just keep asking her if I can put it off until the day he decides not to be an asshole?" He laughs, but there's no humor in it. "I keep telling myself I just need to get through another year and a half, but how can I even think that far ahead when I don't even know if I have it in me to get through the next period?"

Sarah reaches across and squeezes his hand. "You do. I know you can do it."

Jamie stops shuffling papers and stares at her hand around his. "Maybe I don't want to do it anymore." His voice is small, like it's hiding under the desk. The day isn't even halfway over yet, and already he sounds exhausted.

Sarah wants to tell him not to say things like that, but Mrs. Hathaway closes the door, and that's the signal they're about to start. Jamie makes his presentation; it's good, maybe not the best he could do, but once he gets into his topic, he seems able to put aside his anxiety. If only Sarah could put aside her anger half as easily, even for a moment, but she can't, never has been able to. It's been a steady beat of the hammer, this anger, ever since she was old enough to realize life isn't fair, life doesn't care about fairness or whether you don't have a mom. Injustice is ingrained into this life, and there are only three things you can do in the face of it: you can try to work it out, beat flat the imperfections from its surface through brute force; you can discover some way to turn that injustice into power; or you can simply let it bulldoze you.

Jamie hasn't learned the alchemy that might let him transform the raw materials of pain into something more tempered, worth keeping. That takes time, a continuous forging against an anvil of hurt. By the time it's done with you, either you're broken or you're indestructible.

Sarah has always felt indestructible. Jamie has it in him to be as well. But what about Billy?

❖

Now that he's gotten halfway through the day, Jamie feels like he can breathe a little easier. He goes to his locker to put away his English books and get his lunch. His locker is on the hallway off the science wing, an older part of the school where the lockers stand in rows perpendicular to the walls. The teachers don't like the arrangement, since it gives students places to stand out of easy sight, but the district doesn't have the money to replace them yet.

When he shuts his locker, Billy is standing on the other side of it. Jamie lets out a little yelp before he regains control of himself.

"What do you want?" Jamie asks. He notices how eerily quiet the hall is, now that most everyone is either in the cafeteria or in class. No one would notice if Billy decided to beat him up right here.

"That's, 'What do you want, Mr. Dumbass Monkey?'" Billy says, smiling. To Jamie, it's more like he's baring his teeth.

"Leave me alone." Jamie tries to get out of the corner he's in, but Billy dodges to the right and leans against the locker, his outstretched arm barring Jamie's way.

"Say 'Please.'"

Billy lifts his hand and Jamie thinks he's going to punch him or, at the least, slap him, but much to his surprise—and, judging by the expression on his own face, to Billy's surprise also—he places his palm flat against Jamie's cheek. It's almost a caress.

Jamie bats it aside, and he knows he's going to completely lose it if he doesn't get away from Billy soon. "What the hell is the matter with you?" Jamie shouts, and then makes a break for it. He doesn't stop running until he's out of the hallway and by the cafeteria door, and then he looks back. But Billy hasn't followed him.

Jamie has always thought standing up to Billy would make

him feel better. It doesn't. He expected one of two possible outcomes: an apology (unlikely) or a physical assault (virtually inevitable). But the way Billy touched his face... It reminds Jamie of a story his history teacher told about Captain Cook's ship arriving in Australia, how the sight of it was so massive and unfamiliar to the natives they could not comprehend it, so they acted as if it wasn't there until they saw the canoes approaching shore and realized the threat.

Maybe that's how he should treat what Billy just did. Ignoring it, though, isn't the same as unknowing it. He can't make it or Billy disappear. The only thing that's vanished, as far as he can tell, is his appetite for lunch.

Sarah can tell something's happened. Jamie's out of breath when he sits down, and the curling wave of his bangs has crashed over the sweat shine on his forehead.

"What happened?" she asks.

"I don't want to talk about it," Jamie says.

"But—"

"No. I mean it."

His hands are trembling a little as he opens his lunch bag, so Sarah relents. Glancing toward the cafeteria doors, she sees Billy looking in. They lock eyes briefly, and Billy looks away and walks off.

Eventually, Jamie catches his breath, and he and Sarah spend the rest of lunch hour in troubled silence. Sarah may not know the specifics, but she doesn't need details to know that Billy has rattled Jamie again.

Jamie's next class is AP history; Sarah has study hall. She doesn't go to class, though. Instead, she waits for Billy.

Sarah's never actually spoken to him. They don't travel in the same circles, so far as high school can be said to have circles. Tiny circumferences. Archery and AP English don't often intersect with varsity football and wrestling. She only sees him in passing, and she's never seen him get aggressive toward Jamie. If she had, maybe that would make it easier to justify, this urge to put an arrow through Billy's heart.

She won't do anything as violent as that, of course. What she will do is hide in the bathroom after lunch until the bell for fifth period rings, then she'll slip out and go back to the cafeteria, where Billy has the second lunch period.

She watches him. Sitting at a table on the other side of the cafeteria, an apple and a glass of milk in front of her, she tries to stare at him without looking like she's staring. Occasionally, she glances away, catches someone else's eye—they look at her as if to say, *What are you doing here?* Their gazes don't linger too long, though. She prefers it that way. Sarah likes to think she's realistic about her looks: pretty enough for the first glance, but not so compelling as to warrant a second. It's also why none of the teachers stop her in the halls between classes. (A reputation for studiousness helps, too.)

Billy sits just off center at the table crowded with boys in letterman's jackets and girls in cheerleaders' skirts. He's not the focus of attention—that's the quarterback and his girlfriend, who isn't a cheerleader but is rich enough that she's popular without making that effort. More than watching Billy, though, Sarah watches what and whom he watches. After a while, she notices a pattern, unexpected at first, but the more she thinks about it, the more she starts to get it, why Billy is so bent on making Jamie's life a misery from the time he walks in the front doors of the school until he makes his escape to the bus—and probably even beyond that.

When lunch is over, she goes to sixth period, wondering what to do with this new knowledge. Wondering if there *is* anything to do with it. It makes her even angrier than before, makes her actually want to go to her locker and get out her archery quiver, notch an arrow, and zero in on the back of Billy's head.

That thought stays with her the rest of the afternoon, so she's not surprised when, like a target she's been aiming for, she finds herself behind Billy at the end of the day when she walks out of school. He's standing on the curb, kind of apart from everyone, and he's staring at Jamie, who's walking across the parking lot to the school bus.

There's a rock in Billy's left hand, she notices. *Huh, I never knew he was left-handed.* He's turning the rock over in his palm, like a worry bead or a stress ball. He wipes his face with his right hand, and Sarah thinks it's odd, that gesture. He looks troubled or exhausted more than angry. First he glances left and right, making sure no one's watching, but he doesn't look behind. He doesn't see her.

She plucks the rock from his grip as he's winding back for the throw, and she's dropped it into her coat pocket before he's even finished turning around to stare at her, dumbfounded.

"Hi, Billy," she says, trying to keep her voice from rising, even though it feels like there's a fist-sized lump of screaming lodged in her throat just begging to be let loose.

"What do you want, freak?" His voice rises to a squeal, and she can see he's embarrassed by the tone of his voice. He's at least six inches taller than her and he's trying to look intimidating, but it's not working.

"I don't think I'm the only freak around here," she says.

Sarah looks past him at Jamie, who's gotten on the bus safely and the doors have shut. Soon he'll start to wonder where she is, why she's not riding home with him. Later, she'll have to call her dad and ask him to pick her up on his way home, but she'll just tell him she had extra archery practice. He's usually distracted enough to believe whatever she tells him.

Billy also watches Jamie get on the bus, and then turns back to Sarah and sneers. "Looks like we both missed your boyfriend." He flings the last word at her like an insult. She just sighs.

"He's not my boyfriend, dumbass. He's gay. Besides, he's not the freak I was talking about." She pats the rock in her coat pocket. "Jamie's left-handed, too. I wonder what else you two have in common."

"You don't know what you're talking about," he says, but in a brief moment of hesitation, a trembling in his eyes, he verifies her suspicion.

"Wouldn't it be easier," she asks, "if you'd just be yourself?"

Sarah walks away without waiting to hear his answer. That wasn't the point of asking the question in the first place.

The bus hasn't pulled away yet and she breaks into a jog, hoping to catch it before it takes off. She's almost too late, but she bangs her fist against the side of the bus as she comes alongside. The driver opens the door, giving Sarah a sour glance when she boards. Jamie shifts on the bench to let her have the window seat—she likes looking out the window, he likes being on the aisle—and she can tell from his reaction that the smile on her face is too forced.

"What's up with you?" he asks her.

"Nothing," she says, and looks out the window. By this time, Billy has gotten into his car and is pulling out of the parking lot ahead of the bus. Jamie probably knows his car on sight. Given how much Billy has tormented him all year—longer than that, even—Sarah's sure he recognizes everything that could be a harbinger of Billy's approach.

No doubt Billy does the same thing.

Impulsively, Sarah takes Jamie's hand and clutches it against the side of her leg. She puts her other hand on top of his and rubs it, as if she's trying to keep him warm.

"Okay, seriously," he says, "what's the matter?"

"I said nothing," she replies. "What, you don't believe me?"

He glances down at their hands. "At the moment? Not really."

She laughs, more genuine now than her earlier smile. "I'm just really glad it's Friday. What do you want to do this weekend? Want to go see a movie?" She gets out her Oracle and starts to look up show times.

Jamie shrugs. "I have a mountain of homework."

"So do I. It'll keep."

Jamie considers for a moment, then smiles. "As long as you're buying the popcorn."

In his rearview mirror, Billy watches the bus pull out of the parking lot and head in the opposite direction. He's so wound up, he has to pull over. He wishes Sarah had been angrier, had yelled and screamed or maybe even thrown the rock right at him after she took it from his hand. Her cool accusation is more unsettling than rage might have been. Rage, at least, he could understand.

It wasn't a big rock, and it's not like he was aiming for Jamie's head, but now the idea of throwing it brings a wave of embarrassment and shame crashing down on Billy. He leans his head against the steering wheel. What on earth was he thinking when he picked up that rock? What did he even expect to accomplish by throwing it? The envy that filled him earlier that morning is now a hollow ache unlike any hunger he's felt before. He's envious not of just one of them, but both: of Sarah because it's so easy for her to talk to Jamie, and of Jamie because he has someone like Sarah to confide in. Where's Billy's Sarah? What does he have to do to find someone like that? And once found, would they forgive him for what he'd almost done?

The answer's in him, but he doesn't want, he's afraid, to look that deep.

So he lifts his head from the steering wheel. The Kate Bush CD's still in the stereo, "Love and Anger" blaring at him. He reaches over to switch it off, but instead he sits there and listens to the song until he thinks he's finally ready to go home.

STEVE BERMAN's deepest secrets can be found on the last page, under "About the Editor." All right, maybe not deepest secrets. But you might laugh at how he's bossed around by his cat.

I have a gay nephew. Zach. Though I often write about gay themes, I've never been much of an activist. But Zach, he aches to march, to shout, to *do* anything that will help LGBT rights. He loves anarchist bookshops and zines and works as a bike messenger. I remember on a brutally cold autumn night, he convinced me to take him to an outdoor meeting in Love Park, Philadelphia. Part of why I trembled was the wind. Part of why I shook was the enthusiasm rising off the few folk gathered—like the steam that drifted up from our mouths. And that's just one more reason I am proud of the man Zach has become.

Only Lost Boys Are Found
Steve Berman

You're surprisingly normal despite having grown up in a house with an extreme quantity of closets. Every room has at least one. At the top of the steps is a linen closet. Your parents' room has two, a his and hers. Your sister, older and more adventurous, had chosen the other bedroom with two. You don't mind having a single closet; what good is one really? Too shallow, too small. When closed, a closet is like looking at a wall featuring a doorknob. Weird. These days people have chests of drawers to put away clothes. And what guy your age hangs up his shirts or jeans? You sometimes sniff your clothes to see if you can get another day out of them.

❖

Your Closet

What you keep in your closet in no order suggesting proximity or stratum:

A dog-eared paperback, assigned for freshman English class. Your teacher is convinced that every great work of Literature (stress the capital "L") can be turned inside out to reveal a fairy tale. You haven't read much more than the first few pages of the book, bought at a flea market so it's maimed, without a cover. Something about a boy with a flashlight who is climbing down stairs. Or maybe it's a mountain, or stairs set on the side of a mountain. But the boy is scared that his flashlight will die before he reaches the bottom.

A broken iPod, screen cracked in a cool pattern after you dropped it in the school parking lot and fucking Adrian Jesson drove over it. You don't think it was an accident.

A pile that is actually a moss-green corduroy jacket you found at the same flea market as the book and thought might look cool if you ever had the need for a ritzy jacket. Only it's too big and smells…well, mossy.

A shoebox of mixed Legos—ninjas and pirates mostly—that used to belong to Neil Jesson (yes, younger brother to the aforementioned Adrian). You started playing together in third grade. Neil always wanted Hollywood to make a movie where Blackbeard invaded Japan.

A wrapped square box, the dust hiding the shine of the metallic gold paper. A Valentine's Day present for Neil. But he never showed up at school that day. Or the day after or the one after that. You don't remember what the gift is but tearing off the ribbon and the wrapping paper would be something awful, a felony of love, so you keep it way in the back of the closet so as not to glimpse the box too often. You miss Neil.

One thing definitely not in the closet: you. When you turned ten (August, it was brutally hot) you told your parents that inviting girls from school for your birthday party was just okay but you were much more interested in which boys showed. And they knew then the truth and not too much later they had a talk with you so you'd be sure of the truth as well. And they were fine with you.

But not everyone is so lucky. You know this. When Neil never showed, you texted him—at first gentle concerns, then frantic worries. No replies. You dialed and left messages. Nothing. You even called Neil's home wanting to know what happened. Adrian answered both times, the last cursing you out before hanging up. His harsh voice left you feeling like crumpled paper. You are convinced that they somehow found out about you and him and sent him off someplace far away. Maybe to an asylum or boarding school. You feel guilty—you should have been more careful, kept your affection quiet. You should not have urged he come out. Neil was always so shy. You remember how he kissed with his eyes closed and then kept them shut for a few seconds afterward, as if he was afraid to look at you. And you were the one who always began the kiss. Yeah, you feel guilty.

❖

The Refrigerator

You suppose the fridge is sort of like a closet, only cold, icy in spots, and thrumming with electricity. No really, it is "like a closet"—there are even forgotten things at the very back. A jar once for pickles but now holding the remains of a hollandaise sauce made last year. A roll of film from when your sister wanted to be a famous photographer. Yogurt that is no longer alive.

You grab an armful of butter and eggs and bacon and head over to the stove. You leave the fridge door open just in case you need something else.

Neil taught you how to make your favorite breakfast right. He stayed over one night before either of you had decided you were *more* than friends. Your mother always cooked eggs in the pan and bacon in the microwave. But Neil woke a few minutes earlier than you and was already at the stove when you climbed downstairs. His hair was seriously stuck in bedhead mode. But you didn't tease him; calling attention to that would leave Neil silent and withdrawn all afternoon.

He made the most incredible eggs and bacon. And you devoured the plate he made you and insisted right then and there he repeat himself so you could watch and learn. And instead of refusing or complaining, he just smiled and did so. And yes, you wanted to kiss him, the first time you ever felt that way.

Raw bacon goes into the skillet first. Let it bubble and warp as it cooks. Watch out for the fireworks of launched hot grease. When it's shriveled down to crisp strips, ruddy meat and amber fat that all taste of 100% salty nitrite goodness, you lift them onto a plate. Then crack the eggs into the same pan, making two yellow eyes staring back at you, the whites turning brown and black at the edges from the hot bacon grease. And you start shaving fine bits of butter down onto the whites, followed with a dusting of pepper. The eyes will bubble and become jaundiced but they will soon be the best ever eggs imaginable.

Just as you're bringing your plate to the table, you wish, for the thousandth time, that Neil was sitting across from you with a subtle, pleased expression at teaching you so well.

❖

Third-Floor Boys' Bathroom

Did you know an old-fashioned term for bathroom is water closet?

You're heading to the cafeteria when someone grabs you by the collar from behind and shoves you into the bathroom. In the mirrors on one wall you catch a glimpse of Adrian's squared and ruddy face before he pushes you into an open stall. The door slams back and catches shut.

You back up until you are against the toilet. The paper dispenser is empty, broken, and covered in coarse graffiti. You doubt a girl would ever want to do the things someone wrote.

"Listen. I don't have time to repeat this," you hear Adrian say. "And I don't even know if I'm doing right…but maybe you can help him."

You go even more tense at *him*. *Him. Neil.* "Where is he?" you ask.

Adrian's sneakers are both untied, the laces no longer anywhere near white. "I think…I think he's scared and hiding."

You repeat the question, noting the irony that you are a bit scared right then.

"I said some things. I didn't mean to—big brothers tease. We're supposed to, but I think I went too far—"

You hear the bathroom door open and you hear Adrian say, "Get the fuck out of here," followed by the sound of running away.

"I've heard him crying. I'll be in my room and I'll hear him, but when I cross the hall and open his door—nothing. No one's there. I've gone through his whole room, looked under the bed, everything. But the crying doesn't stop and I can't find him."

You think this is the cruelest thing Adrian could ever say to you.

"I can't help him. But maybe you can. And you have to. I can't take it anymore, hearing him cry and not being able to stop it."

You refuse to say anything and finally you watch Adrian's dirty sneakers move out of sight and hear the bathroom door open. He's gone. You sit down on the toilet and rub the sides of your head and wonder why love and siblings are just so awful.

❖

Your Closet

What do you have that would help with a rescue mission?

It's Saturday morning and you're groggy because you couldn't sleep last night because of what Adrian told you yesterday. It's crazy, but, as you lie half-in, half-out of your closet, with the Legos in reach and the gift within sight, you're willing to believe. Because Saturdays are magical for kids, have been ever since the first morning cartoon was shown on television. At fifteen you hope there's still enough of a kid in you to find Neil with Saturday's help.

❖

Your Sister's Closets

She keeps things needed for adventure.

She's still asleep. Does so till after twelve or even one on the weekends. So you twist the doorknob oh so quietly, oh so cautiously. There's more at risk than a pillow thrown at your head. Such a territorial incursion might get you grounded, and you need your entire Saturday to stage the rescue of the boy you love.

Her room smells...well, weird. A bit of pine from whatever gear she takes to camp at the Barrens, the funk from nearly a dozen sneakers, brine ghosts from found shells that should have been better cleaned.

You glance at her lying in bed. Still in jeans and a sweatshirt. The window open, letting in cool air. She must have snuck back in through the window from whatever exploits she's now sleeping off. So step by step you make your way to the first closet, partially open.

❖

Your Sister's Closets—No. 1

Ugh, clothes and clothes and more clothes. Doesn't she own something other than sweats and Lycra? Not to mention more stinking footwear. Aren't girls supposed to have toes that smell like sugar cookies or something? Not like…wet schnauzer.

❖

Your Sister's Closets—No. 2

Shut. At least the doors slide along a track. You worry about a creak, but the left side moves as if freshly greased. Inside is the stuff that would make every extreme athlete, every stunt double to Indiana Jones, drool. Scuba gear. A pile of rope and pitons. An actual grappling hook. A helmet and chest pads. A lacrosse stick. Three different backpacks.

Your fingers are just closing around the molded plastic grip to the nearest backpack when you hear "Stop. Right. There."

You look over your shoulder. She's sitting up in bed. Worse, she's holding a lacrosse ball in one hand, tosses it up once for menacing effect. Her eyes are a bit crusted over with sleep, so her aim for your head might end up at crotch level, not only ruining your day but any chance of reunion celebration with Neil.

"What does that pinhead of yours imagine it's doing rifling through my gear?"

You think fast over your options. Truth? Nah, she'd mock you even if she did half believe you. You don't remember her once consoling you after Neil left. She was always out with her friends or on the phone. She never cared. Better to lie. "I need some stuff to get back at Adrian for what he did to me on Friday."

She grips the lacrosse ball hard. But you know by the thoughtful look on her face, by the emerging smile, you're in the clear. One, she likes the thought of revenge, two, she won't bother to ask for details because she doesn't care that much, three, she hates Adrian (rumors are that he tried to smack her ass as she walked through the hallway at school, further rumors of what happened next range from Adrian chipping a tooth from being shoved face-first into a water fountain to her pantsing him). "Okay. Make it quick. Then get out."

You grab the backpack, look longingly at the grappling hook because it's so cool with the barbed flares, but decide that you'd only risk hurting yourself and possibly Neil if you did try to throw it. But you take the helmet and chest pads. The ball is thrown at her bedroom door just as you're leaving, huffing as you rush out with your hands full.

In the backpack is a heavy flashlight, a laminated but bent sheet identifying *Poisonous Lichens and Mosses of North America,* a couple of packets of instant coffee mix, a screwdriver, and even some wadded-up dollar bills among some loose papers at the bottom (probably her old homework).

In your room you choose your favorite T-shirt, the one with Harley Quinn from the Batman cartoon—the good one, the one you watched with Neil on DVD, not the recent crap—and say in a falsetto, "Right away, Mr. J," before you put on the helmet. Your face quickly heats up.

As you ride your bike to Neil's house, you feel a bit like a knight in modern armor. A knight on a quest to save his prince.

❖

The Jessons' Basement Closet

Actually this looks more like a root cellar. But you need to enter the house and find a way to Neil's bedroom. The driveway is empty, an oil stain on the cement marking where Adrian's pickup once sat.

You use the screwdriver to pry off the simple lock keeping the doors shut. Then out comes the flashlight. You descend the stairs. Much of the basement is utility-oriented: washer and dryer against one wall, rickety metal shelves holding plastic totes of distant holiday decorations along another.

You hear a whisper calling to you. No, more of a hiss. You shine your light at the source: an old water heater that looks like the belly of a termite queen, rounded and immense, the many pipes rising off it like a child's drawing of how a centipede should walk. You take a step closer. You hear water dripping.

The circle of light slips past the pipes and cement walls to find a door hidden behind the water heater. It's small, swollen from the dampness so that the individual boards bulge and gap, and the metal hinges are rusty. You have to bend down to approach it.

❖

The Secret Basement Closet

No handle on this closet, just a round hole where a doorknob should be. A dark hole, too wide to be a safe peephole. You nudge the door open with your foot. Thanks to the flashlight you see it's over a foot drop to some cement stairs coiling down and down. A trip deep into Saturday-morning logic, but one that also reeks of damp things.

The stairwell is slippery and there's no handrail. As you descend, you count slow under the hot breath that fills the helm. By one hundred your feet splash in puddles on the steps, warm water that spills down each. After you've lost count at around three hundred and sixty-five or so, the water is up to your knees; you have the urge to pee.

Soon, you're wading through waist-deep water (and you did pee, several steps ago, because you could get away with it in the dark, but you'll never tell anyone that), your flashlight's beam waves back and forth over the water until it finds a figure approaching on a boat. No, a raft without sail.

You wave and call out. Could it be Neil?

But no, as the raft approaches the stairwell you see it's not your boyfriend. For a moment, you think it's your sister, for the pirate has her features, down to the tiny scar below her lips from when she fell from the monkey bars as a toddler. But not her boobs, which were never really big anyway, which torments her no end. The bandanna she wraps about her neck when jogging hides much of the pirate's short hair. But the pirate is missing one eye. Your light catches movement in the empty socket: a tiny beak, shiny eyes, atop a bit of fluff. At that you gasp.

"So you're the one who's been lighting up the sky," the pirate says, nodding at your flashlight. "Thought the moon had come down below a while."

"What's wrong with your eye?"

"Polite boy, aren't you? If you ever been at sea you'd know that all apprentice pirates must raise their own parrots from a chick before they earn their peg." The pirate—the apprentice pirate, really—makes a soft, clicking sound and lifts an oyster cracker to her missing eye. The beak plucks the cracker in a second.

"Why are you here? It's not syrupy eel season for months," the apprentice pirate asks.

"Uh, no, I don't want any eels."

❖

The Closet-Raft

You shine your light onto the raft and see it's actually a massive closet door, the knob serving as the rudder.

"What's on the other side of the water?"

The apprentice pirate squints her remaining eye. "Danger. Not much else. Not really sure. Other than danger."

"Would you take me across?"

"You have coin of the realm?"

You root around in your sister's backpack for the cash you saw earlier. You pull out some of the papers.

The apprentice pirate catches one before it falls into the water. "Eh, what's this?"

Only one side is blank. On the other is a black & white photo of Neil, a photocopy from his Facebook account, with the words *This boy is missing. We miss him. Have you seen him?* Below that is an e-mail with your sister's name.

You stare at the flier long enough for the apprentice pirate to clear her throat. You always thought your sister didn't give a shit about Neil. She had made fun of you finally meeting a guy in time for Valentine's. But the flyers...dozens of them. You imagine that when you thought she was out with her friends, she was handing them out to strangers on the street. When she was chatting on the phone, she was asking if anybody had seen Neil.

You fall to your knees on the closet-raft. "Damn." You owe her an apology for an accusation never voiced.

"So you're looking for him? Lost boys and pirates don't get along—"

"You're only an apprentice pirate."

"True that." She feeds the parrot chick another cracker. "How did you lose him?"

"I'm...I'm not sure."

"That will make finding him harder."

❖

The Closet-Raft

Bobs along the strange lake. Every so often the apprentice pirate adjusts the rudder. You give her the few dollars you found in the backpack.

When your flashlight—dying, so you only dare turn it on for a minute or so every once in a while—catches sight of a dock, you feel relief.

"Here," the apprentice pirate says, handing you a glass canning jar. It's empty but for a tiny sliver, dark and moist at the bottom.

"It's my last bit of syrupy eel. You might find yourself hungry along the way."

As you hop onto the docks, you thank the apprentice pirate and wish her luck on her PSATs (Pirate Scoundrel Aptitude Test?) or whatever exams she needs to graduate to full pegleg and crossbones.

A flagstone path emerges from the dock. You follow it through the dark, your eyes struggling to see any detail more than a few inches away.

You risk draining the flashlight, now a flickering beam. The glint of metal ahead catches your attention.

A ninja, all dressed in customary black except for a strip of exposed skin around the eyes, is balanced on the heel of one foot, atop a naked katana thrust between the stones of the path. The pose is so damn cool you just stop walking and stare.

The ninja reaches behind his back and pulls out a small chalkboard. Without swaying, he begins writing on the board. His handwriting sucks, so you have to move closer to read it.

You must be lost.

"Not really."

He smears it clear with a hand, chalk dust drifting down to lighten his uniform.

Only lost boys are found beyond this point. So, you must be lost to go farther.

"Does losing a boy count?"

The ninja scratches his head, which soon looks like he has dandruff. *I don't know.*

You attempt to walk past the ninja, but he leaps down from the sword and blocks your way.

"Why can't you speak?"

He pulls down the cloth covering his mouth and parts his lips. Inside it's all rusty red without any tongue. He starts writing on the chalkboard again. *Because I said something terrible I lost my tongue and have been posted here.*

"What did you say?"

The ninja just shakes his head sadly.

You set the backpack on the ground, ready to have a long argument with him over why he needs to let you pass when you hear the *clink!* of glass—the jar of preserved eel. Which makes you think of the apprentice pirate wanting to get his fake leg, which makes you think...

"If I found you a new tongue would you let me pass?" you ask him.

Agreed.

You get the jar and unscrew the top. You have to twist your hand about inside, not as easy as it looks, to get your fingers around the last eel. It's slippery and so cold. But finally you have it out and hold it before the ninja.

His hands move so fast you don't see him grabbing the eel from you. Only a breeze that chills the remaining slime on your palm. As he leans his head back and opens his blood-stained mouth, you're sure he's going to swallow the eel, but no, he drops it in and puffs his cheeks like he's swishing mouthwash.

Then: "Ah, that's so much better." The voice...it's so familiar. Adrian's, though the ninja lacks his bulk.

"You're welcome," you say.

"All lost boys have to go through the Gate. I can lead you to it but I can go no farther."

❖

The Gate

Resembles Neil's bedroom closet door down to the taped poster of the black-and-white *The Invisible Man*, his favorite movie. A pale green lichen has overgrown the poster's title lettering.

You remember sitting on the floor beside Neil late at night as the television flickered and Claude Rains unwrapped his head, the bandages revealing everything and nothing at once. You leaned your head on Neil's shoulder, distracting him so you could steal the bowl of popcorn from his lap. Buttered, salted kernels went flying. He laughed, though, and so you pushed him down to the carpet, your fingers slipping between his and the thick shag. He looked up at you. Half his face was lit by the television. One eye bright, the other dark. Everything and nothing at once. Conscious of his body beneath yours, of how his weak squirms were almost too much to bear, you felt scared, as if kissing him would be inviting disaster.

But you did.

Fine hairs tipped with luminescent beads rise from the lichen when your hand reaches for the doorknob.

"Looks deadly to the touch," the ninja says. He's actually been really chatty the last hour or so you've been walking towards the Gate. Just rambling about how good it will be to taste sushi again. He's also too curious about the pirate—you might have mentioned where you got the eel from—asking whether or not you think he could take her in a fair fight. And if she's pretty.

You're looking forward to losing him.

You take *Poisonous Lichens and Mosses of North America* from the backpack. Your finger traces a chart. Yes to glowing. Yes to eerie. No to blood-red. No to any skulls lying around. *Ephebe crimen.* You struggle to read the fine print by the lichen's glow. "Physical contact with this lichen can be hazardous to the remorseful," you read aloud.

"I think that's both of us." The ninja rubs his chin.

"You're afraid?"

He nods and backs away, lost to darkness.

"I'm not," you lie.

You thrust your hand at the door. Your fingers wriggle through what feels like a bath of acid and glue. Your worry that while turning the knob, your wrist will crack, your hand fall off, swallowed. But you don't let go.

And when the Gate opens, you're shocked not to see Neil's room or even his house. No, ahead of you is the hall of lockers from school. B-wing, the very hall where Neil's locker is.

❖

The Lockers

Are just another kind of closet.

As you walk the darkened hallway, every locker door begins to tremble. You look to your left and see fingertips sliding through the gratings at the very tops of the metal doors. You look to your right and see eyes watching you from within the lockers.

"Neil?" you call out.

Laughter, not giggling but cruel and coarse laughter, comes from the lockers.

"Who's there?"

Down the hall, from around a corner, steps Neil. His head

hangs down, gaze kept to the scuffed floor tiles, his arms hanging limp. He shuffles a bit farther before sitting down cross-legged in the intersection.

You call out his name again.

He shakes his head.

You start to run toward him. Then the lockers rattle so hard that their doors must soon burst.

Over the din you hear Neil's muttering clear, as if he stood behind you, whispering in your ear. "They'll talk about me. They'll stare at me. And laugh at me."

"Neil."

He dips his head, chin tight against his chest, and wraps his arms around himself. "They'll talk about me. They'll stare at me. And laugh at me."

Seeing him so hurts worse than the lichen. "Is that what Adrian told you?" You have to scream the question because of the noise. You reach him and collapse next to him.

He nods.

You remember the kids that teased you in junior high. They thought you were different. Not different in crazy, wonderful ways, how you felt when you ran around so hard you could collapse exhausted but laughing, or while captivated by the adventures of cartoon heroes. No, they wanted you to feel less than them, even though you breathed the same as them, stuffed food into your mouth in the cafeteria like everyone else. You learned to ignore them.

You slip your hand under his. You ignore the next bout of laughter from the lockers. "You can't hide away forever. Even after high school, there may be people who'll stare when I hold your hand," you say, though the words make your mouth taste bitter. You rest your lips against the top of his head. "Or when I tell you how much I love you. No matter what they say, you have the choice to listen or not."

Neil lifts his head a little.

"You can listen to them or listen to me."

You slide your face down, your mouth pressing first against his forehead, then the tip of his nose before coming to stop so close to his parted lips.

"You said you love me," he whispers.

Those lockers have hushed. Or maybe you're no longer paying attention to them.

"I know," you say. You feel breathless and weary yet eager for the next moment.

He kisses you. You might be surprised…maybe not, but you almost lose the kiss to the smile you begin as you stare into his wide-open eyes.

Together, you stand.

The Gate is still ajar and you lead him back through it, stepping over a pile of gauze bandages—Neil's last Halloween costume—and stacks of wool sweaters, past a couple of fishing poles. Shirts hanging in the way are pushed aside until you emerge into Neil's bedroom, where it's bright. Saturday morning streams in through the windows.

"I'd love to make you breakfast. Even if you aren't hungry," you tell him.

He laughs and nods.

"But," he says, "before we do anything else, I need your help."

Working together, your arms often brushing against one another, you start removing the pins from the hinges of his closet door.

ANN TONSOR ZEDDIES wrote *Deathgift* and its sequel, *Sky Road*. As Toni Anzetti, she wrote *Typhon's Children* and *Riders of Leviathan*. Then she returned to write the Philip K. Dick nominee *Steel Helix*, set in the same universe but under her own name. She also wrote "To See Heaven in a Wild Flower" in *The Ultimate Silver Surfer*, "Ten Thousand Waves" in *Magic in the Mirrorstone*, and *Blood and Roses*, a Jayne Taylor adventure.. She spent her first few summers on a mountaintop in Idaho and learned to read while living in a small house near the Black Forest. As a result, she has always loved the wild places, and after living in Kansas, Texas, and Pennsylvania, she is happy to have moved back to western Michigan where the northern forests and the big lake are always accessible. She has four children, a black belt in tae kwon do, and an amazing collection of action figures.

One of my secret fond memories that I don't tell just anyone is of spending a weekend in Provincetown with some friends. It happened to be the very weekend when my gay BFF became an incipient father to the first child of the two women I was staying with. While I was out walking on the beach, a new life began. Now I'm privileged to know that erstwhile baby as a young man of many talents who brings much joy to his family, including his younger sister, who came along a couple of years later. I've always been proud to have been present at the creation. And this family is one of the reasons I know for sure that a family is defined by the people who care for you, not by the rules in anyone's book. GLBT kids can grow up to be anything they want, including mothers, fathers, and loving partners to the person of their choice.

WAITING TO SHOW HER
ANN TONSOR ZEDDIES

Reggie Collins had a private truce with the Catholic Church that ended the day Father Doyle fired Sister Eloise from the music ministry. Reggie didn't know it had happened until she showed up for youth choir practice, late as usual. She kicked her gym bag under the second pew and unslung her guitar case.

A portly man in a dark suit occupied the podium where Sister Eloise usually stood. He turned toward her, tapping his baton irritably.

"Hey, where's Sister Eloise?" she said.

"Let's keep our voices reverent in the presence of Our Lord," he said. "And introduce ourselves before speaking."

Reggie stared at him, unable to fathom what she was hearing.

"That's Reggie Collins," one of the other choirgirls said, to fill the awkward pause.

"Well, Miss Collins, I'm Leonard Mannington. Mr. Mannington to you," the man said. "I've just been informing the choir about some changes we'll be making here. Punctuality is one of our new expectations. Sister Eloise evidently allowed a degree of informality in worship that I don't find healthy."

"Where is Sister Eloise?" Reggie said.

"Doyle fired her," said a voice from the back row.

The man on the podium swiveled his bulk around to glare at the back rows, taking the heat off Reggie for a minute. "That's *Father* Doyle. And the next person to speak out of turn will be paying a visit to the pastor's office."

Reggie was still clutching her guitar by its neck. She hadn't even slipped the strap over her shoulder yet.

"Take your place," the man said. "You won't need your guitar. We're starting on a new repertoire."

Reggie was doing her best to project righteous indignation while sight-reading the alto part to "Sing of Mary Pure and Holy," when she realized she was standing behind an unfamiliar head. The soprano in front of her had long blond hair spilling wispily over a dowdy, Grandma-style blouse with a lace collar. On the other side of the risers, where the tenors, baritones, and the choir's single bass stood, Reggie spotted two more new kids: boys with super-short haircuts and polo shirts buttoned up to the neck.

Oh, great, Reggie thought. Another super-righteous family has joined the parish. She lost her place and earned a glare from Mr. Mannington. Or Manly McManlyson, as she had already started to call him in her mind.

After the choir had blundered their way through a couple of unfamiliar hymns, Mannington waved his baton at the pale-haired soprano.

"Front and center, Miss Mannington. For our post-Communion meditation, we'll have you solo on *'Panis Angelicus.'* Mrs. Myers will be here on Sunday to accompany you on the organ, but for today, just sing it to my time."

"But, Dad—" the soprano said. He rapped his baton on the podium again and made a *tchkk tchkk tchkk* sound that Reggie guessed she'd soon be tired of. Shoot—she was tired of it already!

"No discussion, please. Front and center."

Reggie prepared to suffer. She'd heard a lot of girl sopranos who thought they were all that.

She scrutinized the Mannington offspring as the blond girl stepped up and adjusted the mike. The girl had that faded floral blouse matched with a full, past-the-knees skirt that drooped on her thin body. Underneath, there were either knee socks or tights, paired with scuffed white Reebok knock-offs. The clothes said she was sixty-five. Her face said she was about twelve.

She took a deep breath, and out of her pale, expressionless face poured the most amazing voice. Reggie couldn't take her eyes off the new girl. Her face stayed the same—no smile, no expressive movements—but Reggie could see her chest rise and fall, and when she glanced down, she saw the girl clenching and unclenching her fists in the folds of her shabby skirt as her voice soared.

When practice ended, Reggie scrambled to assemble her load of gear in time to catch up as Mannington herded the girl and her brothers to the parking lot. What she wanted to say was, "Holy shit, you're better than Charlotte Church," but she hoped to come up with something more tactful. She also wanted to say "Girl, what is your name?" Because "Miss Mannington" wasn't anything you could think about. But she'd forgotten to zip the gym bag. A pair of socks and a water bottle fell out, and by the time she'd collected them, the Manningtons had vanished.

"Thanks a lot," Reggie muttered in the general direction of the Infant of Prague statue that smiled by the back door.

❖

Reggie's mother taught social studies at a nearby middle school and usually got home before Reggie. She was in the kitchen when Reggie banged in via the side door. "Hello there, Regina Marie," she sang out.

Reggie rolled her eyes. "Mom, I've asked you before. Could you lose the 'Regina'? Hello, rhymes with 'vagina'? Do you have any idea what it's like to enter public school with a name that sounds like a body part?"

Here mother put down the dish towel to give Reggie a quick squeeze and a kiss on the cheek. "Well, I think it's a lovely name," she said cheerfully. "We named you for the Queen of Heaven."

Reggie mouthed the words along with her. She'd heard them before. Her mom was a comfortably plump woman whose good humor was apparently indestructible. Even when Reggie had come out to her mom with all the dogmatic flair of a rebellious eighth grader, her mother hadn't flinched. Sometimes Reggie wondered if that was because her mother had managed to summon a denial so complete that nothing Reggie said could upset her. But whatever—at least there hadn't been any trouble, and no one had suggested sending her off to Marymount Girls' Academy to have the nuns take the nonsense out of her.

"Mom! Did you know Father Doyle fired Sister Eloise? And hired some massive dork named Mannington to replace her?"

"Oh, darling, I'm sure he didn't *fire* her. But yes, I heard a rumor that she might not be coming back this year."

"Yeah, well, thanks a lot for not telling me. I walked in there and it was like the twentieth century never happened. It's going to be Youth Mass for Grannies from now on. I'm seriously thinking about quitting choir." She rummaged through cupboards as she spoke, and finally settled for a high-fiber bar with "chocolaty" frosting. Her mother was usually on a diet.

"Mannington," her mother repeated vaguely. "Is that the same Mannington as that nice Barbara Mannington I met on the Religious Education Committee a couple of weeks ago? She had a darling pair of twin girls with her."

"That would make five," Reggie said.

"Five what, dear?"

"Five offspring. Five devil spawn. Five *children*, Mumsie dearest." Reggie grabbed a slice of green pepper off the chopping board, stuck it between her teeth, and made a hideous face around it.

"What are you talking about?"

"Manningtons. He had three more with him at choir practice. Two junior dorks and a damsel."

"Really, Regina, I wish you wouldn't talk about people that way. 'Dork' isn't a nice word. It would be kind of you to welcome them if they're new."

"I have to call them something. I don't know their names. What are they called? Do you know?"

"Why not try the church website?" her mother said.

Reggie took a couple of rice cakes, turned on her DVR of *American Idol*, and settled on the couch with her laptop. Her mother was right. Sister Eloise's bio had already been deleted from the *About Us* section—though a *Best Wishes Sister Eloise Coffee* appeared under *Events*. And the personal info of Dork McManlyson had already taken its place. Children: Lily Virginia, Leo Maximilian, John Paul, Therese, Benedict, Gianna Rita, and Maria Rose. And from the looks of the family photo, there was another on the way. Holy cow, Reggie thought. She was guessing that the soprano was Lily Virginia. Oldest of seven, soon to be eight.

Reggie had one older brother, Ryan, who was already a junior in college. She'd often wondered how her parents squared up being such solid Catholics with only having two kids, but she wasn't about to ask.

"Regina! Are you doing your homework?"

Reggie turned off the TV. "Yeah, I'll be up in my room. Doing homework."

She threw herself onto her unmade bed and stared moodily up at her posters of Lady Sovereign and Joan Jett. Lily Virginia was like a girl-band name unto itself, she thought. Reggie had never actually dated anyone. She had a long-standing crush on a junior girl who played bass with a group called Wonder Pets. Her name was Lauren but somehow she'd gotten everyone to call her Dusty, which Reggie thought secretly was one of those things that was so stupid it was kind of cool. Dusty had a lip piercing and right now her hair was jet black and spiky, like a black chrysanthemum. Last year, when Reggie first fell for her, her hair had been petals of lush red. She wore a lot of goth-fairy gear. Fingerless gloves. Reggie spent way too much time thinking about Dusty Phillips's hands in fingerless gloves, but she'd never actually tried to get to know her.

I'm a LINO, she thought gloomily. Lesbian In Name Only. No wonder my parents don't take me seriously. All it means to them is that I don't go out with boys.

She tried to summon the familiar, comforting images of Dusty's hands (in fingerless gloves) expertly wringing noise from her battered electric bass. But what she kept thinking of was Lily Mannington's thin shoulders rising and falling under the faded cotton, and the defiant set of her pointed chin. Not my type *at all*, Reggie told herself. But she still itched to push back those strands of hair that straggled over the limp lace collar, and find out if they felt the way they looked, like frayed silk.

Reggie put on her earphones, cranked the noise up loud, and tried to focus on readings in world history.

Another surprise came when she walked into her first-period algebra class and saw Lily sitting in the front row. Of course it made sense that the Manningtons had to go to school somewhere, but Reggie had expected them to attend private schools, or be homeschooled or something. Lily got called on twice and worked a proof on the board once, and performed impeccably every time. Clean and right on target, like the notes when she was singing.

Reggie tried to catch up with her in the hall, but lost sight of her in the jam-up on the stairs. Lily was there again in fourth, world history class. But she kept her head down and didn't participate in the discussion. It was the last class before lunch.

Ashley and Leslie, Reggie's BFFs since grade school, usually went to China Express for lunch. Reggie wondered how they'd react if she invited Lily along. But, as she watched, Lily took a brown paper bag from her locker and merged into the crowd of losers funneling into the cafeteria. Reggie shuffled along with them, wrinkling her nose at the stale smell of instant mashed potatoes and canned nacho goo bubbling in steam trays. She hadn't eaten cafeteria food since she was a freshman.

She spotted Lily on the periphery, alone at a table, and slid into a seat across from her.

"Hey," Reggie said. Lily looked startled, like maybe no one had spoken to her all day. "Remember me? Reggie Collins from youth choir?"

The reaction wasn't quite what Reggie had expected. A little smirk spread across Lily's face.

"Who could forget?" she said. "Even if I hadn't had to listen to my dad ranting on about the manners of the godless American teenager all the way home."

"So I didn't make a good impression?"

"Not on him," Lily said. Peeling the strings off a celery stick, she shot Reggie a quick look. Is she flirting with me? Reggie thought. Her heart gave a quick thump.

Lily shrugged. "No one makes a good impression on my dad. He's very hard to please." She squinted critically at the celery stick and discarded it in favor of a sandwich wrapped in wax paper. She peeked inside. "Hmm. Cheese. Want some?"

"No thanks."

"Aren't you eating lunch?" Lily took a bite. The bread looked very whole-grainy and seemed to require a lot of chewing. A crumb stuck to the corner of Lily's lips, which were pale pink without any lip gloss that Reggie could see.

"Look," Reggie said, putting her hand over the bitten sandwich, "you really can't eat in here. You might as well tattoo a big *L* on your forehead. You want to toss this shit and come with me?"

Lily froze briefly. "Um...sure," she said. "But...where are we going?"

"What you really need is a friend with a car. But even if you can't drive, you can still get off campus." She shepherded Lily through the knots of smokers outside the cafeteria door.

"I thought we weren't allowed off campus during school hours."

"Technically," Reggie said.

A trail of discarded food wrappers and torn plastic bags stuck to fences marked the way to a cluster of disreputable storefronts a few blocks from the school.

"This place is Frank's, technically," Reggie said. "But most people call it the Candy Ass. Because of the sign." Neon letters glowed dimly behind the grimy front window. They'd once read "Candy And Snacks." Now most of the letters in the last two words were missing.

Lily crossed her arms and shivered. Technically, it was spring. Only a few gray crusts of snow clung to the curbs. But the wind was chilly. Lily wore a cheap-looking teal windbreaker, the kind with a fuzzy white lining in a polyester shell, over her cotton skirt.

"I probably should have said this before," she said, "but I don't have any money. You go ahead and get what you want. I'm not really hungry anyway."

Reggie kept wondering why she was bothering with this girl. She seemed more trouble than it was worth. Lily put her hands up to her mouth and blew on them to warm them. Reggie felt that twinge in the pit of her stomach again. She wanted to capture those thin, pale fingers and hold Lily's hands in her own until they were warm.

"Oh, hey, if I'm going to welcome you to the hell that is Springdale High, the least I can do is buy you a hot dog. Tuesdays are BOGO Coney Dogs. It's not gonna cost me extra."

Lily strolled around the crowded aisles while Reggie made conversation with the counter man. When Reggie handed her the foil-wrapped treat, she loaded relish and condiments onto it until the packet was oozing, and crammed a bite into her mouth before the door had jingled shut behind them.

"Oh my God, this is delicious." She took big bites and chewed with cheeks bulging. Reggie made another note on her Mental List of Things to Know About Lily Mannington: doesn't get much junk food. Reggie had sort of imagined that someone that elfin-looking would be kind of anorexic—tiny bites, maybe stopping halfway through and giving the rest back to Reggie, which Reggie wouldn't have minded because she was still hungry. But Lily consumed the whole thing and licked her fingers. She seemed more animated afterward, a touch of color in her cheeks.

A warm fantasy immediately filled Reggie's mind: she took Lily home with her. Her mother wasn't there. Reggie showed Lily how to cook all her own favorite comfort foods. She expertly toasted a pan-fried Monte Cristo sandwich for Lily, who swooned at its melted, crunchy-gooey goodness. And when Lily turned to thank Reggie, there was a crumb at the pink corner of her lips. Reggie bent to brush it away...

"Want some?" Lily said. Reggie snapped out of it to see that

Lily had pulled a handful of Tootsie Pops and gummy bears from her pocket and was holding them out to her.

"I thought you didn't have any money," Reggie said.

Lily shrugged. "I don't. I shoplifted them. I take things. What? I never have any money. My life is all about the cheese sandwiches. I have to do something."

"You could get in trouble," Reggie said neutrally.

Leslie had gone through a shoplifting phase—a CD, a lipstick, a Hello Kitty zipper pull. She'd thrown her loot in a desk drawer, given it to a friend, or tossed it off the bridge over the railroad tracks. It had been a joke to Leslie, something she did just to prove she could, not because she wanted things. She'd grown out of it. Every once in a while, Reggie came across one of those stolen favors and felt uncomfortable. She wasn't that much of a rebel.

Lily's lips took on a sarcastic twist that Reggie hadn't seen before. "Yes, I suppose I could. So, if you want to be so nice and hang out with me and all, you'll have to think about that, won't you."

Reggie guessed that this wasn't casual fun for Lily. It was something much more desperate. Slowly she picked out a grape Tootsie Pop, her favorite, feeling her fingers brush against Lily's palm. "Thanks," she said, unwrapping it and filling her mouth with the synthetic but comforting sweetness.

Lily pushed the fistful of candy toward her. "Take more," she said. "For later."

"Couldn't you take up smoking or something?" Reggie said as they approached school's C Door and its acrid cloud of smokers' exhalations.

"No, I can't." Lily shifted the Tootsie Pop to her cheek so she could answer. "It's bad for my voice. I want to get a music scholarship. But don't tell anyone that. My parents think I want to be a nun. Anyway, I'd just have to shoplift the butts, so what would be the point?"

"I can't smoke either," Reggie said. "I'm on the lacrosse team. I do a lot of sports. Because I like it, but I hope I might get some financial aid, too. Also my mom would kill me if I was smoking. Hey, I don't have practice today—do you want to come home with me after school?"

"I'm not allowed to hang out with people my parents don't know," Lily said. "And I have to get home to take care of the twins. If my parents see your parents in church enough, then maybe. I'll work on it. Thanks for lunch." She flashed Reggie an actual smile for about half a second before whisking around the corner to her next class.

Leslie and Ashley caught up with Reggie moments later.

"Where were you? We went to China Express for mu shu."

"There was this girl from church. They're new here. I promised my mom I'd be nice to her. She was about to eat in the cafeteria. I had to stop her. We got Coney dogs."

"Who?" Ashley said. "Not that freak in the granny dress who was in algebra? What's her name?"

"Lily Mannington!" Leslie shrieked. "She should be in *Gone With the Wind*! Lawsy, Miss Lily, I don't know nothin' about birthin' no babies!"

Ashley and Leslie fell over each other laughing and smoothing imaginary skirts.

"It's not her fault," Reggie said. "Her dad's some kind of religious nut. He makes her wear that shit, so STFU, okay?"

"Oookayyy," Leslie cooed. "So it's like that, is it?"

"It's *like* nothing. Shut up. Her dad took over the youth choir, and he's a massive douchebag. If you pick on her for her clothes, you'll be doing exactly what he wants, and I hate him. And she has an awesome voice."

Ashley started singing. "The hills are alive…with the sound of music…"

"Okay, Reggie von Trapp…your nun-girl is safe with us," Leslie said.

Sometimes I hate my friends, Reggie thought.

❖

She obsessed about Lily's smile for hours, later, in her room with earphones blasting and the taste of grape-flavored sugar in her mouth. She wished she had someone she could talk to about this. Leslie and Ashley had been her friends since grade school. They'd stood by her loyally when she came out, and she'd listened to endless hours of their drama with one boy after another. They knew about her crush from a distance on Dusty Phillips. But that was different somehow. This was up-close. Everything about Lily felt immediate to her. Every detail pricked her like a tack pressed into the skin, and drew a response as immediate as a drop of blood. It hurt to realize she didn't trust her best friends with a feeling this raw.

As the semester continued, Lily's presence and absence became just a fact of life, like the changeable spring weather— sunny skies one day, back to winter's chill the next. Reggie made a few tries at pulling Lily into the circle of her regular friends, but Lily wouldn't cooperate. The Manningtons' weird rules made most ordinary meetings impossible. After a while, Reggie realized that Lily's instinctive withdrawal made sense. Leslie and Ashley were—what? Jealous? It was hard to believe, but maybe they were. They didn't openly mock Lily in front of Reggie, but she was sure they did it behind her back.

Reggie saw Lily in odd moments: outside on the grass by the church parking lot, while their parents drank coffee after

Mass; in the chalk-smelling chaos of the Springdale High choir room before practice; an occasional clandestine rendezvous at the grocery store when Lily was sent to buy extra milk. And at lunch, as she regularly ditched her normal lunch group to haunt the Candy Ass and other spots where they could split Reggie's lunch and fill up on stolen treats.

They met at Sister Eloise's farewell coffee. Reggie wanted to spend a few minutes with the nun, who was one of the few adults she'd ever enjoyed talking to. But she also wanted to eavesdrop on the Manningtons. Sister Eloise was surrounded by a knot of the parish ladies, and Reggie couldn't get near her anyway. So she watched Lily's family instead.

The three boys stood around like the pint-size, tall, and grande of dorkdom, all wearing the same kind of khaki pants and tightly buttoned white shirts and ties. They leaned on a table in the back of the room with a couple of other kids from the LifeTeen program, a group Reggie had eschewed. The twins ran around and under the tables, with a middle-sized girl in their wake. That must be Therese, Reggie thought. She seemed more robust than her older sister, and had a cloud of dark hair instead of Lily's wispy blond. Mrs. Mannington had taken a seat on a folding chair and was sipping a cup of water, oblivious to her offspring. She rested one hand on her voluminously draped, pregnant stomach. She looked tired. Her skin was pale, like Lily's, but her once-fair hair was mostly gray.

One of the twins fell down and cried loudly as Therese picked her up and joggled her. Slipping from her sister's grasp, she ran to join her twin in clinging to their mother's skirts. "Cake, Mommy, cake!" they beseeched.

Mr. Mannington, talking with Father Doyle on the far side of the room, frowned at Lily across the heads of the parishioners. "Lily! Help your mother!"

Lily collected the twins, boosted them onto the windowsill next to Reggie, and went for more cake. "They're cute," Reggie said uncertainly. Though they were only three or so, both girls wore glasses, which made their round-eyed stares kind of intimidating. She smiled at them, and they immediately turned away to bury their fingers in the frosting on the slabs of cake Lily dealt out to them.

"You wouldn't think so if you had to babysit them twenty-four seven," Lily said. Then she planted a quick kiss on the nearest child's head, as if in apology. "Therese says she likes to, but it's not fair to her to let her watch them all the time. Plus there's cooking dinner and stuff. Mom doesn't feel good most of the time."

"When is the baby due?"

"August. It won't be a good summer."

"But maybe after the baby is born—" Reggie ventured.

"Are you kidding me?" Lily said in a low, bitter voice. She kept her poker face, but she drummed her scuffed shoes against the wall. "Give it a couple of weeks and she'll just be pregnant again."

Reggie was shocked. She couldn't believe she was hearing someone like Lily criticizing her parents' sex life in the church meeting room. She wouldn't have dared. "But there's natural family planning and stuff," she said, lowering her voice as far as she could, but still feeling her cheeks burn. "That's what Mom said the only time I could get her to talk about, you know, the pill or anything."

Lily snorted. "Well, maybe you'd like to talk to *my* mom about that." Suddenly she smiled a thin saccharine smile and solicitously wiped the twins' chins with a napkin. "Talk about something else, Dad's coming this way."

Reggie looked up and smiled, too. "Good morning, Mr. Mannington," she said, trying to win back some of the points she'd lost at their first meeting. His gaze swept over her and rested somewhere beyond the window, as if she were unworthy of his scrutiny.

"Come along, girls. Your mother needs to rest."

Lily threw Reggie an apologetic grimace over her shoulder as she towed the twins away.

This is crazy, Reggie thought. I can't have a crush on someone I can't even hang out with, ever. It's like one of those prison romances where they fall in love on the Internet. She could see Lily, standing pale and brave in frayed gray pajamas against a barbed wire fence. She wanted her more than ever, wanted to fly to her side and save her. There's got to be a way, she thought. There's got to be some way for us to be together.

Sister Eloise was finally alone. Reggie marched up to her before some other well-wisher could take the spot.

"I'm really going to miss you," she said. "Choir isn't the same without you. I hate the new hymnal."

Sister Eloise laughed. "God love you, Reggie Collins," she said. "Don't ever change. You just keep on speaking your mind. But we have to accept that not everyone has the same tastes. If you're serious about making music, that's one thing you'll soon learn."

"But why do you have to go?" Reggie said. "Is it true that—well—" She lowered her voice and looked around for Father Doyle.

"I accepted a position at Marymount," Sister Eloise filled in smoothly, before Reggie could blurt out the dreaded words "you got fired." "I think it was time for a change. We are a teaching order, and teaching is my first love. But I'll miss you and the rest of the young people here very much."

Reggie's parents had had enough bad coffee and gossip. They stood near the door and beckoned her insistently.

"Keep in touch!" Sister Eloise said brightly, waving.

Reggie didn't think she would. She'd had a million questions she wanted to ask. Did you really want to be a nun? Or did you just go to the convent because you didn't want to be with a man? Does God really talk to you, and if so, why doesn't he talk to me? Will he still talk to you if you're gay? But she'd never get to ask her now. People leave and never tell you why. Adults lie and are jerks. Why keep on being nice when nothing makes sense? Reggie felt a kinship with Lily. Better take what you can, because no one listens to what you're asking for.

❖

Lily wasn't in school that Monday. Reggie went to lunch with Ashley and Leslie and felt guilty because it was so easy and fun. At least, until they started talking about Lily.

"No offense, but people think she's a freak," Ashley drawled, while trying to balance a straw on her nose. "Couldn't you get a crush on someone semi-normal?"

"It's sweet that you want to save her," Leslie said. "You'll be her brave rescuer and she can be your pretty, pretty princess. But come on, Regs, do you even know Miss Nun-girl is gay? She'd have to burn in hell for you. That just doesn't seem too likely."

It was true, Reggie had to admit. She didn't even know how Lily really felt. But that didn't stop her from calling the Manningtons' number when she got home. Lily answered.

"Where were you? Are you sick?"

"No, I'm fine. My mom wasn't feeling well, so I stayed home for the twins. My dad had a seminar to go to. I had to fix breakfast and get Therese and Ben off to school."

"What, they couldn't get their own cereal?"

Lily's tone became guarded. "Sorry, I can't talk right now.

Yes, I will be in school tomorrow. Yes, thanks for letting me know about that assignment. Good-bye."

❖

"What was going on yesterday?" Reggie asked her at lunch the next day. "Do they not let you talk on the phone? Should I not have called?"

"The phone's in the kitchen, and there's always someone around. There's no privacy. And I was in the middle of fixing dinner, so I couldn't really talk. I can't ever talk about my parents, because they're always there."

"And they really kept you home from school to babysit?"

"Pretty much. Mom isn't doing well. Someone has to keep things running."

"Someone ought to report them for child abuse. They can't keep you out of school."

Lily grabbed Reggie's arm, squeezing it till it hurt. "Don't even think about it. Please! You just—you can't possibly get it. I have to tough it out and not make waves till I turn eighteen and can get out. I have to be there for Therese and the twins. Even Ben—he's so little. I have to get out and get a place of my own, and then I can help the others. I can't let them cut me off till then."

"Okay, okay," Reggie said. "Chill. I didn't mean I was going to. I was just saying. It's not right. You need to stand up to them."

"Oh sure." Lily's eyes sparked with anger. "Like you do, right? You just go along with your nice parents. Go to Mass, work hard at school, act normal. And then you'll go off to college and do what you want. Your parents don't want you kicked out of youth choir, so you act nice to my dad, even though you can't stand him. And your parents hate Father Doyle—like pretty much everyone else except my parents!—but they won't say anything. Everybody just goes along to get along. So don't tell me what I should do."

It was the closest they'd ever come to a fight. Reggie was scared, but it was exciting too. Did this mean they had a real relationship? It had to be more than a crush if they were fighting.

"I'm not," she said meekly.

❖

Frank's was out of Coney dogs.

"What? How can you run out of hot dogs?" Reggie said. It was like an omen. This wasn't going to be a good day.

"You girls are late. Lunch is over," the bearded Greek guy behind the counter growled. "I got grilled cheese left. You want it or not?"

She had to settle for the grilled cheese, and there was no BOGO, so she paid for two. She was juggling the hot, greasy objects and looking around for Lily when there was a crash in the back aisle.

Lily stood in the gourmet snacks section, hands outspread helplessly. One of the dusty jars of caviar that never got bought lay splintered on the floor.

"I'm so sorry—I didn't touch it—it just fell—" Lily stammered. Reggie knew that wasn't true. Lily had been trying to stuff it into her pocket. And if the Greek guy looked, he'd see the candy bars and jar of olives that already bulged her windbreaker. But he didn't look. One thing Lily could do well was look innocent and helpless.

"Get out," the counterman said. "Get out! You girls are trouble! Don't come back tomorrow!"

Back on the street, Lily popped the top off the olives and fished them out greedily with her fingers.

"Did you see the look on his face?" she said. "I thought I was going to wet my pants." She doubled over with laughter, but it was the fake kind.

"Listen, you've got to stop," Reggie said. "It's not funny anymore." She was beginning to understand that she was in over her head.

"Fine, then," Lily yelled, going from mirth to rage in a breath. "Don't be my friend if that's how you feel about it! My father thinks you're a bad influence anyway. He told me to stay away from 'that Collins girl.'"

"What? Why did he say that? He never even sees me!"

"Oh he sees you all right. He says you're 'defiant' and your skirt was immodest for Mass on Sunday."

Reggie remembered how he'd averted his eyes at the coffee hour, as if she were a hair in his soup. Lily was laughing again, in a hiccuppy way that made Reggie worry she was going to choke on her sandwich.

"He's such an ass, he doesn't understand you're the only good influence there is. You're the only reason I don't go totally *nuts*. Everyone else just thinks I'm a freak."

They walked rapidly, in silence, back toward the school. Lily hunched over, hands in her pockets, sneakers slapping the pavement. Her hair fell forward over her face, leaving the back of her neck bare and vulnerable. At the edge of the parking lot, she halted, staring at the ground.

Reggie nearly went on without her. That would show her, she thought. But she couldn't.

"I'll try," Lily said. "I know it's getting scary. But it's like I just have to do something to take the pressure off. Being in school makes it worse. Seeing how other people have choices, and I don't."

"There's got to be something else you could do," Reggie said.

"Yeah, I've thought about cutting myself," Lily said. "Anorexia is out, because I never get anything to eat anyway. Who would notice? Plus with seven kids and a pregnant woman, the bathroom's never free when I would need it."

Reggie hoped she was joking. Lily was so practiced at hiding her feelings that it was hard to tell.

"Do you ever go to the movies?"

Lily just rolled her eyes.

"Well, TV then!"

"Um…no. We watch PG and religious videos. There was an awesome one about Thérèse of Lisieux. She dies of TB and one of the other nuns loves her so she drinks her spit."

"Eww." Reggie said. "Wait—I've got a brilliant idea. I'll load up some videos on my iPhone. *Glee, American Idol*—you can watch them. I'll lend it to you."

Lily reluctantly shook her head. "No, I share a room with Therese and the twins. They'd find it. And my parents probably wouldn't give it back, even if I said it was yours."

"Oh shit—the bell's ringing."

They had to run for fifth hour. But Reggie was determined to come up with something to change Lily's life, and the fact that they were both late and got a first warning gave her another idea.

"All we have to do is be late from lunch two more times. Then we'll get a detention. You'll miss the bus, and you can come to my house, and we'll tell your parents my mom offered to drive you home from detention."

"What good would that do?"

"You'll get to come to my house. Maybe they'd see it was okay—"

"No. If I get detention with you, my parents will just say I can't ever see you again."

❖

But, as if the thought had made it happen, they were late twice more that week, and were ordered to the cafeteria for detention.

Reggie wouldn't have supposed that Lily could get any paler, but she did.

"Oh my God, this is awful. I'm going to be sick. They'll kill me."

"Here, use my phone," Reggie said. "Just say you have to stay after, and my mom will take you home. Because I know she will."

Reggie was surprised to see Ashley and Leslie arrive arm in arm while Lily was on the phone.

"Hey, what are you juvenile delinquents doing here?" Ashley said. "It's like this is the only time we get to see you anymore."

"What did you do?" Reggie said.

They exchanged glances.

"Got caught driving off campus. Cut the assistant principal off at a red light, so he couldn't really overlook it. You should have been there! He was with Mrs. Swanson from AP German. Do you think he's doing her? They looked really guilty. Oh, sorry, Lily, no offense to your tender ears."

Lily snapped the phone shut. She was so pale she was almost blue, like nonfat milk. "I don't give a shit who's doing who," she said.

"Oh Miss Lily! Such language!" Leslie said.

Reggie had planned to wait to propose her next great idea until she got Lily safely to her house. But she could see that the next hour was going to be awkward unless she could get all four of them into the same head space.

"It's good you guys are here, because I need help. With a fashion-related issue. It's Extreme Makeover time. I'm going to swap clothes with Lily."

"What? No—" Lily tried to get away, but Reggie had a tight grip on her elbow. "Shut up, we're doing it."

"Oh, sick! Like *The Breakfast Club*. I get to be Molly Ringwald!" Ashley snickered. "And Regs can be Emilio Estevez."

"Quick, into the bathroom while he's still taking roll," Reggie said.

Leslie waved at Mr. Stebbins, the monitor. "Excuse us, we have to *pee!*" she called. They hustled Lily into the girls' bathroom.

"Come on, it's something different," Reggie said. "Don't you want to at least see what you'd look like?"

She pushed Lily into a stall, then pulled off her own layers of tank and tee and tossed them over the barrier. "Put those on and throw me yours—hurry up, I'm standing here in my underwear."

She didn't mind changing clothes around Ashley and Leslie—they'd slept over at each other's houses hundreds of times. There was a long pause. Finally, Lily's white granny blouse was laid over the door. Reggie put it on. It was miles too big even for her, and drooped sadly around her shoulders. She took off her skirt and stockings. The blouse hung down almost far enough to be a minidress.

It took several minutes for Lily to sling her skirt over the door and poke her crumpled knee socks and shoes under it. Reggie guessed she was having trouble with the panty hose. Reggie donned the skirt. With that, the blouse, and the shoes, her personality seemed to have been erased. She felt like a little kid playing dress-up with old, too-large clothes.

"Wow, Reggie—you look so…modest." Ashley said.

Lily emerged slowly, head down, looking at the unfamiliar shoes. Her hair still hung in her face.

"Oh my God, you look like a model," Leslie said. "You have great legs. You're so thin. You could wear anything."

Lily frowned at her reflection, a tinge of color coming back into her cheeks. "This is stupid," she said. "Clothes don't change who I am."

"Yeah, but they sure change who you look like," Leslie said. "Come here—I've got a scrunchie. I'm going to pull your hair back. And lip gloss. This is a good color for you. You should be wearing this, too, Reggie. But I guess it doesn't matter in that outfit."

Reggie stopped hating her friends. They were great. Ashley gave Lily hair clips. Leslie put her funky little thrift store necklace around Lily's neck.

"There you go," she said, stepping back. "And ta-da, you look amaaazing. Not like Regs over there. You just can't take her anywhere."

They exited the bathroom in a cluster and grabbed chairs as close to the back as they dared. Reggie felt unexpectedly awkward in Lily's clothes. Oh well, it's a joke, she thought. That's what she'd say if anyone commented. It was only till her mom came to take them home, where she could change and get back to normal. Lily's clothes smelled like Lily. Reggie hugged the floppy blouse against her chest and breathed in the scent quietly. It was bliss, but it would be hell if anyone noticed her sniffing. She'd never hear the end of it. Lily did look great. And she was actually talking to Leslie and Ashley, smiling even. Yes! My great idea! It's working! Reggie thought.

The win lasted till the bell finally released them, and they rushed out to the car line. Reggie saw her mother's car waiting. But before she could steer Lily over there, Lily stopped dead in her tracks, turning white again.

"Oh God, it's my dad."

The dented minivan screeched to a halt. Mr. Mannington jumped out. Reggie could dimly see Therese's scared face at the rear window.

"What the devil do you think you're doing?" he shouted in Lily's face. "What kind of getup is that? Get in the car."

Lily looked back toward Reggie and her friends. "I—I'm sorry," she said. "I'll give your things back—I—"

"I said get in the car. Now!" Mr. Mannington yanked Lily's arm so hard she stumbled and nearly fell. The door slammed, and the van roared away.

"That went well," Ashley said brightly.

"I have to go home and change," Reggie said. "I'll call you." She felt numb. All she wanted to do was hide. Go back home and be normal and safe. Get the hell out of Lily's clothes. She itched to tear them off and could hardly wait till she got home.

❖

"Regina Marie, what on earth are you wearing?" her mother said.

"Lily and I swapped clothes," Reggie mumbled. "It was just for fun. I trade clothes with Ash and Les all the time."

"Oh dear," her mother said. "You know, darling, maybe that wasn't the best idea. You know how…particular her parents are."

Thank you, Captain Obvious, Reggie thought. But she didn't say anything. Her mother was right for once.

❖

Lily didn't come to school the next day, nor the one after. Reggie had an after-school rehearsal for Show Choir, in anticipation of All-City, followed by a night game for the lacrosse team. Lily missed the choir rehearsal. In between choir and game, Reggie called Lily's house. An unidentified Mannington boy answered, and said Lily couldn't come to the phone. He didn't offer to take a message.

Reggie was sure she'd see Lily at youth choir on Wednesday. She had to come to that—her dad was the director. Reggie cut out of lacrosse at the first possible minute and just pulled a dry tee over her sweaty practice jersey, to make sure she'd arrive on time. She was early, but the Manningtons were there. Reggie waved to Lily, trying to convey that everything was all right. Lily was back in her frump outfit, but she wasn't noticeably damaged otherwise.

Mr. Mannington intercepted Reggie as she tried to cross to the choir risers. His nose wrinkled as if he could smell her from several feet away.

"Regina Collins, I'm afraid that until your attitude changes, you will not be welcome as a member of the youth choir." Reggie's mouth fell open. Her mind raced. Had she missed a rehearsal? Had she been late—well, more than usual—failed to learn her part?

"What—I don't—"

"Your defiant attitude is inappropriate and is a bad influence on other choir members."

Light dawned. "What? Is this about me lending Lily some clothes? What does that have to do with this choir?"

"What you apparently fail to realize, Miss Collins, is that

singing at the Most Holy Sacrifice of the Mass is a ministry, not a performance, and as such to be approached in a spirit of service and humility, not one of self-seeking and pride."

Reggie didn't even know what that was supposed to mean.

"If you wish to discuss this matter, Father Doyle has graciously consented to consider speaking with you. Take it up with him. Good day."

Lily, behind him, mouthed silently, "I'm sorry. I'm sorry." But aloud, she said nothing. As soon as he turned around, she dropped her gaze to her music rack.

Reggie picked up her gym bag and shuffled out. Behind her, the choir struck up "O Salutaris Hostiam." With a definite hole in the alto section, Reggie noticed, and something off-key in the sopranos as well.

Reggie had to call her mom to come and get her early.

"What happened? Don't you feel well?"

"No, it's Douchebag McManlybuns who isn't feeling well. He kicked me out of choir."

"Oh, Regina! Why would he do something like that? You haven't offended him, have you? Really, it's simply awful to use such disrespectful language about your friend's father. I'm ashamed of you."

"Oh, give it a rest," Reggie muttered. And then louder, "I didn't do anything! I've worked harder on that dumb choir and his stupid music than anyone."

"Then why would he—Regina! Does this have anything to do with those clothes you were wearing on Monday? Have you done something—well, something inappropriate with—"

"All I did was lend Lily some clothes, okay? It was a joke! Because that stuff they make her wear is a joke! He's making some kind of a big deal out of it because he's *sick*, okay? And no, I did not do anything 'inappropriate.'"

Fortunately, they'd reached the Collins' driveway by then, so Reggie could jump out and slam the door behind her. "And if I'd kissed her on Main Street it would not be inappropriate, because I'm *gay*, Mom, G-A-Y!" she shouted. But not until she was safely in her room and had turned the volume up as loud as it would go.

❖

Lily finally returned to school on Thursday. Reggie rushed to claim her at lunch. Lily shrank back, almost like her first day of school. "I can't go to lunch with you. I can't go off campus. I can't get in trouble again."

"Well, okay," Reggie said, "but what are you going to eat?"

Lily held up a brown paper bag.

"We can go sit by the tennis courts," Reggie said. "I have to talk to you. What happened on Monday? Why was your dad so mad? Are you okay?"

Lily sat on the ground under a tree and handed Reggie half a cheese sandwich and some slightly brown-edged apple slices. "He was furious," she said in a small, constricted voice. "You can't imagine. My mom had to make an emergency trip to the doctor. That's why he came to get me. They needed me to come home and take care of the kids. So he was already upset. When he saw me in your clothes, he kind of lost it. He was driving the car and yelling about my 'trashy friends' and how he wasn't going to have me bringing this trash and filth into the house and corrupting the innocence of my little sisters. I thought he was going to have a heart attack."

Reggie felt sick. "I'm sorry. It was supposed to be fun. I didn't mean to get you in trouble."

"It's not your fault," Lily said. "It's not your fault he's a freak. When we got home, I tried to tell him that—that it was just for fun. I said I'd finally made some friends and we weren't doing anything bad. He said I wasn't allowed to see you again if this was how you were teaching me to behave. And then he started yelling 'Shame on you' and slapped my face. And then I went and changed and he went to the hospital to get Mom." Her voice was dead flat as if it was just the weather report.

Reggie felt numb too. She couldn't even imagine her dad slapping her. "How is your mom? Is she okay?"

"She's fine. The doctor said she was just tired. He put her on bed rest for a few days. That's another reason I was out of school. But If I get in any more trouble, I'm scared they'll make me drop out and get a GED. They're just looking for an excuse. He said if there's one more 'incident' I won't be allowed to do any extracurricular activities, and I have to go to All-City, Reggie, I just have to. If I can't keep on singing, I won't have any way to get out of the house except to go be a nun. That's why I can't hang out with you. You're the best friend I ever had, but I just can't. Please, please understand."

She started to cry. Reggie reached out and took her hand. It was cold, just as she'd imagined. She wrapped her other hand around it to warm it. Lily squeezed back, hard.

"My mom wanted to know if I'd done something 'inappropriate,'" Reggie said. She wanted to kick herself as soon as she'd said it. Lily looked up at her with tears still sticking to her pale eyelashes.

"Do you ever wish you could? Wish you could just do something inappropriate? I wish that all the time," Lily said.

Reggie was close enough to breathe in that scent of Lily, mixed with the smell of sun on the grass and the asphalt of the tennis courts. She leaned closer—or maybe it was Lily's fingers clinging to hers, pulling her nearer. Their lips met. Lily flinched, but then she pressed her mouth against Reggie's. A sweet feeling, like a full-body sugar rush, swept through Reggie.

But when she tried to put her arms around Lily, Lily pulled away.

"No, I can't," Lily said.

"But—but you just kissed me," Reggie said.

"Yes, but I can't! They freak out if I even hang out with you. What do you think they'd do to me if I had a girlfriend? They'd kill me if I dated a *boy*. It's too big a secret. I can't." She started to cry again.

"We'll think of something, Lily. We will."

Lily shook her head, sending wisps of fair hair whipping around her face like dry grass in the wind.

Reggie tried to catch hold of her hand again, but Lily put her hands up, palm out, to ward her off.

"No, please don't. Don't think of any more stuff. I just have to last until I'm eighteen. And then I can leave. But I swear to God, some days I'm just afraid I won't make it."

She picked up the cheese sandwich and threw it as far as she could. "Oh, sorry. Did you want that? God, if I just had a candy bar right now."

They walked silently back across the field to school. Before they parted at the door, Reggie said, "I'm going to keep thinking about this. I'm not giving up."

❖

She couldn't wait to be alone in her room. Yesterday, she'd been miserable and furious. Today she felt stupid with bliss. She threw herself on the bed, hugging her pillow. I kissed a girl, she thought. I kissed a girl and she kissed me back!

She gave herself a few minutes to enjoy her trance. Then she

jumped up and got ready for action. For she'd had two thoughts
on the way home. One required a phone call; the other, a search
of her dresser and closet. The phone call took persistence, but
she finally got through. "Why, Regina Collins," said the voice
of Sister Eloise. "How nice to hear from you. What's on your
mind?"

❖

The other thing she needed was found at the back of a drawer,
and tucked into her bag for later.

❖

When Sunday morning came, it felt strange to be sitting in
the pew with her parents, instead of up front with the choir. She
gazed hatefully at Mr. Mannington's broad rear view and didn't
join in the prayer responses or the hymns.

She didn't think it could get any worse until the sermon
started. Father Doyle cleared his throat and began to speak with
deceptive mildness about the topic of loving the sinner but hating
the sin, and what that could possibly mean.

"When a child, for instance, tells us that they are involved
in an inappropriate relationship, whether with another young
person of the opposite sex, or even of the same sex, it is our
responsibility to stand up for the truth in love. We need to let
them know, for instance, that same-sex attraction is a choice,
a bad choice, a wrong choice, one that can be overcome with
prayer and courage. We must support them in choosing the right
way, the way of purity. It is a false kind of love that supports
'choice' of a destructive lifestyle."

Drops of perspiration popped out on his forehead, and his
fingers gestured nervously. Reggie's cheeks burned. She couldn't

turn her head an inch to look at her parents. She felt as if the priest's eyes rested accusingly on her. She caught sight of Lily staring fixedly into space with eyes round and unblinking.

Father Doyle blundered on, covering abortion and divorce as well. "We all have our crosses to bear…" He paused to wipe steam off his glasses with a lace hankie that he tucked back into the sleeve of his cassock. Yeah, and yours is that you're a hypocrite and in the closet, Reggie thought furiously.

The offertory was taken, gifts marched to the altar. The wine and wafers were consecrated and the congregation knelt in worship. Reggie sat with her arms crossed and glared at her mother when she motioned Reggie to kneel alongside. This was war.

I'm never kneeling again, she thought. She gazed across the church at Lily like a soldier awaiting the firing squad.

Father Doyle came forward with the chalice, and people started lining up to receive communion. Reggie reached into her bag and pulled out the crumpled, rainbow-striped sash she'd retrieved the night before. One boring winter day she had Googled "gay Catholics" and discovered the Rainbow Sash website. She had ordered one to wear on Pentecost for the official protest. But she'd decided the time to take a stand had come early. She looped the sash across her shoulder and proceeded toward the altar, behind her parents.

Standing in front of Father Doyle, she looked him in the eye and held out her hand for the wafer. He jerked the chalice out of reach, as if he thought she'd try to snatch the precious contents. "You will not present yourself for the sacraments while wearing a symbol of your defiance of the Church!"

"I haven't done anything wrong!" Reggie said loudly.

"Take off that sash or get out of line!" he said, in a vehement whisper that sent spit flying. People were looking.

"I'm not taking it off." Reggie turned and walked, in what

felt like slow motion, to the pew, where she remained standing. Her mother tugged at her shirt, trying to get her to sit down, but she stayed where she was until the last hymn was sung and the choir marched out. They cut the hymn short after just one verse, so Reggie knew she had at least managed to fluster them.

❖

Breakfast was a silent affair until Reggie's mom appealed to her father. "Jeffrey! Don't you have something to say about this?"

Reggie's dad looked as if he'd rather be alone with his pancakes. He put his fork down. "Reggie, I think what your mom means is that, well, what was the point of that little display?"

"Yes, why did you have to embarrass your family like that?" her mother said. "Not everybody has to know about your personal problems! Why can't we just get along?"

"Is that what this is to you?" Reggie said. "My personal problem?"

"Oh, darling, I didn't mean it like that," her mother said. "It's just that every parent wants her child to have a nice life, and it's just going to get harder for you if you keep on with this stubborn idea you have."

"This isn't my problem!" Reggie said, slamming her mug down and slopping cocoa onto the cheerful tablecloth. "This is about Father Doyle and his douchebag pal."

"Don't use that kind of language at the table," her father said.

Her mother chimed in simultaneously. "You know the other families in this parish are not like that. They've always been perfectly nice to you. Father Doyle isn't all there is to the Church."

Reggie waited until they were done. "Mom, Dad, I have something to say. People like him? Maybe they're not all there is to it, but they're the official spokesmen. And nobody stands up to them. You don't. You just go along. And it's people like him who make life hard for people like me. And you give them money every week to make my life worse. That's why I stood up today. Someone has to. I just got kicked out of choir and you didn't say a word. Fine. I'm going to the Unitarian youth group from now on. They'll let me play the guitar there. Something has to change, and it's not going to change by everybody just acting nice. That's it, I'm done."

She grabbed a piece of bacon off the plate and ran upstairs with it. She felt all shaky and scared, but nobody followed her to lecture her. When she went back downstairs to get a cinnamon roll an hour later, her parents spoke carefully of other subjects. She felt sorry about yelling at them. They didn't get it—but at least they still loved her.

She brought her own brown bag to lunch on Monday. It was a big bag, stuffed with cold pizza slices, chips, and frosted brownies, and Lily's favorite cream-cheese olives. Reggie figured she needed to get Lily's blood sugar up for what she was about to suggest.

"Why did you do that—that thing with the sash?" Lily said. She refused even to go outside, and they ended up at a table alone in the cafeteria, among the barbarian hordes. "My father had a fit. He said you shouldn't be allowed back in church at all until you'd gone to confession and made a public apology." She accepted a slice of pizza, and a begrudging, sarcastic smile briefly curved her lips. "Actually it was kind of awesome. I thought Father Doyle was going to pee his pants. Oh yeah, I forgot, he doesn't have any pants. Unless he wears them underneath his cassock." She sighed and crunched a chip. "But it does mean I can't ever be seen with you again because you're not even a bad Catholic."

Reggie decided there was no way to work up to it gradually. She had to jump in. "Okay, then you can go to the audition by yourself. I just thought you'd want me along for support. But I can show you which bus to take and I'm sure you'll be fine."

Lily's eyes went as wide as they'd been in church. "What are you talking about?"

"You want to keep singing, and you need to get away from your parents. Marymount is interviewing for admissions next year. I called Sister Eloise. She works in their voice department. She promised to set up an audition for you and be there as one of the judges. We can go there on the bus after school. You're all set."

"But I can't. My father won't even pay for hot lunch! Marymount tuition is huge!"

"Sister Eloise says they'd kill for a voice like yours in their travel choir. It's a big fund-raiser for them, so it would be worth a scholarship."

"But if they found out I'd gone there on my own—"

"Look, I don't know! Maybe Sister Eloise is talking out her ass! I don't know! But I know I stood up in church and made a total ass of myself in front of my parents and everybody because you said nothing would change by just being nice all the time. So could you just get on the bus with me? Please?"

Lily took a big shaky breath. "Okay. I'll call my mom and I'll tell her—I'll tell her something." She smiled her sarcastic, head-tilted smile. "And if I get caught, I'll tell her you're Satan!"

❖

Reggie sat outside the audition room. Lily sang "Panis Angelicus" again. Her voice soared up, then caught, wavered— Reggie held her breath—and soared higher, pure and clear. It was better than before because there was feeling in it. She can't be stuck in a church forever, Reggie thought. She has to get out where that voice can be heard. Whatever it takes.

The song ended, and Reggie breathed a sigh of relief. She looked around at the hallways. Marymount looked pretty posh, an old-money kind of style with thick carpets and gilded woodwork. The girls she'd seen on the stairs had sleek hair, nice wool skirts and blazers, tailored blouses. Reggie wouldn't have liked it. But maybe it would seem like a haven to Lily.

The door opened. Reggie was surprised to see Sister Eloise, who made a "shh" gesture. "Hello, Regina," she said in a half whisper. "They're doing the interview portion. I thought I'd just slip out and let you know she did well. Really well. I can't promise, of course, but I'm almost sure they'll invite her."

"And the scholarship?"

"If the voice department wants her, they'll make it possible." She smiled conspiratorially. "And they will want her, if I have anything to say about it."

"But her father—"

"I don't want you to worry about him. The Marymount staff can be very persuasive. They won't send an old sister like me to talk to a man of Mr. Mannington's...character. It will probably be our chaplain, Father Martin. He's a very serious young man. I feel sure he'll make a good impression."

"I hope so," Reggie said. "Lily has to get in. It's important."

Sister Eloise touched Reggie's shoulder. "Whatever happens, Regina, remember you did a good thing. You're a good friend. Keep in touch. I expect to hear great things about you."

She went back inside, closing the door softly behind her.

What Reggie didn't expect to happen was that Lily would disappear. Maybe Sister Eloise had known. Reggie hadn't. The brave rescuer is supposed to ride off with the pretty princess. She's not supposed to get a quick hug when they get off the bus, and then a breathless phone call to say the princess is in, but she has to go because her mother's taking her to buy a uniform. And then nothing. A postcard with a new address. But a total absence of the smile, the voice, the presence that was Lily. That wasn't how it was supposed to go down. She'd thought Lily would stay at Springdale until the end of the year, at least. Then go to Marymount in the fall, which was a long time away.

But the sisters at Marymount had snapped her up right away. It was a good thing for them—they almost always won at All-City, and they'd be sure to this year, with their new soloist. But it didn't feel like a good thing to Reggie. She sucked on grape-flavored Tootsie Pops and cried. Be careful what you wish for, she thought.

Regina went often to the Unitarian youth group. She'd made a big enough fuss to get there—it would have been feeble to give it up. She saw Dusty Phillips sitting in a folding chair, and it was like catching a clip from an old movie on TV. A movie you'd once loved, a movie that had once made you jittery with anticipation. But it seemed like such a long time ago that she didn't feel the suspense anymore. She just walked over and sat down next to her.

"Hi," she said. The other girl's eyebrows went up. "Hello."

"I'm Reggie Collins."

"Yes, I've seen you around. I didn't know you were a UU."

"I'm not. But I got thrown out of my church and I have a guitar."

Dusty laughed without a hint of sarcasm. She had full lips, and a dimple in one cheek. "Well, do you want to warm up before the rehearsal? Show us what you got."

Simple as that, Reggie was side by side with Dusty Phillips, heads bent together over chording. Dusty wasn't wearing her fingerless gloves. Her hands were capable and slightly plump, with chipped nail polish in every color but pink. And they were warm, as Reggie found out a few days later.

Dusty wasn't what Reggie had imagined. She was a friend. Someone to talk to, someone she could have lunch with, play music with, someone who could drop by her house. Dusty was there to talk Reggie down from her nerves when she played an ensemble piece at All-City. And she understood when Reggie saw Lily from a distance during the Marymount performance and quietly freaked out.

Reggie was out in the hall during the second intermission when she heard a familiar voice behind her. "Hey, Reggie. Regina Collins!" Reggie's stomach twinged as if she'd dropped two floors in an elevator. She turned around.

Lily had her hair cut; now it lay smoothly, like gold wings. In her burgundy and cream Marymount uniform she looked slender and chic. Normal. She grabbed Reggie's hands, smiling.

"Come here, I want to show you something." She pushed open a side door and pulled Reggie out onto the terrace. She started unbuttoning her blouse. Reggie didn't know what was coming next. Lily slipped the blouse down off her shoulder.

"Look—I figured out what to do instead of cutting myself."

She laughed, and Reggie thought she was joking, though as always, it was hard to be sure. "Look."

Reggie stepped closer and looked. Against Lily's pale skin, the fresh tattoos showed up bright and clear. A fleur de lis and a crown. Some weird Catholic thing?

"My aunt sent me some money. I got a demerit being out of bounds without permission. But it's just once, and they don't know what for. Don't look so worried! I'm not going to blow it. But I had to do it."

Reggie ran her fingers over the markings. A shiver went through her at the touch.

"Don't you get it?" Lily said. "It's *us*. A lily and a crown. I still have to make it to eighteen. But I'll never forget you, Reggie. I can't. You're under my skin."

She buttoned up, gave Reggie one of her swift backward smiles, and was gone.

Reggie slid into her seat next to Dusty just as the next piece was starting.

"What's up with you?" Dusty whispered. "You look freaked out."

"I don't know," Reggie whispered. "I'm happy. I think. I'll tell you later." She slid her hand into Dusty's, surreptitiously. "Here—I got you a Tootsie Pop at the concession table. For later."

CHARLES JENSEN is the author of *The First Risk*, a finalist for the 2010 Lambda Literary Award. His previous collections include *Living Things*, which won the 2006 Frank O'Hara Chapbook Award, and *The Strange Case of Maribel Dixon*. A past recipient of an Artist's Project Grant from the Arizona Commission on the Arts, his poetry has appeared in *Bloom, Columbia Poetry Review, Copper Nickel, The Journal, New England Review*, and *West Branch*. He holds an MFA in poetry from Arizona State University. He is active in his local community by serving on the Board of Directors of the Arts & Humanities Council of Montgomery County and in the national community by serving on the Emerging Leader Council of Americans for the Arts.

I had been dating a guy for just a few weeks when I realized I wasn't ready for things to get serious. We broke it off, but decided to be friends. He came with me to the Pride event in town that weekend with two other friends of mine. We had a great time walking around, talking, being casual and relaxed. It was then I knew I would be stupid not to put my issues aside and be with him. He was the guy I'd been looking for: sweet, funny, creative—and he liked me. Near the end of the day, we saw a mechanical bull set up in the park. Rides were only three dollars. I got on, slipping a gloved hand around a rope tried across the bull's back that I would use to steady myself, while the other hand, I was told, should stay in the air, held up like a protestor's fist. I rode that bull for forty-five seconds before I fell off. The next day, my legs were black and blue with bruises, so sore I could barely walk. But I realized something. I was capable of putting my fear aside and accepting the opportunities—fun, scary, new—that came into my life.

DUET: A STORY IN *HAIBUN*
CHARLES JENSEN

Abbott plays trombone in the T-Roosevelt High School Band. He lugs it onto the long yellow bus to the marching band competition like a third leg good for only tripping and stumbling. When he plays, the brass becomes part of his body, an extension of his arms, his lungs. His breath turns eighth notes into fat birds that zip out of his bell and fly drunkenly above his listeners. He named his trombone Paris, a city he'd like to visit someday. He imagines its music is French, or has a French accent when he plays with other trombones. The bus he boards is ripe with the sour smell of vinyl seats and high school boys, most of whom smell like wilting flowers and autumn. He slides into a seat in the middle, where his feet rest up on the wheel well. He glances out the window, where he sees Lancaster get out of his mother's car, pulling his giant tuba from the trunk before she drives off,

> his blond hair burns hot,
>   glinting white like envelopes
>   full of love letters.

Lancaster carries the tuba like a trophy toward the bus. He crabwalks like a drunken fool to make some flute girls laugh, then pretends to stumble over his own feet. The tuba in his arms explodes out of his body like joy, up into the air around him. He nestles it into the back of the bus, climbing around it, walking the aisle. He glances into each row for Abbott's face, wonders where he is waiting for him. Abbott's hand in his between their bodies for as long as they think they can get away with it. Lancaster telling jokes to distract the rest of the band. His body and Abbott's body

> make music with breath—
>> they turn into instruments
>>> played without a score.

❖

The bus lurches forward, coughing a burst of black smoke from the rear. The whole carriage rattles as everyone shouts and laughs and calls back and forth. Abbott looks up and sees his bandmates' words cross over them like footballs not meant for them to catch. Lancaster's hand warm in his hand. The bus puts a shoulder into a speed bump and Abbott's leg, helpless, leans into Lancaster's knee for support. Abbott loves him, loves the way his touch is always warm and generous, loves his big Santa Claus laugh, loves how Lancaster says he belongs to Abbott

> how a pair of shoes,
>> reflections of each other,
>>> share the same body.

❖

Lancaster's dad never asked questions. His mom, though, always wanted to know: *Where are your other friends?*

Lancaster and Abbott up in his room, playing Xbox, playing board games, playing music. She began to test them: barging in without knocking, catching their uncertain over-shoulder looks. But they were up to nothing but being best friends. Lancaster's dad stopped inviting them to watch football. It was a kind of acceptance,

> telling them, *I know*
>   *we are different, but even*
>   *a fox can love hounds.*

❖

Abbott dislikes autumn: everything crumbling around him. Leaves drop from trees like bits of lint, grass starving for water until it sleeps, the birds abandoning their nests for winter homes. Marching band season begins in the swelter of summer but ends long after its warmth does. In three weeks, he and Lancaster will celebrate a year of togetherness, their unworded, unnamed, unquestioned togetherness. Abbott pokes him in the ribs, thinking about it. Lancaster smiles because he knows what Abbott is thinking. Across the aisle, a girl leans forward to ask Abbott about physics class. Instinctively, their hands release,

> letting go like wrens
>   slipping from the nest, their throats
>   heavy with their song.

❖

Lancaster speaks music as if it were his first language: he sight reads better than anyone else in class. Rhythms he counts instinctively. As a kid, he banged pots and pans together until his parents bought a toy piano, then a drum set, then a bedroom that shared no walls with any of their rooms. Lancaster once told Abbott, *When you talk, I hear the notes in your voice before the words, but they mean just as much.* Lancaster counts his steps, counts the taps of the ceiling fan above his bed as it nods while it turns. The world around him adds up to rhythm. He gives back a melody,

> his heart keeps its time
> > like a metronome; his breath
> > > runs arpeggios.

Abbott believes he was born this way, to play a brass instrument, to study the world from a distance, to observe and understand. Music flows into him through his ears, is broken down inside his body into scales and patterns. Abbott explains to Lancaster, *Music is like the universe: it always evens out.* His other good class is physics, where every action has an equal and opposite reaction. He tutors Lancaster in the study of energy: how one thing's potential becomes kinetic; how an object at rest tends to stay at rest until acted upon by something outside it. Abbott knows they were like this, two guys alone in their stillness until they acted upon their feelings,

> making minor chords
> > skew upward, shedding their dirge,
> > > keeping perfect pitch.

Lancaster talks with a guy from the saxophone section about a band they both like. Through the window, he sees the bus zip past neighborhoods, then parking lots, then farms. Then rolling hills. The path they take unfolds its arms until it holds open the entire landscape around them, disappearing on either side of the freeway. The bus has a jazz shimmy to its run, bumping syncopated intervals to the seams in the concrete—ba-dum, ba-dum, ba-dum. A song builds in his mind—it includes a trombone, a tuba. A duet. The deep rumble of the low brass vibrates in his chest and he knows this is both love and music, that Abbott is his friend and his more-than-friend, that around them the bus is filled with people who've never felt this, or have felt it and tuned it out. The kid goes on about the band, but Lancaster can't focus on his words. All he hears is the beat of the road, the light presence of Abbott behind him like a cloud, and the babble of everyone's words bubbling like backup singers

> while the world outside,
>   blurry with speed, is drowning
>   in songs like this one.

Abbott talks *Gossip Girl* with a percussionist who looks a little like Serena van der Woodsen. She plays xylophone, glockenspiel, and bells. Her voice, like her instruments, has a delicate tinkling to its sound, like empty water glasses riding on a small cart. Abbott has been thinking about his future, about colleges, about what it might mean to be apart from Lancaster, even for a few weeks. Lancaster has not yet made up his mind about what comes after high school. He knows his future is in music. Abbott and the girl talk about last week's episode, but his mind is really somewhere else. He does not want to make life-changing decisions just yet. He wants another year of someone else deciding—teachers, parents, etc. He wants another year,

> sequence of measures
>> whose melody remains strong
>>> no matter the pace.

Lancaster's parents had dreams for him. In his father's dream, he carried a football to school, then on a big grassy field in the autumn, across an end zone. In his mother's dream, he carried an architect's sketch pad and imagined beautiful buildings to put people inside. Lancaster's dreams are less clear. *You can't hold off this decision forever*, his mom told him last week. *What are you going to do without a plan?* He'd looked at his tuba in the corner of his bedroom, turned upside down on its bell. *What I always do*, he said. *Improvise.* The tuba, its ear to the ground, seemed it was listening for something coming from a long way away, something only it could hear,

> horses galloping
>> like a timpani's flourish
>>> announcing a change.

Abbott has been planning on college since he started school. His parents led him to believe it was assumed he'd attend. He'd given the decision careful consideration even before the night Lancaster first kissed him in October, in Lancaster's yard, in the dark, the warm yellow gleam from the living room falling onto the grass in flickering shards of light, the shadow of a parent passing across it like a warning. He kissed Lancaster and knew, even still, Abbott would have to leave him,

> fermata of need
>> held until their lungs might burst
>>> with each other's names.

Lancaster, Lancaster. He loves the way Abbott says his name, like something sacred. It enters his ear and drills straight down into his gut, where it ties knots. *Abbott,* he thinks, assigning each syllable its own secret tone: a song of their names. The bus pulls off the highway and curves widely toward the school hosting the day's competition. Lancaster sees a scattered line of long yellow buses huddled near the bleachers like twelve giant horns, all flash and sheen and shine. He leans back into his seat and curls his hand around Abbott's before they must separate into their instrument sections

> the way a whole note
>> becomes half notes, two bodies
>>> of a single sound.

❖

Abbott remembers the steps of the routine and can pinpoint the parts of the music where Lancaster's path crosses his, their big brassy notes shooting out of their instruments, entwining in the air, becoming chords. They weave in and out on the field: first they are a line, then they hinge, swing closed, merge, bend, and curve—all the steps have precision, the way two people who dance must always be in sync,

the way they must know
what their partner plans to do
just as he does it.

❖

Lancaster kissed first, his blond hair bare of its shine in the dark yard, the stars lathered in the sky above their heads, an absent moon. He could not see Abbott's face but moved to where he knew it was, Abbott's tense lips suddenly softening, parting, kissing back. Lancaster, taller, pulled Abbott into his body until they touched. There was no part of it that didn't feel right. Abbott raised an arm around Lancaster's neck, placing his warm hand just atop his shoulder. The kiss broke apart like a rim shot, quick and terse, and neither of them spoke. It was cold. They stayed close for warmth, their bodies shivering

a form of humming,
their chests filling with shared tones
no one else could hear.

❖

After the kiss, they grew closer. It was never something they talked about, that moment, but they knew what they were, what they were to each other. The world was changed for them. They fell into a rhythm of after-school days and weekends hanging out, of telephone calls and study sessions. And then they were in love, but it wasn't a place they arrived at. They looked around one day and they were there. In the hallways at school, there were the two of them, and then there was everyone else. They were apart from it, but it was safe to be in each other's company, this secret perfectly kept, though when they passed each other going to class,

> their inner voices
>   unleashed a silent chorus
>   they sang with their eyes.

Lancaster envies how Abbott's mother has always known: the glint in her eye when he arrives at their door, the weight of the privacy she gives them while they hang out in his room, listening to music or, better, making out with musical accompaniment. Lancaster's mother flips through his yearbook and picks out his girlfriends. *What about this one?* she asks, placing a finger on a clarinetist's face. *She's cute.* Lancaster nods, but says, *It's just not going to happen.* He wonders what she would say if he made her know how much he is spoken for. If she saw the way Lancaster looked after Abbott as he walked down their driveway toward his own house. Abbott once told him, *They will know when they are ready to see it.* And then Abbott rubbed his thigh softly. *And then you can tell them.* Lancaster had closed his eyes, tried to imagine

> his parents' faces
>   holding the shape of "O" in
>   a one-word duet.

Abbott and Lancaster change out of their clothes in the school's dingy locker room. Walls of tiny metal boxes cinched with padlocks are pursed around them, keeping the secret of their own contents away from prying eyes. Abbott thinks this is one true benefit to being with a boy: they share these private spaces with each other, a kind of club. Lancaster's body, naturally athletic, drops his clothing like rain, gentle and graceful. Abbott discovers he's staring when Lancaster snaps his fingers with warning, his eyes playful but cautious. Abbott shimmies out of his jeans like he's catching on fire, then nearly falls to the floor, but Lancaster steadies him with a fast arm, a reflex, as though he expected this,

> the way his fingers
>> turn sheet music into sound
>>> as if he wrote it.

❖

Lancaster knows Abbott will go. He knows that's who Abbott is. He also knows Abbott doesn't know how to tell him. They will have the fall. They will weave toward and away from each other on football fields across the state, their notes will mingle and merge into songs, they will sit next to each other on bus after bus after bus. By spring, Abbott will have a plan and Lancaster will have only impulse, a sketch of something, maybe the time signature of a life he'd like to lead. His measures will be empty of notes; Abbott's symphony will begin the way it always had to. And while Lancaster knows his own song will be beautiful, it will have a kind of fault, an absence,

> a note left unused,
>> a string snapped and silent in
>>> his life's piano.

❖

Abbott and Lancaster share their seat again on the road home, collapse their hands into a single hand. The landscape dissolves into sunset and begins its slow retreat into dusk and twilight. At school, Abbott carries Lancaster's uniform back into the band room, hanging it on the rack next to his own: two identical bodies placed side by side and left to rest together. He joins Lancaster at the curb, where they wait for their parents to arrive by car to take them home. The night, like their first night, is cool and private. Their bandmates have all gone home, and then they hear

> the crickets pick up
>   their tiny violins, play
>   melodies of *yes*.

❖

Lancaster takes Abbott's hand in his hand while they wait. Abbott's eyes meet Lancaster's eyes. *I want you to be the person you are going to be*, Lancaster says quietly. He knows this is another way people love each other, that they become wings instead of weights, ring brightly like major chords. Abbott rests his head on Lancaster's shoulder, feeling Lancaster's breath against the back of his neck. He hugs him a little tighter and says, *I already am.*

> The night, like an ear,
>   absorbs their voices. Their kiss
>   drowns out the crickets.

Abbott sees Lancaster's mother pull into the parking lot and instinctively slides away. As the car pulls up, Abbott stands, ready to say hello to her. Lancaster rises, stands next to him. Lancaster's mother drops the passenger window with a slow glissando of machine-whirr, her face leaning forward to see them. *Hi, boys,* she says brightly. Because he, too, is already who he wants to be, Lancaster puts an arm around Abbott's shoulder. He sees his mother's expression go suddenly slack as he pulls his friend to him, holds Abbott's face in one hand, and kisses him

> the way duettists
>> must breathe in sync, their open mouths
>>> making this music.

SANDRA MCDONALD's debut short story collection, *Diana Comet and Other Improbable Stories*, is an Over the Rainbow book for the American Library Association, a 2010 Booklist Editor's Choice, and winner of a Lambda Literary Award. She is the author of three published science fiction novels and teaches college composition. Read more about her at sandramcdonald.com.

When I taught high school, I had students of all sizes, shapes, colors, and orientations. For Halloween one year, one of my favorite tenth graders came dressed as his church-loving grandmother, complete with hat, gloves, and fabulous purple dress. Surrounded by vampires, rock stars, and sports icons, he caught some flack and went home at lunchtime to change. A few years later I got an e-mail from him and he told me he had moved away to start his male-to-female transformation. I know he will become a beautiful woman, inside and out.

ALL GENDER U
SANDRA MCDONALD

My mother has never objected to my wearing girls' clothes because she thinks I'm her dead sister Linda, reincarnated. She says she knew it from the moment the midwife placed me on her chest—slimy, screaming, waving my tiny fists in protest at being ejected into the world with a penis instead of a vagina. Even as a newborn I knew instinctively that something had gone wrong in the biology department.

Anyway, Mom looked into my eyes and saw dead Linda gazing back—sweet, bookish, never-hurt-a-fly Linda, who died in her sleep when she was only sixteen. Mom named me Linden, which was almost immediately shortened to Linnie and Lin. She put me in frilly dresses and painted my bedroom pink.

So, you see, I never had much chance as a boy anyway.

If you think my mother is nuts for believing in reincarnation, you've never swung through my hometown of Lake Orchid, Florida. We're the oldest spiritualist community in the United States. The big white and green sign on the highway says so. Back in the Civil War, spiritualists were the people who could hook you up with the ghost of your husband or son. Just like Mrs. Abraham Lincoln in the White House, trying to make contact with her dead kid. Séances, spirit guides, mediums, mesmerists, Ouija boards—we have it all. Mom owns the Lake Orchid Mercantile General Store, where the community bulletin board is full of business cards decorated with angels or magic eyes or healing triangles.

Once in a while Mom conducts séances in the back room, but most people who come to Lake Orchid these days are more interested in Reiki, magnetic bracelets, tai chi, chakra counseling, and white-light therapy from the realms beyond. You can learn how to heal yourself or how to heal the planet, how to teleport through multiple dimensions, and how to develop your own clairaudient or clairvoyant talents. We also have weekly bingo.

What we don't have in the middle of sunny, swampy Florida is any kind of college that I can go to and be safe as a person born as a boy who should have been a girl. My best friend Rachel, who got onto the Internet a lot younger than I ever did, told me in seventh grade that I was a transgirl.

"Or you could call yourself a *shemale*," she said helpfully. "Or just *MTF*. Or just *trans*."

Transgirl sounded better than anything else. Like Supergirl, but no leotards. I'm not the biggest fan of my body—the bottom parts are too big and awkward, my chest is totally flat, I have to wax and shave and pluck hair *constantly*—but the idea of surgery and hormone treatments makes me queasy. I don't believe in scalpels or chemicals. I just want to be pretty, and wear nice dresses, and have sex with lots of nice-looking, funny, smart girls. And maybe boys. Because that's all confusing, too—I like both sexes. But I have zero experience. Is that pathetic or what?

I wish someone would build All Gender U, where for four years you can be anything you want and you can have sex with anyone and no one will ever think you're a freak. That would be the coolest college ever.

A few months ago Mom said, "You could go to school online," but she wasn't saying it because of the trans thing. When I leave, she's going to have to hire someone to work in the Mercantile while she runs the Chamber of Commerce, writes the monthly newsletter, handles all of our Internet sales and maintains the community's web, Facebook, and MySpace pages. Mom doesn't actually like dealing with the public.

Meanwhile, the regulars in town love me. The snowbirds who come down each winter and nest in the RV park are just as nice. Give me a tourist lost on her way to Disney World and she'll soon be walking out the door with enough books, healing magnets, and self-hypnosis CDs to open her own store. Rachel says I could sell snow to the Eskimos, and I would, too, but it would have to be snow with glitter—silver and blue, just like the frozen sea.

Male tourists are harder to convince. They immediately distrust my long hair (ponytail, usually, because it's as flat and limp as overcooked spaghetti when I leave it down) and a moment or two later realize there's something rotten going on under my sundress. But this is the Lake Orchid Mercantile, with a rainbow flag flying on the porch, New Age music on the satellite radio, and tarot cards in seven different languages. You come for the unusual, you get the unusual.

Anyway, I'm not going to school online. I want the whole college experience. When I was twelve years old I fell in love with a book written by a Dartmouth graduate about life as a coed in the 1950s—the sororities, the chaperoned dances, the gentlemen callers who signed guest books and waited with corsages in hand until their dates descended from the perfumed, privileged floors above. The book is called *Dartmouth in My Day*. Rachel thought it was crap. Certainly college is nothing like that now, anyway. But that's what I want: ivy and stone, big green lawns, chapel bells on peaceful afternoons, drafty halls, and big libraries with unabridged dictionaries and oak reading tables. I've never been up north but I'm looking forward to leather boots, suede skirts, chenille sweaters, scarves to hide my Adam's apple. My nose will turn pink from the cold and I'll wear black vintage hats that everyone will adore.

Dartmouth was the only school I applied to. But then Rachel convinced me to send in an application to Amherst, too. Better to have a back-up plan, she said. Wouldn't you know that I got accepted by Amherst and wait-listed at Dartmouth. I might not know until July or August if I'm in. And the odds are pretty awful—last year fourteen thousand people applied. Only two thousand got in. Of the six hundred hopefuls on the wait list, not a single one was admitted.

This is where Aunt Catherine comes in. Catherine, who was just as heartbroken as my mother when their sister died, but who did not run away, hook up with a guy, move to a spiritualist camp in Florida, get pregnant, get dumped, and raise a kid on her own. Instead, Catherine did everything properly in her life. She has a lovely home and three sons in Boston, and she not only graduated from Dartmouth but also is some bigwig in their alumni organization.

Aunt Catherine is perhaps the only one who can get me into the college of my dreams.

Aunt Catherine is no fan of spiritualism.

Aunt Catherine is standing in the Mercantile right in front of me, and I'm totally freaking out.

❖

I only know her from pictures, but she looks exactly how someone from the upper echelons of Boston should look: burgundy skirt and jacket, a white silk blouse, expensive shoes, tasteful but lovely jewelry. Her hair is blond and bobbed. She could have just walked off the set of *Mona Lisa Smile*, a movie I've watched only two dozen times. No one in Lake Orchid wears panty hose and silk—you might as well dress up and go sit in a sauna. There's sweat on Aunt Catherine's brow, but it's just a faint gleam. And on her it's not sweat, it's *perspiration*.

"I'm looking for Marilyn Gallagher," she says, pleasant but steely.

"I'm Lin," I blurt out. "Linden. Hi."

Aunt Catherine's eyebrows climb so high they might as well just worm their way over the top of her scalp.

"Linden," she says, the way someone might try out the name of an exotic mineral or zoological specimen. For several moments she studies me. "I thought you'd be taller. Or maybe shorter. Maybe… Well, in any case, I'm your aunt Catherine. It's a pleasure to finally meet you in person."

"Mom didn't say you were coming."

"Your mother doesn't know. I was in Orlando for an alumni fund-raiser and thought I'd come visit."

"Okay, fine," I tell her, which is lame. It's not like she needs to explain herself to me. "We live here. I'll show you."

I'm wearing peach-colored sandals with wooden heels. They match my dress but as I cross to the back door, they clip-clop on the old floor like I'm a big old horse. Aunt Catherine's footsteps behind me are light taps, graceful and lithe. She was probably a ballerina.

I lead her through the storeroom, out back, and across the lot to the house where Mom and I live. It's a shotgun shack from 1937—long, straight, and narrow. Mom's office takes up most of the living room. She's got wooden filing cabinets overflowing with paperwork, a green metal desk rescued from an old army base, and a brand-new laptop. Squeezed in the corner are a sofa from Goodwill and a black-and-white TV that we barely ever watch.

"Mom, look who came—"

She looks up from her computer, squeals with delight,

and throws herself on Aunt Catherine so forcefully they almost tumble through the screen door back out onto the porch. You couldn't tell from their fashions that they share any DNA at all. If Aunt Catherine looks like a sorority mother from the 1950s, Mom is the extra who wandered offstage during a revival of *Hair* and never took off the costume. I've tried to tell her that tie-dye makes her look sallow, but she says that I have my style and she has hers.

Aunt Catherine is being smothered by Mom's hug. She pats Mom's back a few times before breaking free.

"It's been a long time," Aunt Catherine says.

"It's been *forever*," Mom says, and starts moving manila folders and boxes off the sofa. "I can't believe you're here. Sit down here. No, let me move those. Here. Watch out for the springs. Linnie, dear, make us some iced tea, will you? The special kind."

The special kind involves adding sugar, fresh-squeezed lemon juice, and generous doses of rum into the already-brewed unsweet tea we keep in the refrigerator. The kitchen is separated from the living room by a beaded curtain. Through it I can see Mom and Aunt Catherine sitting on the sofa—Aunt Catherine's knees pressed close together, Mom with a sequined pillow in her lap. You wouldn't think they were sisters except for their high foreheads and pointed chins. It's about eighty degrees inside, and that womanly sheen is getting heavier on Aunt Catherine's forehead. They're talking about her drive up from Orlando.

"The rental car company talked me into getting one of those talking navigation machines," Aunt Catherine says. "Very handy."

"Did you see the old steamboat pier? I love fishing over there."

"No, but I saw an antique store your cousin Ellen would like."

"Overpriced and pretentious," Mom says. "What about the Alligator Den? Lin nearly got eaten there once."

"He's very tall."

"Five foot ten," Mom replies. "Heels make everyone look taller."

I carry the special tea in on a blue and yellow tray.

"Don't drink too much," I tell Aunt Catherine, trying to sound casual and cheerful and not like my stomach is full of nervous snakes. "You'll end up on the floor, like Miss Mary, our fortuneteller."

Mom waves her hand. "Don't be silly. Miss Mary had a stroke. Who's watching the store?"

"I guess that's me."

"I guess you better get back there, then," Mom says cheerfully. "Sell lots, we're in the red this month."

So off I go, banished to the Mercantile. If only I'd had the foresight to install secret cameras and listening devices in the living room so I could monitor them from my phone. No busloads of tourists have rolled in with cash and credit cards, so I'm left dusting the Egyptian trinket boxes until Rachel breezes in with her arm in a sling.

"What happened to you?" I ask.

"I was shinnying down the trellis and fell. But I told my dads that I fell off the bike, so that's my cover story."

"Why were you shinnying down the trellis?"

"For practice," Rachel says. "I'm going to break curfew on Friday, which means I'm going to be grounded on Saturday, which means I'm going to have to sneak out on Saturday night."

I abandon the trinket boxes for a display of Native American dreamcatchers. A few feathers, some ribbons, and that sling will be a thing of beauty. "I see a chain of causality here. You could avoid breaking curfew, thus avoid being grounded, thus avoid sneaking out via the trellis."

She flips her long brown hair and clasps her good hand to her heart. "For Matthew Perry, I'd break a thousand curfews."

She means our friend Matthew Perry, not Matthew Perry the Hollywood actor who doesn't do much anymore. Matthew is the cutest boy in school and has been since the fifth grade. He rides a motorcycle. He never brings a pen to class. He drives most of the teachers nuts, except for the ones who'd probably throw themselves in bed with him. His father is the minister at our Lyceum, which is where we go to service and learn about the worlds beyond. Matthew Perry never comes to Lyceum.

I might be a little jealous that Matthew and Rachel started dating, but I try not to think about it too much.

Rachel is totally open to the idea of decorating her sling. While we festoon it—that's a great word, *festoon*—I tell her that the key to my entire future is sitting in my living room, and she thinks I'm tall.

"I told you that you should wear flats," Rachel agrees. "What else did she say?"

"Nothing."

Rachel lifts a silver bell into the air and makes it tinkle. "She wouldn't have come all the way to Florida after twenty years of family feud if she wasn't at least thinking about it."

"She came for a fund-raiser. And it isn't a family feud."

"Twenty years of not talking to each other is a feud."

It's not a feud. My grandparents retired to rural France after reading *A Year in Provence* and haven't been back to America in twelve years. Mom and Aunt Catherine may not talk much on the phone, but they send each other Christmas cards every year. Aunt Catherine's handwriting is precise and beautiful. Mom uses colored markers and glitter. Aunt Catherine's cards always feature her sons on the cover, all of them wearing matching sweaters in front of a fireplace. The one with zits grew up to have perfect skin. The one with glasses switched to contacts and got his teeth straightened. Mom sends cards with Wacky Florida motifs—wrinkled old people on the beach, alligators with beer cans on their nose, that sort of thing.

"Mom should have prepared her," I fret. "Not let her walk in here and get all surprised."

Rachel says, "She's going to love you. Just be natural."

At five I close the store and go back to the house. Aunt Catherine has shed her blazer and her shoes. Mom's headband is hanging from our Goodwill chandelier. They're listening to the soundtrack from some horrible John Hughes movie and going through photographs from a black leather box.

"I didn't even know you had these," Aunt Catherine says, reaching for her drinking glass and nearly knocking it over. Her gaze is slightly unfocused. "Grandma sent them to you?"

"When she sold the house," Mom says. "Oh, look! Here's your senior prom!"

"I can't believe I wore fuchsia," Aunt Catherine moans.

Mom looks up. "Linnie, sit down! Look through these with us."

It's a good opportunity for schmoozing, I guess, but looking through old photos with two increasingly tipsy adults isn't my idea of a good time. "Got to eat, I'm starving," I say, and make a lot of noise in the kitchen with the blender. Cold pumpkin soup may not sound yummy, but chopped-up sweet potato and fresh carrot juice with just a dash of pumpkin spice is good on a hot day and great if you're trying to maintain a girlish figure.

The next time I peek out, Mom and Aunt Catherine are looking at an oversized photo with wistful expressions on their faces.

"I never saw this one," Aunt Catherine says.

"Linda was so excited for you," Mom says.

It's a picture of Mom, Catherine, and Linda at Catherine's college graduation. Linda is the youngest, maybe fourteen or so.

Mom is a little older, wearing a big white hat. Catherine has her black robe on and is clutching her diploma. They're all smiling widely.

"She would have liked it there," Catherine says. "You would have liked it, too. Gallagher women have always been Dartmouth women."

Mom says, "Linnie really wants to go, Cath. I think it'd be good for her."

"Him," Aunt Catherine says.

"Linnie prefers to be called 'her.'"

"Linden can prefer what he wants, but people have to use the pronouns that belong to their gender," Aunt Catherine says. "I know you love and support him, but he can't go to any college campus like he is now, Marilyn. Freakish behavior that's acceptable in Lake Orchid is not acceptable in the real world."

Mom says, carefully, "This is the real world. And it's not a 'behavior.' It's the way she's always been."

Aunt Catherine makes a little *tsk*ing noise. "Everyone has a choice. If he promises to dress and act like a boy, then we have some options. But to send him up there like he is now—Marilyn, they'd stone him in the middle of campus. His personal safety would be in constant jeopardy."

"She can handle it."

"You have to see the world for what it is, not what we want it to be," Aunt Catherine says. "Can I have this picture? I'll make a copy and send it back to you."

"Of course," Mom says. "I wish you'd talk to Linnie about this, though."

Aunt Catherine lifts her glass. "And I wish we had more of this tea. It's exceptionally tasty."

I pretty much hate her by now, so I retreat to my bedroom and hope she chokes to death on a lemon slice.

After another round of tea Mom gets it into her head to go skinny-dipping at the lake. She shouts for me to come, too, but I tell her that I have a history exam in the morning. Besides which, I'm not getting naked in front of Aunt Catherine. Aunt Catherine protests the skinny-dipping plan—no Boston Brahmin would ever be caught dead naked in a Florida lake—but Mom drags her out the door and they giggle their way down the street. The photo of sweet, innocent Linda is left behind on the old army trunk that doubles as our coffee table.

Aunt Catherine knows nothing about me. She thinks I'm just some freak who doesn't know about danger or prejudice or the way people judge you. I'm not dumb. I'm not ignorant. Lake Orchid High School has a lot of kids from our community but also farm kids from other towns. I've had some really helpful teachers, but I've also been bullied and spat at and twice I was hit in the hallways. Mom doesn't know about that.

In my fantasy All Gender U, no one ever gets spat at. Teachers and classmates call you by whatever pronoun you prefer. All the bathrooms are unisex, so you never have to make a choice about which one is safest to use. You never have to avoid the cafeteria because people will stare, and all the sororities and fraternities take you for whatever gender you want to be, not what's been biologically assigned without your permission.

It's all a stupid dream, though. Places like that never exist.

Once there was a famous writer named Truman Capote who was tiny and gay and wrote the book *Breakfast at Tiffany's*. He died before I was born. You can see clips of him on YouTube. Anyway, Dr. Fish is Lake Orchid's version of Truman Capote. He's only five feet tall, he's written some popular books about the afterlife, and in his own words, he's "gayer than a rainbow-covered unicorn licking cotton candy with sparkles sprinkled on top."

Dr. Fish is also the town's best medium. Even Mom will admit it. He can run a séance better than anyone else. Luckily, there's not much demand for contacting the dead on a Sunday evening and he's more than happy to hear me complain about Aunt Catherine.

"It certainly does sound like she's got a stick rammed up her posterior," he says when I'm done. He drinks something clear and vile-smelling from a jelly jar. "Aren't you glad she's just your aunt and not your mother? The offspring of parents who don't understand gender flexibility suffer a terrible burden."

I shudder at the thought of Aunt Catherine as my mom. We're sitting on his back porch, which is screened in against the bugs and shrouded with bushes for privacy. It's dark but for some old hurricane lamps. Dr. Fish is not a big believer in electricity. Insects buzz in the woods and the sky is full of bright little stars, all of them out of reach.

"I need her recommendation to go to Dartmouth," I say. "She's not going to give it unless I dress and act like a boy."

"Hmmm," Dr. Fish says, and sips from his jar.

A girlish shout carries through the night air from down by the lake. Mom, skinny-dipping. Aunt Catherine's high protest, followed by a splash.

"She thinks I'm a freak," I say, and pull out the picture of Aunt Linda that I swiped from the house. "Maybe if she believed what Mom believes...that I'm her baby sister, reincarnated. If I could convince her of that, maybe it would be okay if I'm like this."

Dr. Fish's eyes glitter. "Do you think she believes in reincarnation?"

Well, no. I don't think Aunt Catherine believes in anything she can't see or hear. But I don't have any other brilliant plan. I don't have any plan at all. Just the desire to hit my head against the wall.

"More importantly," Dr. Fish says, folding his hands over his belly, "do you believe you were the sister in a past life?"

"No. I don't know. Maybe." I study Linda's glossy hair and perfect face. I'll never look pretty like that. If I'm lucky, people outside of Lake Orchid will think I'm an odd-looking woman. If I'm unlucky, people will mock or curse at me, or maybe even punch, or maybe I'll lose my job or life.

"You can't convince someone of an idea if you don't believe it yourself." Dr. Fish refills his jelly jar from a large plastic jug. Mom says you could peel paint off a house with moonshine like that. "It sounds like you're uncertain."

"I am."

"Good. If you weren't uncertain, there'd be no reason to spend a fortune on a college education."

"But I'm not going to get to spend it at Dartmouth."

"There are worse injustices in the world," he says.

He's right, but that doesn't make my particular injustice any easier to bear.

On the walk home I try to think of some other plan to convince my prejudiced and narrow-minded aunt that I'm worthy of her sainted alma mater. When I get there, however, she's already snoring on the sofa and Mom is in the bathroom, brushing her teeth. She's still damp from the water.

"Did you have fun?" I ask.

"You should have come," she said. "Where'd you go?"

"Rachel needed some relationship advice."

Mom spits in the sink and splashes water on her face. "Did you hear Aunt Catherine earlier? When she was worried about your safety?"

"I heard her say I'm a freak."

"She didn't say that," Mom says, patting her face dry.

"You think I'm a freak, too," I say.

"Linnie." And that's her no-kidding tone of voice, so I back down. Because of all the people in the world, Mom's always going to be in my corner.

"Sorry." I lean against the bathroom doorway. "She's wrong about my safety. No one's going to throw rocks at me. And if they do, I can throw them right back."

"I'm not sure that's the right answer," Mom says. She reaches over and squeezes my shoulder. "In the morning, over breakfast, we'll have a nice civilized talk about it. I believe in you, and you believe in you, so let's make her believe in you, too."

Which is a wonderful plan, but not very specific. I spend half the night trying to think up persuasive arguments. I make a bulleted list, then a numbered list, and then a pie chart. I rehearse a speech in front of the mirror. Meanwhile, the clock keeps ticking and no studying for my history test gets done. Sometime around four a.m., when all the town is asleep, I fall asleep, too, exhausted and dreamless until my seven a.m. alarm.

Now's my one and only chance to convince Aunt Catherine I'm worthy.

But she's already gone.

❖

"She left?" Rachel exclaims. "That bitch!"

We're sitting in history class. It's ten minutes before the bell and our teacher, Mrs. Harwood, is nowhere in sight. They say she's an alcoholic, but I think after thirty years of teaching she's just tired of getting up every morning and looking at teenagers.

"Her plane was leaving at ten a.m. from Orlando," I say, dejected. "She left a note for Mom, wished me luck."

"That sucks. I'm sorry."

"Not your fault," I say.

Mrs. Harwood shows up, walking as if she's dragging a thousand-pound weight behind her. "All right," she says. "Your last exam as high school seniors. Books and notebooks away, please."

When I move my notebook, the graduation picture of Mom, Catherine and Linda slides out. I forgot to return it last night. I stow it in my book bag beside my shopping list (mascara, moisturizer, new shoes) and hairbrush. The exam isn't hard, but when you've only had three hours' sleep it's hard to keep 10-point Comic Sans MS font in focus.

Finally, it's over. I escape for the outdoor picnic area and see Aunt Catherine standing under the awning by the principal's office.

"Oh," I say, so abruptly that Matthew Perry (my classmate, not the actor) runs into me. My purse falls and I drop my books onto the grass.

"Sorry." Matthew bends down to help. "You okay?"

"Yes," I say, aggravated, as kids detour around us in a blur of noise and sound.

"You don't sound okay."

"It's nothing."

"PMS?" he asks. "I've got some aspirin."

Which is the best thing about Matthew—he doesn't give a crap about what I am. When I started school in first grade, I wore pants and shirts like all the other boys. I hated it. But for all her hippy-dippy beliefs, Mom wasn't quite ready to let me publicly wear the dresses I adored. For years I tried to fit in as a boy but was miserable. On Halloween in ninth grade I came to school dressed as a church lady—hat, pearls, flowered skirt—surrounded by vampires, witches, robots, cartoon characters, TV reality show stars and three girls pretending to be Lady Gaga. The next morning, I put on a skirt and blouse and lip gloss and that was it. Changed my life.

Don't think it was easy—I threw up twice before I even left the house. Rachel saw me and said, "You look awesome," and Matthew walked me around school for two days, glaring at anyone who snickered and threatening two guys who wanted to "show me a lesson." He's one of the few straight guys at school who goes to the Rainbow Club meetings.

"No aspirin, thanks," I tell him as we gather my books. "Do you have a pill that can change people's minds?"

"I'm all out." He gives me one of his famous grins. "Just use your famous sales skills and awesome powers of persuasion."

I'm not feeling any awesomeness today.

Matthew heads off for the gym. I walk to Aunt Catherine and try to figure out if she's mad or disappointed or what. Her face is a mask, though. I've got nothing to work with.

"Linden," she says, and then hesitates. "Lin. Can I talk to you for a few minutes?"

"I have to eat lunch."

"It won't take long. Walk me to my car."

Her rental car is at the far end of the visitor lot, which runs along the narrow blue retention pond near the gym. There's a sign there that says *BEWARE OF ALLIGATORS* but I kind of wish that one would crawl up from the mud and keep this conversation from happening.

"Shouldn't you be on a plane by now?" I ask her.

"Yes," she says. "Unfortunately, I got turned around halfway to the airport."

"By what?"

"My conscience. I woke up this morning promising myself that I would never again drink your mother's special tea. I regret that it makes me say things that are…impolitic."

Things like *freakish behavior.*

I clutch my books tighter to my padded chest. "Does it?"

"Your mother tells me that you're a straight-A student with academic awards, community service, and excellent SAT scores. You could get into any college in Florida. Why trade warm weather and a relaxed lifestyle for the Ivy League in New England? Dartmouth won't be as accepting as you think."

"That's not true!" I stop walking. "It has a Gay-Straight Alliance, and gender-neutral housing, and LGBT classes. It's not just some stuffy college with ideas stuck in the past."

"You're right, they have all of those things." Aunt Catherine studies me intently. "Things which look good on web pages or in glossy brochures, but have you actually visited the campus and talked to the people involved?"

"We don't have the money for me to go visit." I try not to sound too whiney about it.

She tilts her head. "Is that so? Your mother says she offered to take you up over the winter break."

I wish she'd never come here. That she'd stayed in Boston and out of our lives.

After a moment of silence she says, "Your mother also told me you practically memorized *Dartmouth in My Day.* I can't believe she bought that for you. My father gave a copy to each of us when we were young, because he expected us to attend regardless of how we felt about it. When your mother dropped out, it broke his heart."

"Mom went? She never told me."

"Just for the fall term. She hated it. Too much snow and

too much stone. When Linda passed away over the holidays, she couldn't bear to go back. That's when she left home and never came back."

Aunt Catherine starts walking again. Reluctantly I follow. Of course Mom wouldn't like it. She's too flamboyant, too free-spirited. But I'm not her.

"I don't want to go just because of some book," I tell her. "I know it's sentimental and outdated. I did a lot of research and planning and I thought about it a lot."

"But you won't visit the campus."

"I will when they accept me."

"And you'll go regardless of the fact that as an alumna and someone actively involved in school, I might know more about it than you?"

We've reached her car. I want her to get in it and drive away. Not because she's wrong about everything, but mostly because she's right. We both know why I won't visit the campus. As long as it's fourteen hundred miles away, it's perfect in my imagination.

"You don't want me to go because of what I am," I tell her. "But gender doesn't have to be binary. It doesn't have to be either/or."

Aunt Catherine's face softens. "I'll tell you what you are. You're my nephew. Or niece. I don't know which, frankly. But you're my sister's child and I want you to be happy, whether that means wearing a football helmet or a ballerina tutu."

Frankly, I look kind of silly in a tutu. Before I can point that out, Rachel and Matthew Perry show up from behind the gym and ambush us.

"Linnie, Mrs. Harwood needs you," Rachel says breathlessly, grabbing one of my arms. "The Honor Society is having a crisis."

Matthew takes my other arm. "And you need to work on your valedictory speech."

"And the school newspaper's waiting for its interview," Rachel adds.

Matthew gives Aunt Catherine his best smile. "We have to steal her away now."

Aunt Catherine's mouth quirks. "Yes, of course. I can't stand in the way of such an important schedule."

"It's okay," I said, shrugging free of their well-meaning rescue attempt. "We're just talking about me coming up to visit Dartmouth."

"Did you get in?" Rachel asks, excited.

"The waiting list doesn't clear until August," Aunt Catherine says. "I can't promise that a recommendation from me would hold any weight at all. But making a visit would be an excellent first step."

We lock gazes and I nod.

She kisses my cheek and gets into her car. As she backs out of the parking space, I remember the photo in my book bag.

"Aunt Catherine! Here."

She rolls down the window and I hand it to her.

"Oh, this," she says. She gazes at it for a moment and then looks at me. "Your mother has shared her theory that you're Linda, reincarnated. Do you believe that?"

"Not really."

She smiles. "I don't believe it, either. You are entirely your own person, Linnie Gallagher. Helmet or tutu."

After she's gone we head to lunch. Rachel asks, "She wants you to wear a helmet?" and Matthew says, "I've never seen you in a tutu," but I'm still thinking about yes, I'm my own person, wrong body and all. Maybe Dartmouth is in my future. Or maybe not. Maybe one day I'll build All Gender U, full of brick and ivy and people who don't care about what you look like when your clothes are off. Boys and girls and trans of all persuasions will be welcomed.

You can come as you are or as you want to be, but please do come. Everyone's invited.

About the Editor

STEVE BERMAN sold his first short story at the age of seventeen, so he's always considered himself a young adult author. His novel, *Vintage*, was a finalist for the Andre Norton Award for Young Adult Science Fiction and Fantasy as well as named to the GLBT Round Table of the American Library Association's Rainbow Project Book List, which is recommended reading of queer books for children and teens. He has edited the young adult fantasy anthology *Magic in the Mirrorstone* (a *Parade Magazine* Pick), as well as Lambda Literary Award finalists *Charmed Lives* (co-edited with Toby Johnson) and *Wilde Stories*. He regularly writes queer spec fic short stories for teens—his most recent being a lesbian retelling of the Swan Lake story for *The Beastly Bride* and a gay vampire tale for *Teeth*. He has spoken about queer and young adult fiction at numerous conferences around the nation but always returns to New Jersey, as his cat Daulton demands it so.

Soliloquy Titles From Bold Strokes Books

Speaking Out edited by Steve Berman. Inspiring stories written for and about LGBT and Q teens of overcoming adversity (against intolerance and homophobia) and experiencing life after "coming out." (978-1-60282-566-6)

365 Days by K.E. Payne. Life sucks when you're seventeen years old and confused about your sexuality, and the girl of your dreams doesn't even know you exist. Then in walks sexy new emo girl, Hannah Harrison. Clemmie Atkins has exactly 365 days to discover herself, and she's going to have a blast doing it! (978-1-60282-540-6)

Cursebusters! by Julie Smith. Budding-psychic Reeno is the most accomplished teenage burglar in California, but one tiny screw-up and poof!—she's sentenced to Bad Girl School. And that isn't even her worst problem. Her sister Haley's dying of an illness no one can diagnose, and now she can't even help. (978-1-60282-559-8)

Who I Am by M.L. Rice. Devin Kelly's senior year is a disaster. She's in a new school in a new town, and the school bully is making her life miserable—but then she meets his sister Melanie and realizes her feelings for her are more than platonic. (978-1-60282-231-3)

Sleeping Angel by Greg Herren. Eric Matthews survives a terrible car accident only to find out everyone in town thinks he's a murderer—and he has to clear his name even though he has no memories of what happened. (978-1-60282-214-6)

Mesmerized by David-Matthew Barnes. Through her close friendship with Brodie and Lance, Serena Albright learns about the many forms of love and finds comfort for the grief and guilt she feels over the brutal death of her older brother, the victim of a hate crime. (978-1-60282-191-0)

The Perfect Family by Kathryn Shay. A mother and her gay son stand hand in hand as the storms of change engulf their perfect family and the life they knew. (978-1-60282-181-1)

Father Knows Best by Lynda Sandoval. High school juniors and best friends Lila Moreno, Meryl Morganstern, and Caressa Thibodoux plan to make the most of the summer before senior year. What they discover that amazing summer about girl power, growing up, and trusting friends and family more than prepares them to tackle that all-important senior year! (978-1-60282-147-7)

Visit us at www.boldstrokesbooks.com

6 : 28

Feb 2018

PRAISE FOR DAVID KUPELIAN'S

THE MARKETING OF EVIL

"It's often said that marketing is warfare, and in *The Marketing of Evil*, David Kupelian clearly reveals the stunning strategies and tactics of persuasion employed by those engaged in an all-out war against America's Judeo-Christian culture. If you really want to understand the adversary's thinking and help turn the tide of battle, read this book!"

—**DAVID LIMBAUGH**, NATIONALLY SYNDICATED COLUMNIST AND AUTHOR

"Every parent in America needs to read this book. David Kupelian skillfully exposes the secular Left's rotten-apple peddlers in devastating detail. From pitching promiscuity as 'freedom' to promoting abortion as 'choice,' the marketers of evil are always selling you something destructive—with catastrophic results. Kupelian shines a light on them all. Now watch the cockroaches run for cover."

—**MICHELLE MALKIN**, AUTHOR, NATIONALLY SYNDICATED COLUMNIST, FOX NEWS CHANNEL ANALYST

"David Kupelian is one of the very few must-read writers in the 21st Century. He has the insight and wisdom to perceive the true state of the culture and the world, and he has the incredible ability to tell the Truth in a readable manner that helps the reader not only understand the Truth, but to understand how to redeem America's culture as well."

—**DR. TED BAEHR**, CHAIRMAN OF THE CHRISTIAN FILM AND TELEVISION COMMISSION, AUTHOR, AND PUBLISHER OF MOVIEGUIDE

"David Kupelian dares to tell the truth about the overwhelming forces in our society which take us far away from our original American concept of freedom with responsibility, happiness with commitments, and traditional values. *The Marketing of Evil* is a serious wake-up call for all who cherish traditional values, the innocence of children, and the very existence of our great country."

—**DR. LAURA SCHLESSINGER**, AUTHOR AND RADIO TALK SHOW HOST

"Over just a few years, life in America has become indescribably more squalid, expensive, and dangerous. Like the dazzling disclosures in the final page of a gripping whodunit or the fascinating revelation of a magician's secrets, *The Marketing of Evil* irresistibly exposes how it was done. It will elicit an involuntary 'Aha!' from you as you discover who did it, and your soul will soar with optimism as you discover the only way we can undo it. In years to come Americans will acknowledge a debt of gratitude to David Kupelian for his honesty, courage, and laser-like insight in this must-read book."

—**RABBI DANIEL LAPIN**, AUTHOR, RADIO TALK SHOW HOST, AND FOUNDER OF THE AMERICAN ALLIANCE OF JEWS & CHRISTIANS

"Did you ever want to know—I mean really know—how and why America is being transformed from a unified, Judeo-Christian society into a divided, false, murky, neopagan culture? Even if you think you know the answers to those questions, in fact, *especially* if you think you know the answers, you must read David Kupelian's *The Marketing of Evil*. So clearly does it expose the incredible con game to which Americans have been subjected that it offers real hope—because when our problems come this sharply into focus, so do the solutions."

—**JOSEPH FARAH**, FOUNDER, EDITOR, AND CEO OF WND, AUTHOR AND SYNDICATED COLUMNIST